Vermillion Clouds

Vermillion Clouds

A Century of Women's Stories from Bengal

edited, translated & introduced by
Radha Chakravarty

1984 - 2009 25 YEARS OF FEMINIST PUBLISHING

kali for women

women UNLIMITED

Vermillion Clouds
was first published in English in 2010 by

Women Unlimited
(an associate of Kali for Women)
K-36, Hauz Khas Enclave, Ground Floor
New Delhi 110 016

ISBN: 81-88965-51-0

Cover design: Neelima Rao

We have made every effort to contact all authors and publishers for permission to use their stories in this anthology. However, if some have been omitted please do inform us and we will rectify this in the next edition.

Typeset at Sanchauli Image Composers, B-28, Nawada Extension, Uttam Nagar, New Delhi 110059 and printed at
Raj Press, R-3, Inderpuri, New Delhi 110012

To Nono, Nani, Dida, Burididi,
and all my foremothers

Acknowledgements

I am grateful to all the authors who allowed me to translate their work for this book, and to the publishers who gave permission for reprints. I thank the editorial team at Women Unlimited for their painstaking work on the manuscript, and Neelima Rao for the cover design. Most of all, I appreciate the support and encouragement of my family and friends, for without them this book would not have been possible.

Acknowledgement

Contents

Introduction

RADHA CHAKRAVARTY

WOMEN'S relationship with history and literature has never been simple or straightforward. For the women of Bengal, writing is simultaneously creative and political, a literary venture that is also a quest for voice, identity and self-expression. The present collection explores the ways in which Bengali women, over the last hundred years 1900–2000, have negotiated their search for freedom through their experiments with the short story, a literary form ideally suited for this blend of the aesthetic and the political. Bengali women's fiction is not monolithic; rather, it is heterogeneous, fragmented and marked by difference along varied social axes, for differences of class, caste and community offer women uneven access to the literary field. The stories in this volume map this disparate history, a narrative with many disjunctions.

The history of the Bengali short story may be traced back to oral sources such as legends and folk tales, as well as written sources like the *Ramayana* and *Mahabharata,* and narrative poems such as the *Mangalkavyas.* From the eighteenth century onwards, the encounter with colonial culture gave rise to new genres like the novel and the novella. Other indigenous narrative forms prevalent at the time included the churnak (anecdote), akhyan (fable) and naksha (portrait). Although it drew upon all these modes, the short story evolved into a genre in its own right; unlike the novel, it was not a form imported from the "West", even though it was open to European influences. As traditional storytellers, women found this form congenial, for it provided a bridge between the oral and the written word, as well as between private and public realms.

The earliest Bengali short stories were published in the 1870s. The pioneers were Bankimchandra Chatterji's brothers, Purnachandra and Sanjeevchandra, who published "Madhumati" (1873) and "Damini" (1874) respectively. Rabindranath Tagore's first short story "Bhikarini" was written in 1877; between 1873 and 1890, the short story flourished in the many influential periodicals of the time, which both promoted and determined the trajectory of this form.

This period also saw women's entry into the literary domain. In the earlier decades of the nineteenth century, literacy had been denied to upper caste Hindu women, while Muslim women read the Arabic Koran without really understanding it. The reform movements of the second half of the nineteenth century initiated a process of change, drawing attention to the need for women's education. More women now found access to education, some in schools, but others at home, under the mentorship of liberal fathers and husbands. Many conservatives, though, continued to regard women's emancipation as an act of transgression, a violation of "pure" tradition under colonial influence.

The 1860s marked the emergence of the "lekhika" or the woman writer. Several factors enabled this historic development. The social reformer, Vidyasagar, had promoted vernacular education at the primary level, making it possible for women to read and write in the language that they spoke, instead of struggling to learn the classical languages. The rise of print media and the growth of a new middle class readership encouraged women to enter literary culture as readers, but also as writers. The reform movements initiated by Raja Rammohun Roy and others also generated debates about gender issues such as widow remarriage, child marriage, polygamy and sati. This prompted women to question their traditional roles and to demand greater freedom. Periodicals such as the *Bamabodhini Patrika* (1863-1922) provided a forum for them to articulate these questions.

Although several women emerged as essayists and pamphleteers, the pioneer of the short story was Swarnakumari Devi, who not only wrote her own stories, but also edited the periodical, *Bharati,* in which several other women writers published their work. Among the many female forerunners of the modern Bengali short story were Indira Devi, Anurupa Devi, Nirupama Devi, Sita Devi and Shanta Devi. Short stories by women in the late nineteenth century remained heavily influenced by Bankimchandra Chatterjee and Rabindranath Tagore, and tended to reflect the relatively constricted lives of the women of those times. Domesticity, romantic love, motherhood and family relationships dominated the plots. There was also often a strong vein of sentimentality in them, but writers like Hiranmanyi Devi and Sarala Devi used satirical elements to express their discomfort with conservative social norms.

It was in the twentieth century that stories written by women acquired sufficient maturity and diversity to merit consideration as a distinctive category. The transition from the nineteenth to the twentieth century witnessed several paradigm shifts. The rise of the Bengali middle class, the disintegration of the joint family, and changing perceptions of women's role within marriage impacted upon the lives and aspirations of women at the turn of the century. Caught in the clash between foreign and indigenous cultures, tradition and modernity, Bengali women struggled to redefine their identity and their place in society.

In their quest for freedom, women widened the scope of their demands. In addition to education, they claimed the right to travel, to participate in politics, and to consider income-generating possibilities. The debates about gender issues now expanded to include the question of women's role in politics. The demand for women's emancipation was not directed solely at enhancing family and domestic life, it was also concerned with promoting greater self-esteem and self-reliance for women themselves. Women's search for empowerment became more nuanced, and their presence within nationalist discourse often proved disruptive to its assumptions.

The early years of the twentieth century witnessed a flowering of women's fiction that reflected these changing trends. The language of the short story evolved from the formal "sadhu bhasha" to a more colloquial "chalti bhasha" of everyday speech, a move that women found congenial. The publication of *Sultana's Dream* by Rokeya Sakhawat Hossain in 1905 marked a turning-point in the history of women's writing in Bengal. This brilliant radical feminist text shook the literary establishment and ushered in a new era in Bengali women's prose.

This anthology tracks the development of the women's short story in Bengal during the century that followed.

The first Partition of Bengal in 1905 triggered widespread protest and a heightened spirit of nationalism. Women stepped out of seclusion to participate in the Swadeshi movement, and their entry into the public domain was marked by their increased visibility on the literary scene. Yet women had a troubled relationship with nationalism, for they became aware of the patriarchal underpinnings of the national movement and found themselves simultaneously resisting both colonial rule and indigenous patriarchal authority. The colonised subject's struggle for autonomy provided a model that women adopted in their own battle against male domination. Nor was the women's movement homogeneous; Muslim women, for instance, felt alienated from the Hindu revivalist underpinnings of much Swadeshi rhetoric. These new political undercurrents found expression in a range of powerful short stories by Bengali women, where feminism and nationalism intersect, and sometimes collide, for these writers sought to create an alternative space where women could claim a national identity without losing their gendered voice.

Such is the fascinating historical juncture at which this anthology begins. The first story, "Dedication" by Susheela Sen, was written in the aftermath of the first Partition of Bengal. Periodicals had always played an important role in the development of the Bengali short story. One such, *Kuntalin*, was particularly significant for encouraging the Swadeshi spirit in literature. From 1894 onwards, this journal instituted an annual literary competition, awarding prizes for entries that promoted the indigenous products, Kuntalin hair oil and Dilkhush essence, without resorting to overt advertising. The winning entries were published in an annual compilation, and many well-known writers participated in the competition. Saratchandra Chatterji published his first story in *Kuntalin*, though under a pseudonym. Rabindranath Tagore judged the competition in the year 1900. *Kuntalin* also provided fertile ground for women to test their literary skills. So successful were they that male writers began to send in entries under female pseudonyms, hoping that this would enhance their chances of winning a prize! (Prabhatkumar Mukhopadhyay, for example, published a story under the pseudonym "Radhamoni Devi"). In 1901, the organisers of the competition published a warning to male authors that entries submitted under false female names would be disqualified. This phenomenon highlights the changing status of the woman writer in early twentieth century Bengal; it also offers a contrast to the adoption of male pseudonyms by women novelists in nineteenth century Britain.

Susheela Sen's "Dedication", which won the *Kuntalin* prize in 1908, explores the psychology of a woman trapped between her traditional wifely role and her urge to participate in national politics. In simultaneously flouting both colonial and patriarchal authority, the protagonist, Bibha, undergoes an apotheosis and becomes a figure of inspiration for young freedom fighters. In death, she assumes an iconic resemblance to Mother India, the image of the feminised motherland popularised by contemporary nationalist rhetoric.

In Giribala Debi's "Baruni" (1920), a prospective bridegroom demands additional dowry on the grounds that the bride-to-be lacks vivacity. The young girl resents being appraised like farm produce on sale in the market. Her spirited sister-in-law springs to her defence, playing a prank on the suitor that forces him to confront his own double standards. Narrated in a wry, ironic tone, this story exposes the masculine bias underlying the commodification of female beauty.

The early decades of the twentieth century also marked the rise of the Muslim voice in Bengali literature. For socio-historical reasons, Muslim women writers gained visibility two decades later than their Hindu counterparts. The periodicals, *Bangiya Musalman Patrika* and *Moslem Bharat* launched in the years 1918 and 1921, respectively, provided a creative forum that foregrounded the Muslim experience. Well-known literary figures such as Kazi Nazrul Islam published their short stories here, but it was Rokeya who remained a figure of inspiration for Muslim women writers of this period. Her powerful satire, "Fruit of Knowledge" (1922) catapults us from the "feminine" domestic sphere into the public realm of history, subverting Biblical myth to highlight the economic exploitation of the colonies by imperialist forces. This so-called "rupkatha" or fairy tale provides a caustic critique of imperialism, but also of the compliance of the exploited, and their blindness to their own subjugation. The narrative makes the succinct point that women must be allowed their rightful place in national life for a strong, independent society to emerge. This story is striking for its formal sophistication, shorn of sentimentalism, and uncompromising in its critique of patriarchy. It further develops the link between gender and nation highlighted in Susheela Sen's story, written two decades earlier. Rokeya's prophetic narrative anticipates the persistence of the gender bias even after the nation wins freedom from colonial rule.

Following Rokeya's example, Muslim women writers like M. Fatema Khanam, Razia Khatun Chaudhurani and Sufia Kamal also experimented with the short story. Razia Khatun's "Eid Moon", published in *Masik Mohammadi* in 1928, narrates the isolation of a widow robbed of her rightful property by her scheming male relatives, but too proud to seek charity even though she is so poor that she cannot afford medical treatment for her dying son. The link between gender discrimination and economic deprivation provides the groundwork for this story, which also depicts the decline of the zamindari system.

"A Bubble in the Great Wide Sea" (1931) by Radharani Debi graphically depicts society's refusal to acknowledge woman as a desiring subject. The protagonist is a young, headstrong child forcibly withdrawn from school and married off at an early age. She realizes that none of the milestones in her short life have been determined by her own wishes. Widowed at fifteen, she embraces the hardships of her position with a bitterly ironic adherence to orthodoxy, but in her ostensible capitulation lies her rebellion.

Between the two World Wars, the nationalist struggle and the influence of European thinkers like Marx, Darwin and Freud forced a rethinking of modernity among the Bengali intelligentsia. Tagore continued to dominate the literary landscape, but his monopoly was challenged by the self-conscious modernity of his detractors in the Kallol group of writers, and the presence of other literary giants such as Tarashankar Bandyopadhyay, Manik Bandyopadhyay and Bibhutibhushan Bandyopadhyay. Within this context, the stories of Rokeya, Razia Khatun and Radharani Debi represent a striking counter-discourse, inserting the question of gender into current debates about modernity.

In the 1940s and 1950s, women's writings in Bengal revealed a strong awareness of the impact of historical events on their personal lives. The Second World War, the Bengal Famine and the Partition affected women in gender-specific ways. Riots, upheavals, mass migrations and economic hardship forced middle-class women into the job market, and drew many of them into political and social activism in defence of civil rights. Against the backdrop of the Bengal famine, Sabitri Ray's "Nothing New" (1945) presents the stark contrast between a starving woman's desperate struggle to survive, and a well-to-do sculptor's attempt to transform her suffering into successful art. The pregnant woman's losing battle against hunger and death provides the young artist with the raw material he needs to create something new, but he remains distanced from the reality of her suffering.

Ashapurna Devi's "House of Cards" (1947) demonstrates the fragility of the institution of marriage, founded on false, one-sided notions of honour. It takes only a fragment of suspicion to destroy a woman's position in her marital home. For the protagonist, goaded by the jibes and innuendoes of her sister-in-law for having sheltered a male fugitive in her room one night, the husband's mistrust proves to be the last straw. She leaves home, staking her own claim to the "honour" that is customarily regarded as a male prerogative.

"Vermillion Clouds" (1953) by Sulekha Sanyal explores the link between women and history, and the special ways in which women are affected by the economic pressures of war. In the story, both Malati and her predecessor – her husband's deceased first wife – suffer a similar fate, each compelled to barter her body in exchange for the family's financial stability. Their twin secrets are disclosed in a moment of poignant self-revelation that heals the rift between husband and wife, but scarred by history, they can only pretend to be emotionally whole.

In the 1960s, under the influence of Bimal Kar, the Bengali short story acquired greater psychological depth and became more inward-looking. "The Shadow" (1962) by Lila Majumdar invokes the traditional ghost story to present a double image of female transgression: a woman smuggler, and the spirit of a dead man's mistress. While one woman fails to elude the long arm of the law, the other takes the law into her own hands even after death, to ensure that justice is done to another wronged woman, the dead man's destitute wife. The drama is played out in the psyche of Gopen Babu, the story's male protagonist.

The 1970s were a decade of turbulence marked by political events like the Bangladesh Liberation War, the Naxalite movement and the Emergency, and natural disasters such as the floods in West Bengal. Jyotirmoyee Devi's "Kindred Souls" (1973) describes the shared plight of two female refugees during the Liberation War, for though they belong to different religious communities, they realise that they are fleeing a common enemy: man. An instinctive bond springs up between them, but once across the border, they are forced apart by the communal divide that makes it impossible for Hindu and Muslim refugees to be assigned to the same refugee camp.

"Face Up" (1977), Kabita Sinha's densely figurative story, focuses on the squalor of the Kolkata slums. The protagonist, Pulin, leads a cramped, impoverished existence in a tiny room at the top of an ancient, overcrowded building. But he has a secret parallel life on the terrace above his room, where he lovingly nurtures a beautiful scented plant. The plant merges in his imagination with the image of Putul, the young orphaned girl he wishes to protect and cherish. Together, they resolve to fight their circumstances, to pursue, at least in their fancy, their dream of beauty and fulfilment.

The Seventies also marked the emergence of Mahasweta Devi as a powerful political writer. In her hands, the Bengali short story moved beyond middle class concerns to focus on the lives of the deprived and marginalised. Today, Mahasweta is feted as a champion of tribal rights, but her fiction simultaneously challenges persistent gender biases. "Giribala" (1982) offers a strong critique of discrimination against the girl child, regarded by society as dispensable, "Lost if she is dead, /Lost if she is wed." Through the rebellion of an innocent village woman whose husband sells their daughters into the flesh trade to feed his ambition, the story makes a powerful statement against the exploitation of women.

In the Eighties and Nineties, fiction by Bengali women demonstrated a continuing engagement with changing social trends, contemporary lifestyles, urbanisation, and the interface between local and global developments. Stories from these decades indicate the growing literary sophistication and versatility of the Bengali woman writer.

Written in the early 1990s, Bani Basu's story "From Kailash to Kolkata" is a witty retelling of the myth of goddess Durga's annual visit to her paternal home on earth. A troubled mother-goddess faces rebellion from her divine offspring, who have changed with the times and wish to discard their traditional image of her. Saraswati wants to shed her austerity for frivolous attire, Lakshmi refuses to remain a docile domestic deity, Kartika the bachelor god desires a live-in relationship with a woman, and Ganesh wants a divorce. On earth, the Durga Puja celebrations mirror the trends of a globalised world, where the traditional values of devotion, simplicity and honesty have given way to conspicuous consumption, violence and greed.

"Playing with Dolls and a New Love Story" (1994) by Ahana Biswas is a bold tale of same-sex love that derives much of its effect from its parody of the male voice. This story represents a new trend in Bengali women's fiction, writing the body in ways that break societal taboos about "appropriate" subject matter for female writers. The story also explores the disruptive undercurrents within a joint family in a rural setting, and exposes the collective exploitation and scapegoating of women by the male members of a locality.

One of the most gifted voices in Bengali fiction today, Nabaneeta Dev Sen, for instance, ranges effortlessly between styles and genres. In the course of her long writing career, she has always remained in touch with changing social scenarios. Many of her stories are distinguished by their use of humour, an element relatively scarce in short stories by Bengali women. Her story "Proprietor" (1996) addresses contemporary issues such as divorce, single parenthood, an educated woman's bid for freedom and her eventual recognition of the centrality of her maternal identity. As the title ironically signals, the textual rhetoric hinges on notions of ownership, belonging and proprietorship that underwrite family relationships.

Joya Mitra's "Copper Goddess" is distinctive for its use of the internal monologue, its powerful evocation of atmosphere, and its constant yet muted undertone of violence. The narrative focuses on the liminal, and the abject, probing the social underpinnings of so-called "abnormal" psychology. A penetrating study of the way emotional violence can lead to other forms of violence, the story locates woman as both the source and the ultimate victim of this vicious circle.

"Mindscape" (2005) is an unusual story by the versatile feminist writer, Suchitra Bhattacharya, for it uses the inscrutability of death as a trope for the elusiveness of identity. Four friends on their way to a morgue to identify the bodies of a couple of friends killed in a road accident, realise how little they really know about the man and woman who have died. Evoking an eerie, haunting atmosphere, the narrative reveals the hidden prejudices that colour our relationships, which inevitably remain partial and incomplete.

"Within the Furnace" (2005) by Anita Agnihotri explores the tensions of a father-daughter relationship through the memories of its protagonist, Nandini, as she confronts the statue-in-the-making of her father, once a public figure. When her father repudiated her for marrying outside her caste, she suffered an internal vacuum that left her emotionally impaired. Only while watching the swarming crowd of labourers struggling to pour molten metal into the statue mould, does she break out of her mental prison to experience a sense of her connectedness to the general mass of humanity.

As the stories by Bhattacharya and Agnihotri demonstrate, the Bengali woman writer of the late twentieth-early twenty-first century has come a long way from the nineteenth century "lekhika" struggling for a voice. Together, the pieces that make up this anthology chart the stages of this success story. Today, women's writing in Bengal is recognised as a literary force to be reckoned with. The writers in this anthology experiment with a range of fictional modes, including realism, romance, sentimentality, satire, parody, fable/fairy tale, internal monologue, and occasional use of the supernatural. They demonstrate the elasticity of Bengali using a spectrum of styles, from the formal to the colloquial, including the poetic, the abstract, the dramatic, and in some cases, a mix of dialects. The stories tackle a wide range of subjects, including nationalism, family, domesticity, marriage, motherhood, widowhood, sexuality, old age, trafficking in women, environment, economic change, migrancy, commodification of women, the clash between tradition and modernity, forms of discrimination, women's creativity, and the struggle for survival. While many of the stories are not overtly feminist, most of them express an awareness of the ways in which gender impinges on women's lives. Feminist scholars have also done much in recent years to promote greater awareness about women's contribution to Bengali literature, and literary forums like Soi (the West Bengal Women Writer's Association, of which Nabaneeta Dev Sen is founder-president) promote a sense of sisterhood among creative women.

The Bengali short story today is a vibrant, varied genre, full of possibilities; but there remain hierarchies within hierarchies, and not all women writers in Bengal enjoy the visibility that they deserve, even now. While some women have succeeded in breaking into the male-dominated publishing arena to carve out their own niche within the mainstream, there remain many others who continue to write from the margins, largely ignored by the reading public. Some deliberately distance themselves from the establishment. A few rare figures, such as Mahasweta Devi, transform the margin into a space of empowerment, both for themselves and for the "others" they represent; but there remain many talented women writers whose voices are still unheard, and it devolves upon the discerning reader, critic or translator to draw attention to their work. In this collection, I have tried to incorporate some of these neglected voices, placing their work alongside that of established women writers.

The anthology, though, is not an exhaustive compendium or encyclopaedia; rather it is an attempt to map the bold contours of a broad and uneven terrain. The focus is on representative writing rather than what is conventionally regarded as "good" writing, for many of the stories displace established notions of what "good" writing is about. Omissions are inevitable in a project of this kind. Nineteenth century women writers, the precursors of the modern Bengali short story, do not figure in this anthology due to constraints of space; Bengali writing from the north-east by authors like Minakshi Sen or Jaya Goala, could not be included for the same reason. Other talented contemporary voices, such as Kana Basu Misra and Tilottama Majumdar, had to be left out of the present collection; dalit women's writing, emerging as a visible trend in Bengali literature, did not find a place in this anthology because the short story is not the preferred form of these writers; they work more extensively with poetry and autobiography. In the years that followed Partition and the Liberation War of 1971, Bengali literature was bifurcated into twin streams, one centred in West Bengal and the other in Bangladesh. Despite many overlaps, the disparate histories of these two regions also produced divergent literary trends. The story of Bangladeshi writing is a narrative that demands its own proper space, and has therefore not been included in this book. Texts already available in translation or those that are widely circulated have also been excluded in favour of material less familiar to the informed reader. Instead of Rokeya's well-known *Sultana's Dream*, for instance, I have included "The Fruit of Knowledge", which expresses her incisive views on gender and nation. Mahasweta Devi tends to be pigeonholed as a champion of tribal rights, but "Giribala", included here, reveals the often ignored feminist potential of her work.

In translating the selected stories I have tried to preserve the flavour of the original Bengali texts, while rendering them in readable modern English for today's reader. This is not easy, for the style of the older stories reflects a more formal, old-fashioned use of Bengali, while the more recent stories adopt a range of registers in modern Bengali, from urbane sophistication to colloquial dialect. To capture these variations in English is notoriously difficult, as is the translation of cultural terms for which there are no English equivalents. In many instances, Bengali terms have been retained, allowing their meaning to emerge from the context or embedding brief pointers to their meaning within the translation itself. Kinship terms, names of months and seasons, and of common items of food and clothing, have been retained wherever possible. That the cultural and linguistic transfer is not always smooth reminds us that it is the translator's role to promote understanding by bridging the gaps between languages, cultures and periods in history, but not to erase these differences altogether.

Working on this collection has been a learning experience, and an immensely rewarding one; for it is empowering to feel that, alongside the woman writer, the woman critic, literary historian and translator can also make a difference.

February 2009

Dedication

SUSHEELA SEN

BIBHA'S husband had gone to England to prepare for the Civil Service examination. Married to Jatish at twelve, Bibha was now seventeen. Her husband was to return that very year. Bibha's father Shibchandra was a devout Brahman, as profoundly learned and philosophical as he was peace-loving, dedicated and liberal. He used to tutor a few M.A. students in Sanskrit, and that was sufficient to support his household. He had not approved his son-in-law's plans to visit England.

"Our country's soil is so fertile that it yields gold at the merest scratch," he used to say. "Similarly, our countrymen's hearts are so full of humility and tolerance that they can easily absorb all sorts of ideas and sentiments of the highest order. Travelling to foreign lands, especially to England, destroys the minds of our young men. They return with an attitude of heartless indifference and contempt."

Shibchandra was deeply patriotic. Offering hospitality to guests and service to the poor, he had kept the atmosphere of his home pure and blissful, like an ashram, a holy hermitage. Shibchandra's loving wife was his true soulmate in this matter. At the sacred hour of dawn, when Shibchandra, dressed in handspun silk after his early morning bath, sonorously recited his prayers in the puja chamber, it seemed as if those distant days of the past had returned, when these silent skies of the Indian nation, Bharatvarsha, had resonated with Vedic mantras chanted by Arya sages.

Despite his father-in-law's disapproval and all sorts of other obstacles and hindrances, nothing could stop Jatish. Using all their savings, selling their belongings, borrowing money, he left for England. His old parents, now destitute, retired to their village. Jatish was their only son. Come what may, they thought, if our son returns a well-established man, all our sufferings will be worthwhile.

Sheltered by the affection of her paternal home, Bibha passed her days in tranquility and bliss. She was her parents' only daughter. Shibchandra had three sons, and Bibha was the youngest child. Her parents and brothers doted on her, and Shibchandra had given her a good education. Sometimes, he would send Bibha to stay with her in-laws, and there, too, she would be pampered and looked after.

In Kolkata at that time, the Swadeshi movement was in full swing. Shibchandra himself had always been "Swadeshi". Long before the movement began, he was using swadeshi or indigenous items. Bibha's dadas, her elder brothers, became actively involved in meetings, boycotts, and the like. One day, the eldest of them, Bibha's Borodada, bought a picture of Bangajanani, Mother Bengal, and put it up in the room where Bibha and her mother slept. Though painted by an inexpert hand, the picture touched Bibha very profoundly. In the shape of goddess Annapurna, the Motherland, was offering rice and cloth to her offspring. Failing to recognize her, her own children were passing her by, ignoring her loving gift. The unhappy Mother was gazing at her hostile offspring with yearning, tender eyes! Bibha would look at that picture for long moments, her eyes filling with tears.

The 30th of Aswin was an auspicious date. Bibha's mother decided that all of them would bathe in the river Ganga that day, followed by a meal of fruit. What a scene met their eyes on the Ganga shore! Hordes of boys, young and old men, were marching barefoot, singing:

Bengal's soil and Bengal's water, bless them;
Bengal's air and Bengal's fruit, bless them;
Bless them, bless them, bless them, O Lord!

After bathing in the Ganga, they tied rakhis on each other. Bibha felt that day as if some divine presence was manifest across land and water, in the glow of that fair dawn, on the river-shore. It was almost as if they could glimpse the Mother's smile in the rays of the rising sun. With an inexpressible sweet sensation in their hearts, they made their way back home.

"Bibha, you have become a great devotee of Swadeshi," some girls of the same age would remark, observing Bibha's "Swadeshi" leanings. "But when your husband comes back wearing English boots like a saheb, what will you do with all your rituals and customs?"

"However much he may dress like a saheb, the son of a Bengali will always remain a Bengali," Bibha declared.

"Well, that remains to be seen," laughed her female companions.

Attired as a saheb from head to toe, having educated himself in flawless sahebi etiquette, Jatishchandra came back a Civilian. Immediately on his return he took Bibha off to his assigned place of work. At the time of their departure, he purchased countless English provisions from an English shop, even the cooking implements were English.

"Why are you buying so much foreign stuff?" Bibha gently expostulated. "All these things are available in desi versions, after all. My Baba doesn't buy a single foreign item."

"By the name of Rama, does any civilized human being buy desi stuff?" responded Jatishchandra in a tone of deep contempt, without even removing the cigar from his lips. Bibha was left speechless at his reply.

4

At Sirajpur, Bibha was exiled in a gigantic bungalow in the sahebs' compound. She asked that her father- and mother-in-law be invited there, but Jatish dismissed her request. After their son's return, his parents came on their own to see him once, then went back to their home in the village. They now began to receive some money every month from their civilian son, as a divine reward for all the virtue they had accumulated! Bibha well realized that they would not have survived very long in this place. How could they, amidst such indulgence in poultry and meat, such depravity? Her own inner soul rebelled against it, against the frivolity and lack of spirituality, but she could say nothing. Jatish had always been dominating, but now, having become a Civilian, he had grown even more autocratic. Bibha silently feared her husband. She would secretly use some utensils and desi items that her mother had sent along with her. Once, when he saw Bibha tying her hair with a broad desi ribbon, Jatish yanked it off and sent for silk ribbons from the market. From that day on, Bibha gave up braiding her hair with ribbons.

For some reason, Bibha found it difficult to pass her time in the enormous rooms of the bungalow, surrounded by lonely fields. But she found it hard to say what it was she lacked, what made her unhappy. Jatish never mingled with the local Bengalis, so Bibha, too, had developed no particular intimacy with her neighbours. Every evening she would go for an outing with Jatish in their phaeton. Partying here today, there tomorrow, there was no end to the glamour and merriment. But Bibha did not enjoy such things. When Jatish left for the courthouse, she would sit silently at her bedroom window. Before her stretched a bare grassless field, right up to the horizon. In that desolate hour of noon, gazing at the field, Bibha remembered the loving parental home she had been familiar with all her life, recalling her mother's tireless devotion to service. She would personally sweep and clean her father's puja room. Bibha also remembered, again and again, that image of the Motherland on the wall of her own room. Standing beneath that picture, she had made a tearful vow one holy morning that in the course of this humble life of hers, she would dispel the Mother's grief. But where had that vow vanished? Her husband had been carried away on the powerful tide of "civilization". Who could draw him back into the field of duty by telling him of the Mother's sorrow? If only Bibha were capable of that!

The Pujas were around the corner. Bibha's mother had sent clothes and other gifts for her absent daughter, and on her outing that evening, Bibha wore the new sari her mother had sent.

"What sort of clothes are these?" Jatish demanded as soon as he mounted the carriage. "Why aren't you wearing silk? And what's this awful perfume you have applied?"

"Ma has sent this sari for me," Bibha replied in a trembling voice. "She also sent me a bottle of Dilkhosh with it, I've added a few drops to my handkerchief."

"Why do you use these obnoxious things?" Jatish protested. "I don't touch anything besides English fragrances."

"But I don't like English perfume," Bibha said, rebelliously, but it was not easy to argue with Jatish, and she fell silent.

Again, the 30th of Aswin came around. The day would be fruitless, thought Bibha despondently, for Jatish would surely dismiss such matters as nonsense. From daybreak, Bibha saw groups of young men on the march, singing songs, even in this place. A few boys gathered at her doorstep, singing. Jatish had gone out after his morning tea. A little boy, the youngest in the group, entered the house and touched Bibha's feet.

"Ma, today is the 30th of Aswin," he pleaded. "Today our Mother requests all of you to refrain from lighting your cooking stoves. Let every Bengali survive on fruit."

Bibha's eyes filled with tears. How could she convey to them that she too was a Swadeshi just like them, that though she followed an anglicized way of life here, she had been deeply committed to Swadeshi at her parental home! Without elaborating, Bibha handed five rupees to the boy and said: "I donate this money to your Swadeshi committee here, but I request you not to disclose my name to anyone."

The boys agreed and went on their way. Bibha took some rakhis from them which she sent to her dadas in Kolkata. In that cheerless house, that auspicious date, 30th Aswin, came and went without being noticed.

That night, the wind dropped and it became very warm. To make things worse, the punkha puller kept dozing off. His sleep disrupted, Jatin repeatedly scolded awake the coolie. Ultimately, losing patience, he got up and thrashed him soundly, flinging him from the veranda onto the courtyard below. Striking stone, the poor man's forehead split open and blood poured forth. Wiping himself with his faded garment, the docile coolie came back and resumed pulling the punkha, back and forth. Bibha felt as if her own body had borne the brunt of this violence. Sleepless and still, she lay on the bed. Ultimately, when she saw that Jatish was sound asleep, she rose silently and went to the window. The field stretched to the horizon, flooded with faint moonlight. In the distance, a couple of trees stood motionless. The night breeze rustled through the leaves. In a nearby house, boys were singing, and Bibha heard a boyish voice:

Coming close, then turning back in tears, who are you?
Gazing at my face in futile hope, who are you?
Alas, my Mother, it is you!

Tears streamed from Bibha's eyes. She felt as if their Mother, disgraced and abandoned, was walking away alone across that moonlit field, leaving her children behind. As if the night breeze was blowing through her loosened tresses and her white aanchal. Mother, please don't go away! Forgive your foolish children and return!

From that day, Bibha's health began to decline sharply. Hearing of her indisposition, her father brought her home. She had come back home after a year, but she was not the same Bibha anymore.

"How thin you have become, Bibha!" her mother exclaimed.

"I don't know why, Ma," Bibha replied. "Perhaps I could not tolerate the water and the atmosphere of Sirajpur."

In the joy of returning home, Bibha spent a couple of days in high spirits, but gradually took to her bed. Examining her, the doctor pronounced her illness incurable.

Lying in her sickbed, Bibha's thoughts and anxieties seemed endless. Each day, her dadas would bring her a different set of bad tidings. Some days they would tell her that so-and-so had been jailed for no fault of his own. Other days they would say a terrible famine had broken out, with countless numbers dying of starvation. Hearing these things, Bibha would gaze vacantly at the sky, her entire being dissolving with the sorrows of her Swadesh, her own nation.

One day Bibha noticed her brothers hastily gulping down their food in order to rush off somewhere.

"Where are you going?" she asked them curiously.

"Haven't you heard?" they replied. "Last evening, at Goldighi, there was a violent clash between the police and our boys. An old woman was trying to make her way through that crowd, the police superintendent deliberately shoved her so she fell. A couple of boys who were close by tried to help her and came to blows with the police. They have taken the boys into custody. The trial will take place today."

8

For the next two or three days Bibha's brothers went in and out, then one day they returned, looking downcast.

"What is it, Dada, what's happened?" Bibha asked them.

"Both have been sent to prison. Unless they pay a hundred rupees each, they will be jailed for a month."

"Can't they raise a hundred rupees?"

"Impossible! Both are very badly off."

"If we inform Baba he will immediately donate all he has, but after that he'll run into severe financial difficulties," said Bibha's Mejodada, the second of her elder brothers. "That is why we have kept him in the dark. He will never borrow."

As her brothers prepared to set out again, Bibha called out to them.

"Listen, Dada, I have a pearl necklace worth almost two hundred and fifty rupees. Sell it set the boys free."

Their sister's words brought tears to the brothers' eyes, but they protested: "No, Bibha, if Jatishbabu gets to hear, you will be in trouble."

"No, no, he will not get to know," she assured them.

The ailing Bibha made such tearful entreaties that just to please her, her dadas agreed to take the necklace.

That night Bibha slept well after a long time. But from the following day, there was no hope of her staying alive. Once she coughed up blood during a prolonged bout, and that caused a sharp drop in her pulse-rate. Her parents and brothers gazed at her frail, beautiful face, suffused with an other-worldly tranquility. Once her mother heard her say something indistinctly. Bringing her ear close to Bibha's lips, she heard her say, in a faint voice:

"Ah, don't beat him, don't beat him anymore, or he will die!"

Once again she spoke, in a hoarse, inarticulate voice:

A new sun will rise that morn,
A new life shall then be born,
No dream, nor idle tale, is this,
For it will come, that day of bliss!

That very day, Bibha's soul departed for its heavenly abode, fleeing the cage of this broken body. At exactly the same moment, a group of singing boys came to the doorstep, with the two boys, released from jail, who had come to thank Bibha. Her brother invited them upstairs to see her. Bibha seemed to have fallen asleep, cradled in the lap of a limitless peace. The eternal, immortal beauty of the Mother's image adorned her countenance with extraordinary grace, even in death. Hearts filled to overflowing, eyes full of devotion, they gazed upon her. Not once did they feel that they were standing beside a dead person. It seemed that this divine image had been created by the Maker, that the breath of heaven would instantly bring it to life. Slowly, with reverence, they touched the dust from Bibha's feet to their own foreheads and went back, singing in tear-choked voices:

In serving you, let our days on earth pass by;
O Ma! Let 'Bande Mataram' ever be our cry!

Jatishchandra received the news of Bibha's death with profound sorrow. As he could not afford to take time off from work, he had not been able to visit Bibha. To dispel the emptiness in his heart, he soon married the daughter of a gentleman just back from foreign shores.

Translator's Note: *Swadeshi*: a movement that involved boycotting British goods in support of indigenous products, to promote self-sufficiency, during one phase of India's struggle for Independence; the word means "of one's own country".

Annapurna: goddess of bounty, another name for Parvati, who went from home to home seeking rice when Shiva visited her in the guise of a mendicant. *30 Aswin*: on 30 Aswin 1312 (16 October 1905), the British Government split Bengal into two parts, sparking widespread protests. *Rakhi*: the holy thread tied by sisters on their brothers' wrists to celebrate the bond between them, during the festival of the same name; during the agitation that followed the Partition of Bengal, people showed unity by tying rakhis on each other's wrists. *Dilkhosh*: an indigenous fragrance associated with the Swadeshi spirit. *Punkha puller*: person who manually operated an old-fashioned ceiling fan by pulling on a rope.

Baruni

GIRIBALA DEBI

FATHERLESS and motherless as she was, when he took the orphan Baruni away from her rich paternal uncles and brought her to his own home, Prakash Majumdar, who earned fifty rupees a month, had not dreamt that he would see stars when it came to marrying off his maternal cousin. At that time he and his wife, Shailabala, were convinced that hearing Baruni's pathos-filled life story, and attracted by her large, dark, heavy-lashed, melancholy eyes, some educated, large-hearted young man would marry her without a dowry and take her home. But as Baruni grew older, their illusions began to disperse. They realized that their imagined utopia was for her a distant dream. In the hope of relieving himself of the encumbrance that his female cousin had now become, when the distraught Prakash asked the elders of the neighbourhood – Nilkhudo, Harida, Choudhuri Moshai and the others – for advice and suggestions, they unanimously counselled him: "Send for a carriage and deposit your burden where it belongs. The girl has kakas. They can marry her off or let her remain a spinster, as they please. Why is it any concern of yours, bapu?"

But Prakash showed no sign at all of dispatching his burden to the place where she belonged. Rather, his anxiety about finding a match for her continued to increase. Where there was no likelihood of a combined profusion of gold and jewels materializing, the fathers of prospective grooms (and sometimes the grooms themselves) showed not the slightest interest in seeing the prospective bride.

At Prakash's importunate request, the fathers of some would-be-grooms, and even some would-be-grooms themselves, did come to inspect the sacrificial beast; but beyond praising Dinu Moira's rasgullas and Bhim Nag's sandesh, Prakash did not hear them utter a single positive word. Yet the man had such amazing patience that he would not lose heart. Night and day, tenaciously, he haunted the doorsteps of the bhadralok, the civilized gentry. Seeing no way out, some of them irritably sent word though their attendants from the inner quarters: "Babu is not at home, you can't meet him now." Some others, in an excess of generosity, informed him: "If the girl had been a little fairer we would have had no reason to object. Our son has told his friends he will not marry unless the girl has a milk-and-roses complexion," and so on. One marriageable young man, casting a bleary glance through his spectacles at Prakash's agonized, anxious countenance, smiled: "What's all this talk of money, Moshai? If the girl met our approval, would money be a problem? Not that this girl of yours is not to our liking, but then, how shall I say it, her face is not exactly oval like an egg. And her eyes are not quite almond-shaped. Otherwise … but let that be. Keep trying, and you will surely find a groom."

The bottom line was that nobody was crying out to be married without the prospect of gaining a single cowrie – was it their bounden duty to marry her? If neither father nor guardians had the wherewithal to offer the equivalent of the girl's weight in cash, why entertain fantasies about marrying her off, baba? Was a bridegroom some throwaway scrap to be picked up casually from the roadside?

2

Although prospective bridegrooms did not cast a second glance at Baruni's unappreciated looks, youth did not pass her by. Like spray cast up by a moonlit river in the monsoons, burgeoning youth unfurled its flag, showering radiance upon the graceful limbs and rosy cheeks of the flower-like maiden. The surging waves of this youthful voluptuousness perturbed Baruni even more. Why such a splendid flowering of youthful beauty in the body of an unfortunate orphan? And was Age, wretched creature, also about to announce her fifteenth year, consigning her fourteenth to the womb of the past? Baruni grew desperate to somehow conceal herself from the world's mocking gaze, but without success. The neighbours' inquisitive eyes, at noontime gossip sessions on the secluded sun-warmed terrace, recalled the grace of the lotus blossoming in the pond. Standing in the shade, Bindu of the Dutta family called out to Nirada on the terrace opposite: "Have you heard, bhai, that the unfortunate Majumdar girl couldn't find a customer even today?"

"Aha, what's the hurry!" Nirada responded enthusiastically. "Barely twenty-three! In time, so many things will happen – even homely sweetmeats will grow wings!"

The Chatterjees had no staircase leading up to the terrace so the women had to stand at their windows to join in the gossip. The Chatterjee matron stuck her head out of the window. "Who will marry her off?" she asked in a voice full of mockery. "Their family ties are so tenuous after all. Can't a girl be palmed off in the marriage market if one tries hard enough? Truth be told, …" Breaking off, she glanced at her companions and smiled a deep mysterious smile.

It did not take long for this snide insinuation to reach Shailabala's ears.

"By hook or by crook, we must get Thakurjhi married within the month of Baisakh itself," she insisted to Prakash. "I'll give the ornaments I'm wearing, and you must go to her kakas to arrange for some money. Her father had some substance after all, by law she is the rightful heir to that: don't forget to mention it."

"It will be futile for me to go there, Shaila," said Prakash, smiling a little wanly at his wife's suggestion. "Her father's younger brothers had already declared: 'If these people take her away as a show of family rivalry, let them also face the music when it comes to getting her married.' Still, I think I shall pay them a visit. When the responsibility is mine, how can I afford to not swallow my pride? Today, having heard of a possible match, I dropped in at their place as well."

"What is the man's name?" demanded Shaila, her voice full of emotion. "Where does he live, the prospective bridegroom? What does he do?"

"Spare me Shaila! Let me answer all your questions first, before you ask any more," Prakash smiled, seeing his wife's agitation. "His name is Manohar Sanyal. He stays in the Potoldanga Street Mess and is a third year student at City College. He has in-house dining arrangements. He is his own guardian, and if he likes the girl, will not ask for money. But ..." Prakash paused.

"Why did you say 'But' and stop?" cried Shaila anxiously. "Is the young man not of good moral character then?"

"No, my dear, that's not the problem, I have checked that out with the mess, his moral character can't be faulted. But still, you will not like him."

"A young man of good character, well educated, why wouldn't I like him? Are my tastes so very peculiar?" demanded Shaila angrily. "Have I said that you must not marry your sister off unless you find the son of an Emir from Kabul?"

Upon seeing his wife's rage, Prakash could not contain his merriment.

"Why are you so angry, Shaila?" he asked, his laughter resounding through the house. "It's because I know your tastes are of a very high order that I am somewhat hesitant to speak of this young man. He has no other fault, but his appearance is not at all attractive. His complexion is extremely dark, and he has protruding teeth."

"If his appearance is not attractive, is he to blame for that?" responded Shaila after a moment's careful consideration. "One's looks are not made to order after all: the Almighty has a hand in that. He is educated, of good moral character: what more can a man boast of? How do looks matter in a man, or symmetry in a pearl!"

Prakash was somewhat reassured to hear Shaila say that it was not necessary for a man to be attractive. He had no desire to consign his orphan sister to an unknown fate; even though it was not in his power, he was trying to find a match for Baruni where the girl could live in peace and happiness. But when it came to ensuring happiness for her sister-in-law, so dear to her heart and the living image of her brother, Shaila's eagerness far exceeded Prakash's own. She did not easily like anybody; now, seeing her being so kind about an unattractive young man, Prakash was very surprised. Fearing that any delay might cause Shaila to change her mind, he wasted no time in trying to arrange for a viewing of the bride-to-be.

3

At noon, as soon as they were done with their daytime meal, Shaila started dressing Baruni for the occasion. This afternoon, the bridegroom Manohar Babu was coming to approve his would-be beloved. Shaila was decking her out in a manner designed to ensure that at very first sight, Baruni would win the heart of this young man, this B.A. student who craved beauty. Having draped Baruni in a turquoise sari and arranged her heavy, shampooed tresses and secured them with a red ribbon, Shaila began to grind khoir to prepare catechu paste. Adorning her sister-in-law's body with some of her own choice ornaments, placing a khoir dot on her forehead, turning Baruni's beautiful, abashed face this way and that to gaze at it adoringly, Shaila playfully recited in an undertone:

'Midst a host of golden lotuses, upon a coral throne
Sat the beautiful Baruni, braiding her hair
With pearls; therein he appeared ...

Turning her face away from her sister-in-law, Baruni gave a little smile.

"What's come over you today, Boudi?" she asked. "Why recite such highflown verse, as if from *Meghnadbadh* itself ?"

Shortly before dusk, sporting an immaculate hairstyle, suffusing the air with the tender fragrance of ittar and rose, Manohar Babu made his auspicious entry into Prakash's abode. From her secluded vantage point, observing the groom's twisted, Ashtavakra-like figure, Shaila's shining lamp of joyous enthusiasm was extinguished with a single puff. Is this the bridegroom then? The one with whom my golden statuette must be united? It was like placing a necklace of pearls around a monkey's neck! Did it not occur to her even once that he too might turn his face away in dismissal and leave? Dark and hideous he might be, but he was the bridegroom, after all, and a B.A. to boot! Could Shailabala afford to slight him? Despondently, she repeated a poem to herself learnt by rote in childhood, in order to discipline her mind: "What do looks matter bapu, if there are virtues aplenty?" Her rebellious, agitated mind was somewhat calmed by these words of authority, but not entirely set at rest.

After silently scrutinizing Baruni for a long time, Manohar Babu rose to his feet, emerged from the room, and pronounced his opinion in sombre tones: "The girl is beautiful, no doubt, but nothing extraordinary. And I detect a flaw: an extreme lack of liveliness and sparkle. She seems strangely lifeless."

Prakash was left in no doubt that this was a pretext for

demanding money. But Shaila's jewellery was their only asset, where would they find more than that? They had hoped that in exchange for a few of Shaila's ornaments, Baruni would be rescued from her predicament, but now the import of Manohar Babu's words cast a dark shadow of depression on their countenances. Simultaneously, screened from public view, another heart began to burn with pain, sadness, shame and contempt, consumed by a deep private agony. That heart was Baruni's.

4

Approaching Baruni's kakas for financial help for her wedding, Prakash came back humiliated and wounded to the heart. Shaila felt she had been pierced with a poison-tipped dart. Her husband may be poor, but he didn't deserve to be dishonoured. Was this his reward for offering a place in his household to someone else's daughter purely out of pity? For trading all they had in exchange for a single person's happiness? All Shaila's rage and antagonism were directed at Manohar Babu. For someone as ugly as a ghoul to demand money by finding fault with another's matchless beauty! To think that my godlike husband should be insulted, but not the devil who is capable of making all sorts of excuses for rejecting such beauty, along with ornaments worth a thousand sovereigns! Tossing and turning all night, tormented beyond endurance, Shaila was unable to sleep. Prakash knew his wife well, so even in the midst of such suffering he couldn't help being amused.

The next day, once Prakash had left for work after his morning meal at half past nine, Shaila was ready with her entire plan of action. Firm resolve radiated from her youthful countenance.

Casually entering the bedroom Shaila found her eight-year-old son Bikashchandra arranging his books and preparing for school.

"Biku, can you do something for me?" Shaila asked him tenderly.

"Can't I just, Ma!" said Bikash enthusiastically, "I'm grown up now, after all. Just the other day Baba couldn't find you any chocolate coloured thread for your sewing, but I got it for you!"

His mother smiled broadly, hearing her son speak of his age and experience.

"Yes, Biku is now very grown up indeed, and he can do all sorts of things," she agreed, feigning amazement. "Do you know where Manohar Babu and his companions live? If I give you something, can you deliver it to his mess?"

"Of course, I can, Ma. The mess is opposite our school, and the other day I went with Baba right up to Manohar Babu's room, didn't I?"

"Today is Saturday; at two o'clock, when Kishan goes to fetch you, I'll send something with him. Leave Kishan downstairs and go up to deliver the packet to Manohar Babu, then come away. Understood? said Shaila.

Nodding acquiescence, Bikash left for school.

5

After school, carrying the book-shaped, paper-wrapped package, secured with red ribbon, that their servant Kishan had brought with him, Bikash arrived at Mahohar Babu's door, barely concealing an irrepressible urge to see what was inside the wrapping. In the room he found, instead of Manohar Babu, another young man of about twenty or twenty-one, handsome, attractive and fair-complexioned, on a chair, reading the newspaper. He was the son of a zamindar from East Bengal. His name was Anilchandra Roy, and he had recently graduated from medical college. Looking in amazement at this unknown young boy, Anil asked him:

"What is your name, khoka? Where have you come from?"

"My name is Bikashchandra Majumdar," replied the boy, confidently. "My father's name is Srijukta Prakashchandra Majumdar. I have come to meet Manohar Babu."

Bikash's words reminded Anil that a match was being negotiated between Manohar Babu and Prakash Majumdar's daughter. He was now curious about why this little boy had come to Manohar Babu in the afternoon. Drawing Bikash close affectionately he asked with a smile:

"Has your pishima approved Manohar Babu, khoka?"

"Why do you call me khoka as if I'm a little boy?" protested Bikash, somewhat offended because he felt this mode of address belittled him. "My name is Bikash, isn't it?"

"Yes it is, and I made a mistake. Your name is Bikash, not Khoka. Now tell me, Bikash Babu ..."

"Wrong again!" interrupted Bikash. "Why do you call me Bikash Babu when I am so much younger than you?"

"I shan't go wrong again," promised Anil, charmed by the boy's simple statements. "Why have you come to see Manohar Babu?"

"I have come to give this to him," Bikash declared, showing him the package.

Anil privately concluded that this must be the girl's doing, now beyond the sanctioned age for marriage. What gift had she sent her would-be husband this afternoon through the hands of a young boy, unbeknownst to everyone at home? Unable to gauge the nature of the gift from his interrogation of Bikash, Anil asked him eagerly:

"Tell me, Bikash, has Manohar Babu taken a great fancy to your pishima? And what did your pishima say after seeing him?"

"What is there for pishima to say? Yes, she did say once,

that evening when it was raining heavily, pishima said to ma, if someone can accept me into his own home without a price, without sizing me up like a bottle-gourd or a pumpkin from the garden, I will worship him like a god even if he is lame, ugly and blind in one eye. You see, my pishima is very good-looking, just like you, but still Manohar Babu has said that her appearance lacks animation."

Anil couldn't keep from laughing as he listened to these wise-sounding words so gravely uttered by Bikash.

"Anil Babu, have you summoned up a flood of laughter in your room today? Whom are you laughing with?" asked Manohar Babu as he entered. Then, seeing Bikash, he stared at him in amazement.

"I have come to deliver this to you," Bikash informed him, handing over the package.

"What does it contain?"

"Go ahead and open it, Manohar Babu, this boy can't tell you what it contains," mocked Anil, before Bikash could speak. "It must be something nice, your would-be wife has sent it as a gift."

Manohar Babu's countenance brightened and his heart overflowed with imagined bliss. His prospective bride had sent him an amorous gift because she was attracted to him! What could it be? Perhaps a book or a notebook full of poems, or a photograph. Face flushed, heart aflutter, Manohar Babu began unwrapping the package.

Peeling off layer after layer of paper, the object that revealed itself did not please Manohar Babu at all. It was a beautiful mirror, notable for its elaborately ornate frame. The first image it reflected was his own face.

Manohar Babu turned red with shame and humiliation. Unable to quell his rage, he flung the mirror to the floor where, with a resounding crash, it shattered into a hundred fragments.

It was already three in the afternoon, and many students had returned from college. Hearing the noise they gathered in front of Manohar Babu's room. Reading Anil's sign language, it didn't take them long to gauge the actual state of affairs. A smile flitted across the lips of some, while a few collapsed laughing on the ground. Shaking with mirth, his head on the table, Anil caused a new diversion by tipping over an inkpot close at hand.

Senseless with rage, Manohar Babu declared in a voice trembling with anger, "What! To insult me so! If my name is Manohar I swear I will be avenged. What presumption, to send me a mirror! Brazen, shameless hussy! For such people, it's best not to stay at home, but rather …"

At this point Anil intervened. Patient and restrained, he said: "Manohar Babu, why fly into such a rage? There is nothing to be angry about here, rather, there is cause for shame. Nowadays we make so many unjust demands on unwed girls; isn't there a limit to their patience as well? This girl who has sent you a mirror, we can see her intelligence and courage. Just as we have preferences, can't they claim the same as well? Whatever our appearance may be, we try to find fault with theirs. That's what they find intolerable."

At the very mention of appearances, Manohar Babu flared up like an ignited flame.

"To speak of appearances about those who behave like whores …" he screamed, his voice trembling with rage.

"Be silent, Manohar Babu!" roared Anil, like a lion roused from slumber, before Manohar Babu could finish. "You have no right to insult the women of a genteel family in such degrading language."

"No, I have no right! And you do, I suppose? How long have you known them, Anil Babu?"

"Don't utter another disrespectful word, Manohar Babu, not one!" retorted Anil sharply. "I shall go personally to Prakash

Babu and beg for that girl's hand in marriage! If they agree, I myself will marry Prakash Babu's sister."

6

It was already four in the afternoon. Finding that Bikash had still not returned, all sorts of fears surfaced in the anxious mother's mind. Realizing how outrageously she had acted, in a fit of rage and without her husband's knowledge, Shaila was overcome by the scorpion sting of remorse. Her cheerful countenance was overcast with gloom.

"O Bari, where's Biku?" Prakash called out, as he settled down to his evening snack after coming home from work and changing into fresh clothes.

Although she could not fully comprehend the whole story, Baruni had a fair idea of what her sister-in-law had done. So without responding to her brother, she rushed from the room in embarrassment.

"I have done something terribly wrong today," confessed Shaila with quaking heart, tearful eyes, lowered head and remorseful voice. "I sent Biku somewhere without telling you."

"Oh, I understand, you sent him to watch the bioscope didn't you?" guessed Prakash, looking inquiringly at his wife.

"No, my dear husband, not to the bioscope."

Shaila said no more. Looking at her despondent face, Prakash was about to say something when Bikash's elated voice was heard in the courtyard.

Hearing him, Shaila's face brightened with joy. Rushing out, she drew him close and said tenderly: "Come and have something to eat first, Biku, we'll talk afterwards."

"I have eaten already. Come with me, Baba," sang Bikash, almost leaping with joy as he dragged his father by the hand towards the outer portion of the house.

Entering the sitting room, Prakash was surprised to see a handsome young man on a chair. Seeing Prakash, the young man rose to his feet. Folding his hands in a namaskar, he humbly declared: "My name is Anilchandra Roy. It is you I have come to meet."

"Yes, I saw you the other day at Manohar Babu's mess, they told me who you were." With these words Prakash offered Anil a chair and took one himself.

Some time passed. Observing Anil's silence, Prakash asked, after some hesitation: "Is there anything I can do for you?"

"Yes, sir, I have come to you with a request", admitted Anil diffidently. "You have a sister of marriageable age. If you don't find me unworthy …" Anil couldn't continue.

"How can I consider you unworthy, Anil Babu!" exclaimed Prakash, bursting with joy. "May the Lord bring you happiness, but I am very poor and without any resources."

"It is because you lack resources that I have come to you, Prakash Babu."

"You can say such a thing because you have a lofty mind. But will your father agree? I don't wish to offend your parents just to relieve myself of my burden."

"You need have no worries on that account," Anil responded gently. "When you meet my parents you will realize that they are unworldly in the extreme. You say I have a lofty mind, but compared to them I am utterly base. I can only try to emulate their ideals, but without success. If I take this step they will be pleased, not offended."

Prakash's eyes filled with tears of joy and gratitude.

"You are a divine soul!" he declared, his voice choked with emotion. "What can I say to you, my dear boy? My blessings upon you – may you live long! Shall I go and fetch Baruni then?"

Anil was very keen to see her once before leaving. A girl so brave, so unafraid, who knew how to return an insult when she received one, how beautiful she must be! But suddenly he remembered Bikash's words: "Pishima said, if only someone can accept me into his own home without a price, without sizing me up like a bottle-gourd or a pumpkin from the garden..."

"No, Prakash Babu," Anil said in a low voice, overcoming his temptation. "There is no need for me to see her."

7

It was a bright, moonlit night in the warm month of Baisakh. The wedding pavilion was redolent with the fragrance of massed blossoms. A southern breeze went wild with the fervour of ardent emotion. Amidst the sweet strains of the Sahana on the shehnai, it was the moment for shubhodrishti, when the bride and groom look at each other for the first time. Baruni, at the repeated urgings of the women of the house, opened her eyes like a pair of blossoming buds and saw an attractive, handsome, godlike young man, his forehead adorned with sandalpaste. He looked at her eagerly. Their eyes met. At the very first glance, the young girl yielded her heart's offering of amorous prayer-blossoms and closed her eyes in an effusion of bliss.

The Fruit of Knowledge[1]
(a fable)

ROKEYA SAKHAWAT HOSSAIN

ADAM and Eve lived in the Garden of Eden. As guests of the Almighty Lord, they led a blissful life in Heaven, free of want. The Almighty had only forbidden the pair to taste the fruit of one particular tree.

One day while wandering the beautiful, saffron-embellished paths of the celestial garden, Eve found herself under the shade of the forbidden tree. Enchanted, she gazed at the loveliness of the garden. While listening to the sweet chirping of birds on the branches, she absently plucked some fruit from the tree and tasted it.

As soon as she did so, Eve's intellect awakened. It was as if her mind's inner eye had opened. She realized that despite their royal lifestyle as guests of the King, her predicament was such that she did not even have a scrap to cover her nakedness. She immediately spread her almost-knee-length tresses over her entire body. Her heart felt weighed down with sorrow, filled with a strange, novel yearning.

At this juncture, Adam appeared on the scene. Eve offered him the fruit she held in her hand, and upon eating the fruit of knowledge plucked by his wife, Adam's intellect too woke to life. Now, in every fibre of his being, he began to feel the wretchedness of his own existence. Was this heaven then? A loveless, inactive, idle life – was this heavenly bliss? He realized too, that he was a royal prisoner, without the power to step outside the boundaries of the Garden of Eden! He lived in a magnificent palace built of gold and silver bricks, cemented with coral and powdered pearl, yet he had not a cowrie's worth of possessions that he could call his own. In fact he did not even possess a piece of cloth to wear! What manner of royal luxury was this? Shattered was the dreamlike ignorance that masqueraded as heavenly bliss. He felt the awakening of knowledge, sharply and clearly! Delusion and complacency were replaced by awareness and agitation.

"What magic kept us deluded for so long!" he exclaimed to Eve. "How happy we were in that state!"

"Indeed!" responded Eve. "This exquisite land of beauty, where the ground is carpeted with a fragrant bed of saffron flowers; this wanton creeper, bejewelled with diamond blossoms; these lotus-hued flowers, blooming on tree-tops adorned with emerald leaves – such things please the eye, but do they fulfil the heart's desires? The honeyed waters of the pool of ambrosia quench our thirst no doubt, but do they satisfy the craving of our souls? What need have we for such heavenly luxuries?" The couple grew desperate for an unknown transformation.

Strolling in His garden, the Almighty saw Adam and his spouse hide behind a tree when they spotted Him. He called out to them, but their hurt pride and embarrassment prevented them from approaching Him. The all-knowing Lord of the Universe was aware of the facts.

"So you want independence, do you?" He demanded in fury. "Away with you, then! Go down to Earth and find out what joy independence has to offer!"

That very day, Adam and Eve suffered a Fall and found themselves on Earth. Here, overcoming all sorts of trials and contradictions such as need-and-abundance, grief-and-rejoicing, sickness-and-health, they attained true conjugal bliss. Eve loved her daughters; she blessed them, announcing that her female descendants would live long; enjoy happiness and peace at home; and that their hearts would store an endless wealth of love.

On the other hand, Adam favoured his sons, but because he did not possess such powerful desires, he imparted no special boon to his male offspring.

In accordance with Mother Eve's blessings, her multitude of daughters grew at twice the rate they were born, and attained longevity at a quadrupled rate! Adam's beloved sons were so pampered, they would fall ill twice as fast as they were born, and die four times faster! If they did not die of natural causes, they died fighting and killing each other on the battlefield! One group would rot in prison, while the rest suffered all sorts of afflictions!

The half-eaten fruit of knowledge that Eve had flung down on Earth when cast out of Heaven, seeded in the eastern part of the world and from it grew an enormous tree. In time, it was laden with fruits and blossom, but the people of that region did not know then how to take proper care of the tree. Heaps of ripe fruit would lie at the foot of the tree; foxes and crows would eat their fill. The leftover fruit would accumulate on the shore of the Shanta river, and a few roll over into its depths.

In due course, the waters of the river, mixed with the juice of the knowledge-fruit, merged with the great ocean, at the other end of which lay Pareestan, land of the fairies.

The people of Pareestan were very attractive, but they had little to boast of beyond their physical beauty. Their land was forested with makal, a wild plant with beautiful but foul-tasting fruit. There was an acute shortage of edible foodstuff. Despite their various manouevres, and all their effort and trouble, the jinns could not harvest suitable fruit from their harsh, infertile land. The parees, fairy women of Pareestan, lived in pleasure-houses comparable to Amaravati, surrounded by luxury items of all kinds and a profusion of wealth. Even so, they were plagued by heartburn – such are the tricks played by destiny!

Once a few jinns, driven to desperation by hunger, swallowed some of the salty water of the Enormous Ocean while they were bathing. As soon as they drank it, the veil of ignorance that enveloped them was lifted and they could easily solve the complex, hitherto unsolved problem of procuring sufficient food. Enlightenment showed them the way out.

On that day, the jinns decided that they would travel to various countries and engage in mercantile activities. Thereafter, loading their ships with makal fruit, they set out on the pretext of trading. After roaming various destinations, the jinns' ship arrived at a port in Kanak Dwip, the Golden Isle, off the shore of the Enormous Ocean. Kanak Dwip was inhabited by a race of golden-bodied people.

The jinn merchants gazed wide-eyed at the prosperous main city of Kanak Dwip. They had assumed that there was no country wealthier than their own, that their mere touch turned dust to gold. But the land of Kanak Dwip seemed like a virtual treasure-trove! The trees bore many varieties of delicious fruit, chief among them the mango. The cultured, saintly people lived mainly on fruits. If only we could once delude these people! thought the jinn merchants.

In exchange for makal, they took some varieties of mango – sonamukhi, andharmanik, and so on – from Kanak Dwip's inhabitants. In this way, every year, they brought a shipload of makal and carried off a shipload of mangoes. Gradually, their trade began to flourish, but as their business grew, Kanak Dwip began experiencing a shortage of mangoes.

The following year, noticing a scarcity of mangoes in the market, the traders grew worried. Abandoning the cities, they began scouring the provinces for mangoes. In the villages they found the autumn fields full of golden paddy, the farmers happily carrying loads of it home. "These people don't know what pangs of hunger are!" sighed the jinns when they saw them. After some hesitation, a trader asked a farmer for paddy in exchange for makal but the farmer didn't understand what he said. A group of sturdy boys and girls surrounded the jinns in amazement and began inspecting their beautiful faces. "How ironical!" the traders thought to themselves. "It seems we have become a curiosity for these farmers' children!"

The traders somehow communicated their request to the farmer. He was unwilling to give them paddy in exchange for makal at first, but his son said:

"Give it to them, they are starving. We have so much paddy to spare."[2]

In Pareestan, so advanced in knowledge and science, the number of trading ships multiplied by the year. Now there was no shortage of food, the parees suffered no hardships of any sort. As the fancy took them, they would travel to Kanak Dwip from time to time on their magic chariots. A close intimacy developed between them and the women of Kanak Dwip, and as a result, the latter tried to imitate the attire and adornments of the parees. It only remained for them to copy their fairy wings!

Formerly, a shipload or two of makal fruit would be supplied, just once a year; but later, countless shiploads began to arrive at Kanak Dwip, several times a year. And masses of paddy were exported to Pareestan. Such was the magic attraction of makal that the farmers could no longer restrain themselves. They stopped storing enough paddy for the whole year. Gradually there came a time when the rice the farmers harvested from the field today would be sold tomorrow in exchange for makal. And so a rakshasi arrived at Kanak Dwip, the demoness called Famine, and made her home there.

While all this trade in makal was going on, something

special took place. On the shore of the Enormous Ocean grew an exquisite guava tree. Nourished by water in which the juice of the knowledge-fruit had mingled, the guavas acquired some of its qualities. The jinns and fairies would carefully collect the guavas for themselves, but one day, while the merchants were loading makal onto the ship, a few guavas happened to fall off the tree onto the ship. They were brought to Kanak Dwip along with the makal, and sold.

A few fortunate inhabitants of Kanak Dwip ate the guavas from Pareestan and from the seed of this fruit, a guava tree took root in Kanak Dwip as well.

More than a hundred years passed.

Thanks to the guavas, a few civilized gentlemen of Kanak Dwip now awakened from their dreamlike state. After hundreds of years of enchanted slumber, what a rude awakening that was! Once blind, they now gained sight only to find themselves plunged into intense darkness! They gazed all around them in wide-eyed amazement and saw that the jinns had robbed the land of all they possessed in exchange for nothing but useless makal. Like leeches, the jinns were sucking the remaining blood from their bosoms. Their hearts broke at the sight of the poverty and misery of Kanak, shattering into a hundred fragments.

Gone was the mango orchard; no fruit remained on any fruit tree; no golden grain in the fields; the womb of the land, once replete with treasures, was full of dust. In every home rose the cry of despair: "O for rice! O for some rice to eat! Alas!" The farmer no longer looked hale and hearty; his frame had become skeletal and all he wore was a tattered scrap of cloth. The inhabitants of Kanak Dwip were left with nothing but makal and more makal. In the city, lining both sides of the main street, were market-stalls full of makal; in village fairs and bazaars there was makal, and in the village sweet shop, more makal.

The Kanak Dwip dwellers had received a boon disguised as a curse, for along with the makal they had also acquired the knowledge-guava. It did not take them long to think of a solution. They vowed not to accept any more makal. One and all, men, women and children, they took a vow to never again be deluded by the magic of makal. Their enthusiasm and tremendous strength could never have come to pass if they hadn't suffered the makal plague. And so, with hearts full of gratitude, they thanked the jinns a hundred times.

The jinn merchants duly arrived at the port with shiploads of makal, but this time it did not sell. When masses of attractive-looking makal began to rot, the merchants had no choice but to break the bad news to Pareestan.

In the Pareestan chamber of commerce, the news caused a great upheaval. The tide of turbulence even stirred the deep and tranquil waters of the Enormous Ocean! Ultimately, a toothless, white-haired old man declared: "Go and investigate why the inhabitants of Kanak Dwip have grown indifferent to makal."

Travelling to many parts of Kanak Dwip, from diverse popular sources, the merchants gathered that the makal-opponents were those who had tasted the guava. They transmitted this news to Pareestan by magical means, and that very day the chief of merchants decreed:

"Tear up the guava tree at Kanak by its very roots."

Once again the merchants sent their leader a magic message: "It is impossible to uproot such a gigantic tree. What then do you order us to do?"

"Sever the tree-trunk at its base," the leader replied immediately.

Hundreds of sharpened axes rained blows upon the base of the guava tree. Seeing this, the inhabitants of Kanak Dwip were at first surprised, then understood what it was all about! First they tried to politely prevent the merchants from cutting down the tree, then they fell at their feet and wept, begging them to desist. But the jinns would not be dissuaded. Now a great outcry rent the air in Kanak Dwip. Flames of turbulence flared up in different parts of the peaceful land. Still the jinns remained obdurate, in fact they tried to convince the golden-bodied people:

"Since the Lord has forbidden the human race from tasting the fruit of knowledge and it was the crime of having consumed this fruit that caused our original mother to be cast out of Eden, know for sure that this fruit is extremely harmful to mankind. It is for your ultimate benefit that we are expending so much effort to fell this tree."

But the people of the land had attained enough knowledge and awareness not to be deluded by hollow rhetoric anymore!

"Why do you eat this fruit then, all of you?" they argued. "Go and cut down the guava trees in Pareestan first, before you destroy our tree. And if our original mother sacrificed heavenly bliss in exchange for that fruit, it is easy to guess the fruit's value. A fruit procured from heaven must certainly be nurtured with the utmost care on this earth." But was anyone willing to listen?

For a while, a great controversy raged in Kanak regarding the felling of the tree. At this juncture, a learned octogenarian intervened:

"Why engage in futile quarrels for the sake of this distorted guava tree? It is merely an altered version of that original fruit of knowledge. Search for that primal tree, the one planted by Eve. The scriptures inform us that it is to be found in the eastern part of the world. Come, let us look for it."

Following the old man's advice, everyone abandoned the present and set out in search of the past! But the learned old man did not accompany them.

After many days of travel, crossing many rivers, streams, human settlements, mountains, fields and forests, the Kanak dwellers arrived at the appointed place and found themselves near an enormous dead tree. After consulting many holy texts and listening to many traditional tales, they reached the conclusion that this dried-up tree was indeed the primal tree of knowledge. Now their hearts were torn asunder by bitterness, by profound sorrow and despair. After tremendous effort, sacrificing food and sleep during their long absence from home, enduring great suffering, had they travelled this far for the sake of a dead tree? The local inhabitants informed them that it had been dead for over two hundred years.

"At least you were kind enough, all of you, not to have consigned it to flames as firewood," responded one of the visitors.

What was to be done now? By what means could the tree of knowledge be revived? Some said, water it profusely; others said, water it with tears; still others suggested donating blood; there were sundry other proposals in a similar vein. In fact, if the sacred tree could be brought back to life in exchange for a couple of human lives, they would not even shrink from considering such an eventuality.

Everyone began tending the withered tree in all sorts of ways. Streams of tears, streams of blood – they held back nothing. But when have the dead ever been restored to life? When all their effort, all their endeavour proved futile, they were heartbroken and vented their grief in diverse ways.

Exhausted with weeping, one of the men was lying under a tree and as he dozed, he dreamt of a sanyasi.

"My dear son!" the ascetic said to him, "it is no use weeping.

Let alone just one or two, even two hundred thousand human sacrifices will not revive the tree of knowledge. It is two hundred years since the shortsighted, selfish, stupid pundits of this country forbade women to taste the fruit of knowledge. In time, that prohibition came to acquire the status of a social law, and men monopolized this fruit for their own consumption. Barred from plucking and eating it, the women were unwilling to cherish and nurture the tree. Gradually, deprived of the care of tender female hands, the tree of knowledge withered away. Go, return to your own land, go now and sow the seeds of that guava. Let the jinns cut down whichever tree they wish. Instead of obstructing them, collect the seeds secretly. All of you now, men and women together, should nurture the newly-planted guava seedlings; then your efforts will bear the desired fruit. Be careful, though! No longer must you deprive the female sex of guavas! Always remember, women have full rights to enjoy the fruit of knowledge that a woman had obtained!"

When he awakened, the man narrated his dream to his companions. Upon hearing what he had to say, all of them said in one voice: Come, let us return then.

"Indeed," observed one large-hearted gentleman, "men taunted the crocodile after they crossed the river: they deprived women of the knowledge that women themselves had acquired. Witness the consequences of that!"

The enthusiastic boys of Kanak Dwip cleared a space in a corner of the garden and marked it out. Then, addressing the girls, they said:

"Come, sisters! You too must come and join us, all of you. Let us prepare the soil with hoe and shovel while you sow the seeds with your own hands! What an auspicious day this is! From now on, we shall have trees of our own."

The jinns were left staring at the scene in stunned silence, unable to stop the Kanak-dwellers in their auspicious endeavour.

Inspired by new fervour, not even giants had the power to obstruct the Kanak-dwellers!

Henceforth Kanak Dwip was abundant with wealth and sustenance, and twice or thrice as prosperous as before. The inhabitants began spending their days in supreme bliss, no longer deluded by any form of magic! For now, the women were in charge of the garden of knowledge.

Like nectar Kanak's tale has power to revive,
Hearing it the dead man comes back to life!

---

1 The events described in the Quran-Sharif or the Bible have not been followed here (Author's Note)

2 Alas! You accepted famine in exchange for your rice, giving it away to others on merchandise! (Author's Note)

Eid Moon

RAZIA KHATUN CHAUDHURANI

"AMMA, give me some water …"

"There's not much water left, baba, and we can't even fetch more before dusk, there's such a crowd of people …"

"Why the crowds, Amma?"

"It's Eid today, that's why."

"Oh … I had completely forgotten. What happened to the achkan and zari cap Baba once bought me for Eid, Ma?"

"I gave them away when you outgrew them."

So they chatted, mother and son. Outside, at that hour, the sun was weaving a border of golden rays for the blue nilambari sari of the evening sky.

"What did you eat today?"

"I had what was at hand – why do you need to know so many things?"

"So Amma, tell me the truth …"

"There was a bit of muri, that's what I had."

"Why, isn't there any rice?"

The mother didn't answer. Gazing at the distant horizon, her eyes filled with tears. After all, it was not so long back, just five years ago, that she too had cooked a variety of dishes for a lot of people on this occasion; today there was not even a fistful of rice at home, no proper diet for her ailing son. There, before them, stood the zamindar's mansion, the very mansion she had once entered in bride's attire. The present zamindar had been a mere boy then, with a headful of curly hair and large eyes. The chubby young lad of twelve or fourteen had come up close, gazed with a mixture of suspicion and anxiety at the bundle wrapped in a red Banarasi sari, and called her "Bhabi." The sixteen year old girl had found in the boy's face a resemblance to the brother she had just lost. Parting the folds to peep at him through the ghomta that covered her head, she felt they looked exactly the same.

"Amma will scold me if she sees us because it's forbidden to enter your room," the boy said, in a low voice. "Please say something."

Tears poured like a waterfall from the young girl's eyes. "Sit down, bhai," she said in a trembling voice.

A portly maidservant appeared suddenly. "I swear to god!" she exclaimed, tilting her head to press her hand on her cheek. "Here I was, hunting high and low, and this is where you've been? Don't you remember what you were told?"

The boy's face fell, but he put up a show of boldness for the new bride's benefit. "Go away, don't be so cheeky!" he declared.

"So it's me who's cheeky, is it? Very well, I'll tell Amma, then."

Without another word, the boy silently followed the female attendant out.

Such episodes were frequent, but despite that the two of them could be seen sitting under the cool shade of a tree on a hot, sunny afternoon, making short work of sour jujubes and unripe guavas procured by various means. Some days, the sister would lovingly prepare all sorts of delicacies and wait for her brother, casting the odd furtive glance in the direction of his house. The mischievous boy would arrive like a gust of wind, brimming with mirth.

"Apa, how I've fooled Amma!" he would laugh. "She wouldn't let me come otherwise, so I told her I was going to the toilet. I came out carrying the *badna*, then left it in the toilet and disappeared."

With mock severity the young sister would admonish him:

"Bhai, you shouldn't deceive your mother. Allah will be angry if you lie to her." The boy would look at her with frightened eyes, and she would relent: "Achchha, Allah will forgive what you did today if you beg his mercy, but never do such a thing again."

There were so many little incidents like this. Her husband Azahar was actually quite pleased, because he had no other relatives of his own, and as for his bride, she was utterly alone in the world.

When he was dying, Azahar's father had very trustingly left his son in his brother's hands. Well, the paternal uncle did not fail in his duties; he withdrew the boy from school when he was only in the second grade, saying: "He's a zamindar, son of a zamindar, why should he struggle to educate himself? Let him learn to handle his own affairs." So Azahar was removed from school and enthroned as the superintendent of his establishment, but his officials were secretly instructed not to show him any financial documents. The boy used his own wits and realized very soon that his own possessions did not amount to much; the rest were to be auctioned off to settle unpaid taxes, but that nephew-loving uncle of his was clinging to them unlawfully.

Some more time passed, then suddenly a storm broke out one day. When the zamindar saheb expressed grief for his departed brother, the young Azahar protested sharply: "No more false tears, Chacha Saheb! In your grief for my father, you have made a pauper of me."

Shortly afterwards, having saddled his nephew with this bride, an orphaned, penniless girl of aristocratic descent, the uncle gave him a house beyond the mango orchard and a few land deeds, and went around saying: "Nobody would do so much for others, nowadays. Because my brother left him in my care, I have educated him suitably, got him married, and helped him settle down."

"True enough," agreed everyone.

The boy-zamindar's zamindari was ruined within six months, for he didn't have much of an estate to begin with. Just a month after he took possession of it, his property had to be auctioned off, for how else could so much money be found?

"What am I to do?" the uncle complained. "He is not destined to enjoy his property. After all, I explained everything to him in great detail, but how can these callow youths maintain a zamindari?"

The following year, like a blessing from Allahtala, Farhad was born, tiny and beautiful like a flower. The young mother looked at her husband, blushing shyly. "He's so beautiful!" she said wonderingly, laying her cheek against the young father's, her heart full of newly awakened love. The next day, Atahar, who was like her brother, came by.

"O, Apa!" he exclaimed loudly, "what a lovely baby, just like a doll! He's mine, I'll take him ..." A little while later, he asked petulantly, "You won't love me any less now, will you?"

"Na re, no, you silly boy!" she assured him, stroking his head affectionately.

But since then, they had been through very difficult times. Atahar had left to study in Kolkata. Azahar earned ten rupees a month handling accounts in a shop, and struggled to make ends meet by tutoring a few boys. Still, how happy they were! Which had triumphed then: seeming hardship, or the comforts of plenty? She was not unaware of the answer.

Sixteen years went by like a mere sixteen seconds. In parting, Azahar had grasped both her hands and said: "Time's running out, Meher, I've spent this life in great happiness. Always depend on Allahtala, he is all-powerful, all-knowing and merciful. He turns nobody away. Farhad is asleep, don't awaken him. Try to raise him as a proper human being, however you can. Without medical treatment, my life has come to an untimely end, but I had everything, and still do. Don't depend on human beings, don't seek anyone's charity, especially not from that family. Such hopes you had pinned on Atahar, but he too forgot everything in the intoxication of wealth. Promise me you will not ask them for anything, not even if you are dying of starvation."

In a flood of tears, Meher promised. Azahar's face had broken into a blissful smile.

"Amma? Ma?"

The beautiful Meher of the past vanished into the world of fantasy, and the prematurely aged mother answered, like one in a trance: "Why, baba, what is it?"

"Will you go hungry all day like this? Why don't you call Rahamat's Ma and send her across to the other house?"

Sparks seemed to fly from his mother's eyes. "Farhad!" was all she said, her voice very sharp.

"Isn't it Eid today …?"

"Who says so?"

"Last night nothing could be seen for the clouds, everyone thought the moon had risen, but today there's a wire from Kolkata declaring it's Eid tomorrow. Tonight, the moon will be sighted."

"All the pulao, korma, firni and zarda that have been cooked – what will happen to them?"

"Arre, as if anything will be left!"

"Achchha, if it's not Eid yet, why not let them go and exchange some of their clothes?"

"What is it they must exchange now?"

"They've bought a pale yellow sari for Hena, but pale blue or green would be better because she's fair. And Sheuli is rather dark, but for her they've got a dark blue sari. They should get a pink one."

Zamindar Saheb was chatting with Begum Saheba. Begum Saheba was not bad looking either, quite fair, buxom, about twenty-three or twenty-four years old. As she was about to leave, she suddenly turned to say:

"Oh no, I had quite forgotten. I'm told, Farhad over in that other house is very ill, but let alone medical treatment, even a proper diet is beyond their means."

"Why should it be beyond their means? His father quarrelled with Baba and squandered so much of our wealth and property, but wouldn't the mother have some savings to fall back on?"

"I don't know the real state of affairs. It's only in this house that they have a bad reputation, otherwise all the people in the village speak well of Bhai Saheb, and Apa doesn't seem such a bad sort, either."

At the mention of Apa's name, a ray of early morning sunshine seemed to flood the closed chamber of Atahar's heart. A memory from so long ago! A sister and a brother! That same Apa, so tender in her love, so harsh in her adherence to duty! Farhad, that flowerlike doll! These days he did not even remember them, their memory buried under a heavy layer of garbage. Apa didn't ever ask after him either; was she sulking then, had her pride been wounded, her feelings hurt? That sister of his, so proud and sensitive, would she not come if he called her to him?

"Farhad."

"Ma!"

"Can't you sit up, baba?"

"No Amma, I feel very weak. Shade my eyes from that light, the darkness is much better. O Ma, look how the fireflies wink in that forest, how the crickets chirp, as if calling, 'Come, come!' as if I have left something behind. 'Come and find it!'

they call. If I die today will you leave me in a forest like that? The cemetery is rather overgrown."

"Farhad! Baba, don't you know how it hurts to hear you say such things?"

"So let it hurt a little. Pain is what I have always given you, what else can I offer you now in parting?"

"Will you go before me, then?"

"If my time has come, what is there for me to do? You are fated to suffer, Ma! After Baba left us, how you struggled, how you passed the days planting these trees and shrubs with your own hands, taking up sewing. You got no help from me, I only concentrated on my studies and thought that was enough to dispel your misery. Now I realize it was a false illusion. Do you know why men become thieves, why they go in for robbery? If I live, I'll slash the stomachs of all those who are pot-bellied from stuffing themselves with the korma and pulao they have got by cheating others, I'd snatch the money from their bellies and give it to unfortunates like myself – call it wrong or whatever you will. Why should some people throw pulao and korma down the drain while others get nothing to eat for as much as three days in a row? I have always been told that there is nothing unjust in the Creator's decrees, but …"

"O re, it is faith that gives us contentment and peace."

"Maybe, but it doesn't give us rice, that's for sure. Everywhere, there's this cry of pain, 'Give us rice!', 'Give us clothes!' – why are these things not for us?"

"They will be ours when the time is right. It's not right yet, that's why we can't have them."

"That's very true! A few people have so much money that the burden of wealth stifles them. Yet, before their very eyes, countless living beings are headed for the grave, crying, 'Oh, for some rice, some clothing!' So when will the right time come?"

"When the time was right, they must have misused their power, then came bad times and a reaction set in. The day people learn to understand the value and proper use of power and time, many sufferings will come to an end."

"Quite right."

"That's all I have understood from my experiences. Now no more useless talk, baba, there's no point feeling dejected. Become a proper human being yourself. If each person tries to dispel the misery in his own home, it will put an end to all the scarcity and hardship in this world."

"No, Amma. One should try to dispel others' misery as well as one's own. I've become very troublesome because I keep arguing with you na? Achchha, say no more, just move your feet closer. You are on your feet all day now, but they are still so soft, like a cluster of flowers! Ma, your eyes are like the stars at dawn."

Before them lay a stretch of wasteland, with a few old trees, almost withered. Immediately beyond that were extensive rice fields, and far away, one or two twinkling lights. That was where the mother gazed as she stroked her son's hair. Wisps of rough, unkempt hair streaked his face. Like the evening star, his eyes had grown dim with sorrow. She was thinking about the things her son had said, indeed, why should some people in this world enjoy excessive comfort and others suffer excessive misery? Why? All human beings were brothers but why did no-one bear that in mind?

"Amma?"

Again her train of thought was interrupted. "What is it, baba?" she responded.

"Put your hand here, touch my body ... You seem to be sitting very far away from me today. Didn't you say you used to be very fond of Chhoto Chacha, who lives in that other house? Can't we ask for his help?"

"No, baba, when in need, one can't bear to accept help from one's relatives. Easier to ask people outside the family. There was a time, when he was small, that he used to say that when he grew up he would take all of us to live with him in his house, get you married to a bride as lovely as a fairy – he used to say all kinds of things. Another time, about ten years ago, when your father took ill, he tried very hard to persuade us to move in with him …"

"Why didn't you go?"

"The time was not right, that's why we didn't. My husband said exactly the same thing then: it will be time for us to go when Atahar acts like a younger brother, erasing all the tangles in his mind, forgetting family rivalry. Anyway, even if that day never comes, all I ask of Allahtala is that we should never have to beg anyone for favours."

"That day will never come, Amma. The poor can never claim family ties with the rich if they don't have the strength."

"Where did you learn so many things, re?"

"Must even this simple truth be learnt from someone else? Here before our very eyes is your eminent brother, but despite his wealth and assets, Baba died without medical treatment, and I am in the same situation today. Yet more than half the estate in that zamindari belongs to us."

"I know all that, but what can I do?"

"Let it be. You will be left with no more ties after this, so why be lured by false attachments? Even if Chacha wants to help, you must not accept his beggarly alms."

"Achchha re, so it shall be. Now stay quiet for a while, or your throat will run dry. Here we are, prattling away, and it's dark already. Let me say my namaz prayers …"

"Just hold me close, Ma."

"Why, re? Have you become a baby again today?"

Placing his head on his mother's bosom, he gazed fixedly at

her face, as if that look would sustain him through a long journey.

"Some water!"

"Here it is … O re, what's this? … What's the matter? … Why is the water leaking?"

"It's nothing, Amma, just raise my head, nothing is the matter … You remember *inna lillahe wainna elayahe razeun* don't you? One day everyone must go to Him, so what is there to grieve about?"

"Baba! … Farhad!"

"O Ma, has it grown dark? Open the window in front … I want to see the sky … it's Eid today, after all … the Eid moon has come for me tonight, na, Amma …"

The woman's heart lurched. "Farhad!" she called out piteously.

Dusk was descending on Farhad's eyes, as night descends gently and silently upon the desolate desert. A single tremor shook Farhad's entire body. His trembling hands reached out once towards the sliver of moon, then collapsed. An ocean of tears surged and roared within Meher's heart.

Just then, an indistinct babble, like the sound of cheering, was heard in the distance. Through gaps in the fence a light became visible, then drew closer. The visitor reached the door, then stopped short. Pausing briefly to listen for sounds from within, he entered the room and spoke in a low voice:

"Is Farhad asleep then? Let him be. I have sent someone to town to fetch the civil surgeon at dawn. After Farhad recovers, I want to take him, along with you, to the other house. We must make proper arrangements for his education … Why are you staring at me like that? … The Eid moon has risen, so I have come to offer my salaams. On this special day, will you forgive me, Apa? Is one supposed to remember a younger brother's lapses? … Surely it's your affection I'll receive today, in exchange for the disrespect I've shown you all these days? Isn't it time?"

The mother gazed fixedly at her son. As soon as she raised her sorrowful eyes, the moon's curving line caught her gaze. The Eid moon! Eid, alas!

Across the ages, those timeless words, full of pain, rang in her ears: "The poor can never claim family ties with the rich if they don't have the strength."

She did not have the strength of body or mind. Her dues had been settled after all, now why trade with an empty treasury? In an indistinct voice, she responded "Forgive? I forgave you long ago bhai, but in this life I do not have the time to take your help anymore. Go back. My journey is almost over. Don't make me lose my way now. Try to remove the miseries of the unfortunate, that will be your service to me."

Slowly the moon sank into the depths of night.

Translator's Note: *Badna*: a small pitcher with a slender spout. *Zarda*: a saffron-flavoured pulao.

A Bubble in the Great, Wide Sea

RADHARANI DEBI

EVEN when the girl was very young, her mother would say: "She's destined to suffer. Being female, she ought to be feminine, soft and gentle; but no – she wants to be equal to men in all things. So obstinate, so proud! Such spirited behaviour is not a good thing."

"That girl is slightly crazy," the father would smile affectionately. "Anyway, it's good to possess some spirit. It's not good to be like your spoilt, effeminate Narugopal of a son."

"Wait and see!" the mother would declare in fury. "I tell you, that headstrong daughter of yours is destined for great misery. She will have to suffer for the flaws in her own nature."

"Yes," the father would affirm gravely, "considering the way you repeat these words every day like a magical mantra, how could your prediction fail to come true? ..."

"I say it for her own good. It is she who will benefit by mending her ways. And if she doesn't, it is she who will suffer."

Without responding, the father would leave the inner quarters of the house.

"Good thing she's my own daughter, born of my womb," the mother would grumble to herself. "Had she been my stepdaughter, people would accuse me of witchcraft."

The girl had numerous siblings. About eight or ten.

Of the four sisters, the third daughter Bindu was the source of her mother's anxiety and disaffection. Such a stubborn, headstrong girl.

The youngest, Indu, was much more wayward and mischievous, but she was not as difficult as Bindu. Indu could be persuaded or diverted, brought under control and made to comply somehow, but with Bindu that was impossible. Ever since she became aware of things as a child, nobody had managed to get their own way with this self-willed girl either through flattery or clever arguments. She was neither utterly unreasonable or unduly sensitive like her eldest sister, Rebati, nor lazy and deceitful like the middle sister, Rohini. Or restless and talkative like her youngest sister Indu; and yet, their mother was extremely unhappy about Bindu. In the face of her keen intelligence and sharp gaze, her mother – even though she *was* her mother – would sometimes feel rather uncomfortable. Whether Bindu said anything or not, she understood everything – that was probably her greatest crime, and it was exactly what her mother disliked about her.

Bindu was then about seven or eight. Gold bangles in a mustard-blossom pattern had been ordered for Rohini, along with four saris in nilambari and striped designs.

"I want saris and bangles, too!" implored Bindu. "Just like didi's."

"She's right," the father said. "Giving things to one daughter and not the other, what sort of system is this? … Look, she's almost in tears!"

"Let her cry, then," retorted the mother angrily. "Don't teach her to demand an equal share at this early age. She's a girl. If she marries into a large household, will she be able to demand her share in this way? Jealous of her sister now – will she envy her sisters-in-law later? That's all it would take for her in-laws' home to resound with cries of glory in praise of your daughter."

Then, less angrily, she resumed: "There are proposals pouring in for Rohini's marriage. That old, worn-out pair of bangles doesn't suit her any more, so I ordered new ones for her. Those matchmakers are constantly dropping in to see her; that's why I've bought her four saris for everyday wear. When it's her turn, Bindu will get the same things."

Bindu was easily appeased. Not for a moment did she doubt that she too would receive bangles and saris when she was grown up. Her dark-complexioned face aglow with a cheerful smile, she enjoyed examining her mejdi's new bangles and saris, making no further fuss, no more petulant demands.

At school Bindu excelled in her studies. Her teachers would give this headstrong girl lessons to prepare and ask her the toughest of questions. They were delighted by her wonderful answers. All of them were happy with this extremely diligent pupil. But she had barely turned twelve when her mother tried desperately to withdraw her from school. Rohini had been married off; now it was Bindu's turn. The girl was almost twelve: it was no longer proper for her to attend school.

Bindu raised a storm of protest. She was unwilling to give up school under any circumstances.

"Why confine her to the house?" her father demurred.

"Why continue sending her to school?" her mother retorted angrily. "She's not going to become a judge or a barrister with her education, is she? Since she's going to be married off, she'll spend her life handling dhama-kulo-handi-kolshi for the kitchen, and jhinuk-kantha for her infants! It makes no difference whether she marries into aristocracy or the professions – a woman's life doesn't revolve around pen and ink, books and ledgers."

Defeated, her father said, "Then let her study at home," in a tired voice. "Master moshai comes anyway to tutor her in the morning, I'll ask him to come by twice a day for her lessons. She's eager to learn, has a head for her studies, it's not a good idea to stop her education completely."

"A grown up girl," said the mother in disgust, "immersed

in books day and night, learning no household skills! When she goes to live with her in-laws it is me they will blame for this! What do you care, anyway?"

The father offered no reply.

When she was withdrawn from school, Bindu wept, refused food, and made a great fuss. For almost a week, she did not eat, and her eyes and face were red and puffy from constant weeping. She spoke to no one at home, just lay in a corner of her room, fasting. Helping her younger siblings dress, running errands for her mother, arranging her father's clothes for the courthouse – she didn't perform any of these tasks. Even the elderly private tutor, Prasanna Babu, came twice a day only to be turned away; Bindu simply refused to take lessons from him, lying rigid in bed, her face stuffed into her pillow.

She recalled how, when she was only five years old, she had been forced to join school against her will, in exactly the same way. Her daily stream of excuses, protests and tears had proved just as ineffective in the face of her guardians' unshakeable will. Nothing had changed, the situation remained the same. She wasn't surprised, she only struggled with the fact that her wishes, her likes and dislikes, made no difference to the course her life would take.

Time heals all wounds.

Gradually Bindu resumed her meals and immersed herself in household duties. But she gave up her lessons with the private tutor. Her father knew exactly what her refusal signified, but her mother was actually rather pleased. Still Bindu couldn't continue like this for very long. Little by little, she took up her studies again. Not in school or with a private tutor, but on her own. She would go to her father or her elder brothers to clarify the difficult bits. In this way her studies progressed faster than before. A year later, she decided to take the end-of-school matric examination as a private candidate, but meanwhile, something else happened. Their mother bought a Banarasi sari, blouse and petticoat for Bindu's younger sister, Indu.

"Won't you buy one for me, Ma?" Bindu demanded.

"Why, if we find a groom for you today, you'll be married off tomorrow," her mother replied. "We'll have to give you lots of clothes, Banarasi and all, for your wedding. Why buy them beforehand?"

"But it wasn't like this for Mejdi's wedding," protested Bindu, affronted. "Whenever I ask for anything, you say, 'I'll give it to you for your wedding.' Why? What if I die before I marry?"

Indeed their mother had not ordered anything for Bindu recently, because everything would be bought for her wedding.

"Always jealous of Mejdi, aren't you ashamed of being jealous of your little sister now" she said angrily. "I'll do as I please, give everything to Indu, not to you."

Stunned, Bindu shrank back, suppressing her tears. Didn't Ma know how much she loved her little sister? Why didn't she think twice before making such an ugly accusation? In shame, disgust and humiliation, Bindu vowed that she would never again ask anyone for anything, however justified her demand.

When no match was arranged for her even after a year's effort in Allahabad, it was decided that Bindu should move to her maternal uncle's house in Kolkata. Once her marriage was decided, her father would take leave and go to Kolkata to organize the wedding.

This time, Bindu went straight to her father and made clear her strong objections to this plan.

"Baba, I won't go to Kolkata," she declared, shaking her head vigorously.

"Why, you silly girl", her father asked gently, smiling affectionately. "You'll see a new city, new sights! Why don't you want to go?"

"I've decided to take the matric exam privately next year,

Baba," she informed him. "Moving to Kolkata would ruin everything. I'm not going."

Her father lapsed into a worried silence. Before he could reply, Bindu buried her face in his lap and said, in a tear-choked voice: "Baba, I beg you, please don't get me married now. I don't care for such things at all."

Her father smoothed the scattered strands of her hair lovingly. "That's not possible, ma!" he soothed, "I'm growing old by the day, am not in good health, either. Who knows when something might happen? You don't know how relieved I'll feel if I can leave you and Indu in good hands." Then lightly, he continued: "It's because your exams will be affected that you object to marriage, isn't it? Very well, you can continue studying on your own even in your mama's house in Kolkata, just as you do here! Ask your uncle and the others for guidance whenever required. It's not as if your wedding will be fixed right away, either. And if the date falls before your exams, I'll bring you back to Allahabad with me after the ceremony, instead of sending you to your in-laws' place. You'll come back here for your exams!"

"Don't get me married at all, Baba!" begged Bindu again, "or I may not survive!"

"Quiet, you mustn't say such things," her father admonished her gravely.

At her uncle's house in Kolkata, Bindu found it was not at all convenient to study.

Here, the daughters and daughters-in-law of the household did not study at all. There was no secluded space anywhere in the house where Bindu could study by herself. The women of the family spent all day bathing, braiding their hair, changing their saris, dressing up, going to the theatre or the bioscope, and avidly exchanging opinions about what they had seen.

Nobody cared much for books, and the few that they read were trashy Bengali novels.

It was an affluent household. All the housework was handled by cooks, attendants and housemaids. Bindu realised there was a huge gap between herself and the young women of her uncle's place. She even gazed in wonder at the maids who worked there, the young Subashi and the elderly Shashi, at their bright, wide-bordered saris, their jewellery, their impeccable hair and attire.

The women at her uncle's place rose from their beds at eight or eight-thirty, sometimes even at nine. They enjoyed a long nap in the afternoon. They spent all their spare time talking about their husbands or about the wealth of their natal or marital homes, discussing the latest fashions in clothing, exchanging all sorts of intimate female banter, replete with sign language and innuendo. It did not take her long to realize that their jokes and gestures often exceeded the limits of propriety.

Sometimes Bindu was their target. Though she didn't understand the meaning of every word, she could sense the implications.

"What's this!" the young women would say, the whole lot of them rocking with mirth. "She's the very image of Kapalkundala, the forest maiden! Our lady's such an innocent, she doesn't know the ways of the world!"

Bindu would flush with shame, humiliation and disgust.

A suitable match was found.

The bride was seen and approved, cash transactions were negotiated. Jewellery, bridegroom's attire, items for donation – once all this was settled and the final viewing of the bride had taken place, the first stage of preparing for the wedding was complete. The date and time for the ceremony was fixed.

Accompanied by her mother and siblings, her father came down from Allahabad on a week's leave of absence, to organize Bindu's wedding.

One day, when they were alone, Bindu begged her father: "Baba, I beseech you, please put a stop to all this! I don't know why, but I'm feeling suffocated. Believe me, Baba, I haven't the slightest desire to marry."

"Shame on you," said her father, affectionately. "You mustn't say such things. This wedding can't be called off now."

But Bindu persisted, "When you return to Allahabad next week, promise that you will take me along."

"Achchha," her father consented, "I'll ask your father-in-law. My views won't matter any more, for now you will become their property! Only if they consent and are willing to send you to us, can I take you away with me."

"Can't you take your own daughter with you, if you wish?" exclaimed Bindu in agitation. "Why not? Are you selling me off to them, Baba?"

"I'm not selling you off," said her father wanly. "I'm giving you away, relinquishing all my rights over you. I can no longer exercise any claims on you."

"I beg you, Baba," Bindu pleaded desperately, "please don't give me away to other people in this way. I will not go!"

"You mustn't say such things now," her father reprimanded. "You are grown up now. As you can see, a woman's real home is with her in-laws. No woman stays on forever in her natal home."

At the appointed time, the wedding ceremony took place in the prescribed manner.

Afterwards, as her father, mother and siblings prepared to depart for Allahabad, Bindu created a fuss. "I'm going with you," she insisted obdurately.

But her father-in-law and his elder brother refused to send

her so far away, so soon. It seemed they had selected a grown girl for a bride precisely because they could not allow her to spend much time with her parents. Their household lacked a mistress to manage it. Her mother-in-law had passed away, so Bindu would gradually have to assume "charge" of the household.

When her parents left, Bindu shed no tears at all, remaining dry-eyed and calm as she bade them farewell. Her female relatives whispered meaningfully in private: "Just wed, but look how intimate she is with her new bridegroom! Parents and siblings left – and not a tear did she shed!"

But that was not why Bindu didn't weep. Whatever she really desired would be denied, and what she didn't want would come to pass – that was what she had experienced all her life, ever since she became aware of things. It seemed obvious to her that her desperate wish to visit Allahabad should be thwarted.

Her studies came to a standstill. Her dream of taking the matric exam vanished.

In her marital home, Bindu became a tireless, docile daughter-in-law. Head covered, she immersed herself in her duties, attending upon everyone's pleasure, from her father-in-law's elder brother, to her brother-in-law's wickedly naughty two-and-a-half-year-old son, even the maid who had served there for many years.

Seven months went by swiftly. Bindu seemed to have settled down, to have accepted her existence as a daughter-in-law. Everyone at her in-laws home was impressed by her talents. Her husband remained at a hostel in Kolkata, pursuing his studies, returning home on the odd holiday. Basking in his love, she had forgotten the frustrations of her previous life.

Suddenly, one day, came the utterly unexpected news that Bindu had become a widow. Her husband had died of Asiatic cholera in his Kolkata hostel. It was as if the entire family had been struck by lightning. Immediately, young and old alike set up a heartrending wailing, in a tremendous outpouring of grief. Bindu stared fixedly at them, frozen with disbelief.

Her husband's paternal aunt, also widowed, came forward to perform the difficult task of bathing Bindu and transforming her into a widow. As she rubbed off the bright streak of sindoor in Bindu's parting, the woman struck her own forehead and exclaimed tearfully: "Alas, not even fifteen – just a tender little girl! Married less than a year, to be struck by misfortune already, what an ill-fated woman ..."

Bindu gazed wide-eyed at her widowed aunt's dried-up body, hard as a man's, at her head of short-cropped hair, her charmless face, her unadorned, calloused, work-hardened hands. Then suddenly, she burst into a flood of tears and cried out, shaking her head in violent denial: "I can't be turned into a widow! Please let me go, Pishima! Don't make me look like you – I want to stay just the way I am."

Her preferences had not mattered the day that streak of sindoor had been applied to her parting, the day she had been decked out in a beautiful sari and jewellery. Likewise, today when she entered the room after her bath, her unadorned body clad in a plain white length of fabric, her desires proved utterly futile at the inaugural moment of her new image.

Admission to school and withdrawal from it, the transition from adolescence to married life, from wifehood to widowhood – all these had happened to her against her will, despite all her resistance. This time she was told that the burden of widowhood was the gift of the Almighty God Himself.

Perhaps that was why Bindu began observing the rituals of widowhood silently and without protest, adhering strictly to orthodox rules. Some felt sorry for her, others commiserated, and some even began to object: "Why go to such extremes from the very beginning? Change your ways gradually."

Bindu only smiled frostily in response. This time she had decided that she would make it a point to seek the exact opposite of what she really wanted. To see if her desires would be fulfilled in being thwarted! Perhaps her wishes would come true – granted by flesh-and-blood human beings or whimsical fate, she didn't care.

With unwavering concentration, Bindu began to follow the sundry rituals, vows and fasts of widowhood, going without water on ekadashi, living on the sundried sacrificial rice designated for widows. Chopped off all her heavy, cloud-like mass of hair. Wore only a length of plain white fabric.

Now she had resolved to her fate. Punishing herself mercilessly, she smiled to herself and wondered: Who has brought this upon me? God or man? It's my life, I must undergo its joys and sorrows – and yet, it is determined by everyone else! What is the meaning of this? Why should I not take the responsibility of determining what's good for me and what isn't? If I have to suffer, I'll embrace suffering with my own hands, of my own free will – why should others decide for me?

All her kinfolk tried to placate her: "There's nothing to be done. After all, these things are beyond the power of human beings, it's your fate … destiny …"

Bindu did not utter a word, positive or negative. Only fifteen, and her whole heart seemed to rise up in rebellion against someone, no matter who! Against people … the Almighty … society … or destiny …

Translator's Note: *Kapalkundala*: the eponymous heroine of Bankim Chandra Chatterjee's novel, she is brought up in the wilds and innocent of social mores.

Nothing New

SABITRI RAY

A large house it was, occupying a large tract of land. English dogs on the south veranda, tennis lawn in front. Kitchen at the back. The domain of the cook and the domestic staff.

Foaming starch strained from cooked rice would flow down the kitchen drain. The rich man's female cook was so careless that a fair quantity of rice would also disappear into the drain along with the starch. And that was why, exactly at ten every morning, a crowd assembled beside the narrow drain. Such a pushing and shoving there would be that some people would fall face down into the stinking drain. Many hands would grab and pounce where the thick foaming starch mixed with rice lay. For no apparent reason, one woman really lost her temper and sank her teeth into the tough, long forearm of one of the men in her rage. The man, in turn, grabbed the woman by her hair in a firm grip.

"O, you'll be the death of me!" the woman wailed. A flood of unsavoury, incomprehensible expletives burst forth.

At the same time the kitchen window also burst open. With supreme arrogance, a Hindustani-speaking servant admonished them: "*Ai! Chillao mat, bhago yehan se!*" (You there! stop shouting, get out of here at once!)

"*Baapre baap!*" the cook piped up. "Enough to deafen one – a bunch of good-for-nothings, all of them!"

By now, the kitchen drain had been cleaned out. In an instant everyone vanished from sight. The man looked around and found everyone gone. Releasing his grip on the woman's hair he said: "Hey, don't go away, wait a bit." He said this quite easily, with a smile.

"Aha, isn't he amorous!" said the girl, spitting in his direction.

"Why, it was you who bit me first," he pointed out, wiping the spit with his left hand.

"Why did you grab the rice I had my hands on?" she flashed at him.

"Oho, I'll let you have some of it," he assured her, and so saying, he undid the knot at the end of his loincloth and took out two pieces of stale hard roti, many days old.

The girl pounced on the roti, snatching it from his hand. Then, stuffing it into her mouth, she cast a sidelong glance at him.

He was still grinning, displaying his hideous teeth.

A few months later. The jostling near the drain was considerably reduced. A couple of people still came there occasionally and would insert their hands into the drain, just beneath the outlet from the kitchen. Sometimes they would find a scrap or two of roti, at other times nothing.

But that girl just would not move from the spot. The daughter-in-law of the single-storey house next door would open her back door and pour some rice and starch into the girl's handi every day.

A strip of empty land lay between the rear walls of three houses, with a broken bullock-cart in one corner. Just above, on the balcony of the first floor flat in an adjoining block, Shobhan was lost in thought about his forthcoming exhibition. Indoors, within the room, a heap of soft clay was piled up in a corner.

Shobhan was a sculptor. The clods of clay took shape and form at the touch of his fingertips. Gazing at the clay lying in a pile, his head flamed with extraordinary excitement. Before his eyes rose an image of the heroic expression on the face of a Greek man with a spear, or of the undulating tresses of a Hellenic female. Shobhan was finding it hard to decide what would appeal more to connoisseurs of art: Minerva, or a paired image of Shiva and Shivani.

Suddenly, a flapping noise disrupted Shobhan's train of thought. Glancing down he saw a skeletal dog gnawing and snapping at the sores on its mangy body. And when from time to time it shook its whole body, it was accompanied by a hideous sound – flap, flap, flap. Beside the dog was a girl of about seventeen or eighteen or maybe a little more, sitting with legs outstretched, eating something from her lap. She was dressed in a short piece of cloth that did not even reach her knees. On one leg was a festering sore, blood oozed from it. And large flies were settling down, now on the sore, now on the girl's face and eyes. In great irritation she flapped the flies away with her left hand from time to time, while with the right she lifted the food and stuffed it into her mouth. The matted, unoiled locks on her head looked like the bedraggled feathers of a crow in a storm. A bit of cloth was wrapped haphazardly around her body – from a long accumulation of dirt the fabric had acquired the colour of the mud.

For several days in a row Shobhanlal saw the girl sitting in the same spot. Sometimes a man, even more rough in his appearance,. would bring some rice or stale bread from somewhere, and the two of them would sit and feed themselves. Afterwards they would drink water from the tubewell by the street.

When it rained they would take shelter under the broken bullock-cart. Rain water would wet their pieces of cloth, which would then dry on their bodies.

Every day Shobhan observed this scene.

One day, after a shower of rain, the sun shone with full

force. Shobhan broke out in a sweat, the humid heat of the month of Bhadra disrupting his concentration. Rising, he went and stood on the balcony and looked down at the same girl. Suddenly he noticed a change, something new, in the girl's appearance. He observed her very carefully, every part of her body, from head to toe. His eyes began to shine. Entering his room, he began to sieve the clay. In just a few days, the statue took shape. Seeing it, Shobhan realized that it was a perfect likeness. It bore the marks of a would-be mother's unspoken agony. As he compared his half-naked image, its ribs exposed, with the girl's appearance, a friend of Shobhan's entered the room. A contemptuous sneer on his face, he observed mockingly:

"When there are so many gods and goddesses around, how did your eyes light upon a beggar from the street? Is this a puja in aid of the impoverished?"

"Well, let even the children of the soil receive some homage, no harm in that" retorted Shobhan, stung.

"I wonder whether this figure, your daughter of the soil, might not end up covered in dust after all. She may never gain admission into an affluent home."

Agitation gripped Shobhan. What if that were indeed to happen? Who could tell? And he needed the money. In a disturbed frame of mind, Shobhan rose and went to the veranda. The last few days the man had not appeared. Now, three days later, here he was again with some rice knotted in the end of his loincloth. He was happy today, and the girl had cheered up, too. Her face, her eyes, shone with joy. The man fetched a matchstick from a shop at the corner of the alley. In a short while, the rice began to boil inside the clay handi placed on the stove made of three bricks. They bent over it, checking the rice again and again, their faces brimming with joy.

Shobhan was still standing on the balcony …

"See how fragrant the rice is?" asked the man.

"Where did you find it?" the girl replied, restless with anticipation.

"I went far beyond the railway station. On the rail-tracks were entire carriages full of rice. So many people were probing the cracks and openings in the carriages for it – I'll go there again one day."

That very evening, on the balcony next door Shobhan heard the husband telling his wife: "Today a military vehicle had an accident, a couple of beggars were killed. One of them looked like that man who used to live with that girl down below. Never mind, the only casualties were beggars after all."

Shobhan noticed that the girl was sitting in exactly the same posture as before, legs outstretched, eyes fixed on the alley. Every now and then she would glance at her own body. She seemed to have grown even more haggard, collar-bones even more visible. There were dark smudges at the corners of her eyes. Meanwhile, the gentleman's voice could be heard once again:

"How can we afford to be sentimental, tell me. Some unknown beggar dies, and we are supposed to grieve for him? Seems we must hold a condolence meeting even for that dog, all skin and bones, if it dies." The gentleman was a doctor.

A few days later, late at night. The surrounding houses were deep in slumber. Shobhan was still at work, applying plaster to the female form. Suddenly an agonized moan floated up: "Oh, Ma – Ma, my own Ma!" From some unknown source, a pathetic wail wafted across, quivering on the breeze. Gradually, it turned into the sound of weeping, an agonized cry of unbearable pain.

It was the girl who wept. Rising, Shobhan went out onto the veranda. The girl was clearly visible in the moonlight. Crouching with her face between her legs, she was screaming with pain. "Ma – Ma-go, Ma, Ma-go!" The dog who kept her company let out a bark from time to time. The housewife in the adjacent flat had woken up, too. In a sleepy voice her husband was saying: "To wake me up so late at night, and for this? You can see for yourself what's going on!"

Still the wife persisted: "Please go and take a look, just give her an injection, if nothing else. Put her out of her agony."

"Yes, I must scrabble in dirt at this unearthly hour, I suppose!" grumbled the doctor. "It's nothing new. Just go to bed."

From down below the cries could still be heard: "Ma – Ma-go!"

Now even the window of the single-storey house to the right flew open. An incensed male voice could be heard, saying: "What a nuisance, in the middle of a civilized bhadralok colony!"

Once again, all the windows slammed shut. Shobhan stood there in silence, unable to sleep. The girl's helplessness filled his mind with pity and sorrow. His veins seemed to grow heavy with a futile agony. From time to time the girl's cry floated to his ears: "Ma – Ma-go – Ma – Ma-go!" As he stood there, Shobhan kept thinking that early next morning he would see the wailing woman clasp a newborn babe to her bosom. And blossoming on her exhausted lips, the first smile of motherhood …

The sound of the motorcar horn awakened Shobhan from his slumber. The day had dawned. Quickly he went to his balcony, but looking down, got a shock. A short distance away the girl lay dead. Next to her lay the body of a newborn baby.

Before Shobhan's frozen eyes rose the remembered vision of the previous night. In his ears rang the dismissive, contemptuous voice that said:

"Oh, that's nothing new, nothing new at all."

The House of Cards

ASHAPURNA DEVI

IT was Tarangini who raised the subject while chopping vegetables in the morning. Placing the handi on the flaming stove, Mamata came running up to her and cried: "You're chopping vegetables into the basin meant for washing rice, Thakurjhi! Here, please give that to me."

Paying no attention to Mamata's words, her husband's sister wound the fibrous strands of banana pith around her fingertip.

"So, how late was it when Dada came home last night, Bou?" she enquired.

"He didn't come home at all last night, bhai," replied Mamata, startled. "It's not easy to catch the nine o'clock train after the hullabaloo of a wedding feast! He mentioned a train that leaves at around dawn, so perhaps that is what ..."

"Dada didn't come home last night?" asked Tarangini, amazement writ large on her face. "What are you saying, Bou! With my own ears I heard ..."

"Heard?"

"A heavy voice, I thought maybe he was hoarse because he had caught a chill. At around two or half-past two last night. I went back and said to Himi: 'It's probably your Baba, back home again, right Himi?'"

Mamata's elder daughter, Himani, was close at hand, sorting greens. She neither responded to her pishi, her father's sister, nor raised her head.

Glancing at her, Mamata said with mild irritation: "Leave the fantasies for later. Now let me have the basin will you, the water for cooking rice is boiling."

"What's more," Tarangini persisted, displaying no anxiety about the rice, "I clearly saw shadows cast from your window onto the wall of Bhabani's room. Shadows of two figures – right, Himi? Oh, she's just gone for a drink of water, has she?"

The way she repeatedly asked her daughter to bear witness, it struck Mamata that this was not mere curiosity on Tarangini's part. It was more like a probing interrogation. Rage inflamed her from head to toe.

"Then you must have seen a ghost, Thakurjhi. Be careful! Don't lose the amulet with Rama's name on it to protect you!" Looking furious, she picked up the basin and stormed out.

For the moment, the matter rested there. The problem could have been resolved if she had allayed all suspicions before she left, but Mamata was not keen to let the story spread. There was not much difference between confiding in Tarangini and publishing the news in the daily newspaper. Where was the time anyway? Sejo Deor, the third of her husband's younger brothers, took his meal of rice at eight in the morning, Himu's school bus came for her at eight-thirty. So it went on, one thing after another, and she had no time to breathe until half past ten. Once the boys had been sent off, they were free. Then it was possible to spend a couple of hours relaxing with legs outstretched, drinking tea and gossiping.

It was almost nine when Tarangini's dada, her elder brother, arrived on the scene. Extracting a bundle of *Preetiupahar* pages from his pocket, he flung them in his sister's direction.

"Taru, give me a little oil, I'll have a bath," he said. "I can't stay long enough for a meal. But in any case that's not required, we had such a late night yesterday. My word, would any civilized person go by train to attend a wedding feast? May Lord Rama help me! Where is my gamchha?"

The moment he arrived upstairs, after a half-minute bath he could be heard calling:

"Where are my clothes? Khoka, can you tell me where my clothes might be?"

Sticking her head out of the kitchen window, Mamata called out: "Khokon, please tell him his narrow muga-bordered dhoti is on the alna itself, on the clothes rack where it should be. He is always in such a hurry!'"

She was tempted to go upstairs on this pretext: she had not seen him for almost eighteen or nineteen hours, and she certainly missed him, but she was embarrassed. Compared to her youth, the embarrassment of advancing age was an obstacle even more insurmountable. Sudhangshu though, had come downstairs by now, having located another garment. Another half-minute over his plate of rice, and off he rushed at great speed.

But the Maker of our destiny has a whimsical bent of mind. Looking upon this peaceful, harmless household with its simple way of life, his instinct for stirring up mysteries was aroused.

Mamata's younger sister's bhashurpo Nimai – the sister's elder brother-in-law's son – arrived there looking woebegone.

"Bodo Mashima, Ma has asked you to come at once," he announced. "Khudima is in a lot of pain."

Dropping the work at hand, Mamata rushed to him. "Is that so?" she cried. "Since when, Nimai? She's in a lot of pain, is she?"

"I think so… Ma has sent me to fetch you."

Mamata's sister Sabita's marital home was not far away. Her elder sister-in-law was of a timid cast of mind. It had been decided beforehand that she would send for Mamata at the time of delivery.

"Then please call a rickshaw, baba," said Mamata, wiping her damp hands on the gamchha.

"But Chhotokaka is here with the car! After taking you to our home he will go to the doctor's house. Come, let's hurry."

"Then please come here for a moment, Thakurjhi," Mamata

called out. "Everything is done, only the thick-grained rice needs to be prepared, and the charchari is still cooking, take it off the fire when ready. Ma is probably at her prayers, tell her about the developments ... I can't say when I'll be back ... Let's hope all goes well. Where are you, Nimai? Let's go baba. Durga! Durga! May everything go well."

"Loose woman!" muttered Tarangini, indistinctly to herself as she threw a piercing glance in the direction of her departing sister-in-law. Yet, a few hours earlier, Tarangini would not have dreamt of uttering such words.

"Where has Bordi gone, Thakurjhi?" asked Bijoli, seeing Tarangini in the kitchen when she came to fetch her son's bowl of milk.

Thakurjhi was straining tea for herself and her mother into a pair of large stone tumblers. Without raising her head, she replied: "It's hard to keep track of everybody's comings and goings in this household, Mejobou! Doing so would cause trouble, too."

She had not yet digested the sarcastic remark about seeing ghosts.

Although Bijoli did not understand the significance of Thakurjhi's comment, she had no time to linger for her son was wailing.

At last, done with her prayer rituals, Sushilbala now came downstairs. Squatting near the stone tumbler, she enquired: "Why is it I don't see Borobouma here?"

"My word, I'm tired of accounting for Borobouma, this eldest daughter-in-law of yours! She's gone to her sister's house; her younger brother-in-law came with the car to fetch her."

It was rumoured about Sushilbala that she loved her daughters-in-law more than own daughter. That she had a special soft corner for her Borobouma was not untrue. She was not alone in this. No one, either at home or abroad, could help loving this ever-smiling, never idle, dutiful daughter-in-law whose virtues knew no bounds. When it came to cheerful conversation, warm hospitality or the care of invalids, she was matchless. Perhaps she was somewhat lacking in modesty and demureness, but "shameless" was too strong an epithet for her simple, unaffected behaviour.

Sushilbala couldn't help smiling at her daughter's annoyance. "So you are jealous, are you" she asked. "Is her sister in labour? Poor girl, then she must go to her. Mothers and sisters, as the saying goes … the mother gone, the sister so near at hand, why should she not go there?"

"So must she rush off with anyone who comes her way? It is your encouragement that has ruined her character. The sheer brazenness of it!"

"Don't say such things, Taru, my Bouma is an angel," declared the mother, putting her empty tumbler down with a sigh of satisfaction.

"We don't need such angels! If you knew about your angel's talents …" Tarangini pulled a face.

Subsequently, those "talents" were revealed. All day, taking advantage of the culprit's absence, a storm of adverse comment raged within the house. Bijoli apart, almost everyone had no hesitation in believing – hard as it was – that Borobou's nature and moral character were not above suspicion. Unfortunately, such indisputable evidence was discovered, that it could not be overlooked.

In a single moment's thoughtlessness, Mamata managed to sink the loaded cargo-boat carrying all the respect and devotion, love and admiration that she had accumulated over these eighteen years.

Himangshu was cautioning his wife: "It won't do for you to run after her calling 'Didi! Didi,' seeking her affection so blatantly.

If she isn't careful, I shall have no choice but to look out for her."

"O Ma, have you gone mad, all of you, in this house?" cried Bijoli in agitation. "Can you really believe this of her?"

"I didn't want to, but there's no trusting a woman."

Bijoli's face flushed. "Then why don't you throw me out as well? How can you trust me? I'm nothing but a woman after all!"

"I can do that too, if necessary. I'm not Dada!"

Sudhangshu's reputation had always suffered because he was rumoured to be excessively devoted to his wife.

Bijoli could not contain her annoyance. "Had you been like Dada, you would have found your salvation by now. Anyway, your sister is also a woman, not a man, so there's no trusting her either, right? What if she was lying about this?"

"What would she gain from lying?"

"She has always been jealous of Didi."

"She found those garments out of jealousy, I suppose?"

Bijoli could not think of a retort.

The whole thing was indeed a riddle.

And as for Sabita, what lack of good sense on her part to choose this day of all days, to go into labour! If Didi had been here, Bijoli would have wept and pleaded until she succeeded in getting to the bottom of this mystery. But that was not to be. The One who entangles us in webs of trouble was busy at his task, weaving away. Who could ever unravel those knots!

"I knew right from the start that this girl would bring disaster upon us one day!" cried Sushilbala, striking her forehead. "For a girl to be so talkative! Flinging off the covering on her head to sit and gossip with all and sundry, laughing out loud, not heeding who is family and who is not! Serving tea to anyone who comes along, offering them water, overflowing with warmth and hospitality! Can it ever be a good sign for a woman to be so friendly?"

Mamata's son was fortunate to have gone to visit his Boro Pishi, his father's elder sister, now that his matriculation examinations were over. But nobody thought of veiling their remarks in Himani's presence.

As for the subject of this tumultuous controversy, after a whole day of anxiety and fasting, once the tussle between life and death was over and this poor woman left mother and child in the nurse's care to come back home after bathing in the Ganga, it was quite late at night. She was supposed to dine at her sister's house before returning home, but on the way back it was Mamata who insisted on being dropped off at her own doorstep. Along with a hint of delicate reproach against her husband, she also felt a certain apprehension. She had been sure that when Sudhangshu came home and heard the news, he would rush to Sabita's house. Who knew whether he was feeling well after last night's excesses!

The same person, Sabita's younger brother-in-law had come to drop her off.

"As you can see, Mamatadi," he smiled, "nobody needs you at home. Having eaten their fill, everyone has gone to sleep without a care in the world. Serves you right – you will get nothing to eat here. Not a sip of water all day! Boudi will be very unhappy, I can tell you."

"Tell her not to be angry or upset, bhai, one day I will visit her to be fed on demand. Just let Sabu recover first."

As soon as the attendant opened the door, Mamata's eye fell on someone sleeping on a camp bed.

"Who is sleeping here, Subodh?" she asked in surprise

"Borobabu, madam."

"Borobabu! Why downstairs?"

Subodh didn't know why, either; he had merely followed

instructions to carry the bedding downstairs. Thinking hard he said: "Maybe it's because he's expecting you."

"Don't be silly, you idiot!" she smiled gently, handing him her wet clothes as she entered. Groping in the dark, she placed her hand on the sleeping person's back and asked: "Did you give up hope, then? It almost turned out that way – they were adamant about my not coming back. But you know me, I can't stay away from my old man at night. I came away, ignoring all their jibes."

Sudhangshu merely shifted his back, shrinking from her touch. He didn't say a word.

"You can sulk, I must say, even in your old age!" persisted Mamata, leaning forward slightly. "You didn't even come to their house. How your 'Sabi' suffered! Gave birth to a lump of a girl, ultimately, but she went through no end of pain for that."

Surprised at not receiving any response to her remarks, Mamata sank down at one end of the bed. Drawing her husband's hand into her lap, she asked tenderly: "What is the matter, are you not feeling well?"

"Go inside Don't pester me." Pulling his hand away, Sudhangshu turned his back on her.

Deeply hurt, Mamata rose to her feet. What was the reason for such anger! Couldn't a woman visit her own relatives in their time of need? But it was not her husband's nature to demean himself at his age by making his anger and offended pride public. What could the matter be? In an even more gentle tone she said: "I'm going, but surely you are not really going to sleep here? Get up, let's go to the bedroom."

"I am neither inclined to enter that room, nor to talk to you. Go! Go away from here."

Hungry and exhausted, Mamata eyes filled with tears at her husband's unexpected harshness. But without revealing her distress she asked:

"Please let me know what I have done wrong."

"I don't feel like discussing anything with someone who pretends to be naïve and innocent after harbouring evidence of her guilt within her own room. You certainly trained yourself in cunning ways, but ultimately couldn't pull it off."

At last it struck Mamata that there might be some connection between all this and Tarangini's questions that morning. But – for shame! Staggering up the stairs like one inebriated she looked around for proof of her guilt, then suddenly noticed, lying in a heap beside the bed, a mud-stained, faded khadi dhoti, and a kurta in a similar condition. … Like a hunted animal, pursued by the police, the boy who had taken shelter in this room for a few hours last night … Mamata herself was not aware that at some point he had changed his clothes to protect himself. Perhaps when she had gone to check if anyone was awake, before letting him out of the house …

The state in which the frozen, immobile Mamata stayed up through the night, was something known only to the One who remains invisible, keeping a tally of everyone's joys and sorrows.

Listening with bated breath, Bijoli was completely taken aback.

"What are you saying Didi, was he your maternal cousin, son of your mother's own brother! The missing Nikhilesh implicated in the bombing case? Broke out of prison, did he?"

"Yes."

Flinging her arms around Mamata, Bijoli started weeping loudly. "Why should you keep quiet Didi, why can't you tell everyone? Why punish yourself for no reason?"

"Yesterday I could have explained everything to them Mejobou, but today it is no longer possible," answered Mamata with a wan smile.

"Why not, Didi, isn't there something called religion after all? Why should this unjust accusation go unchallenged?"

"Then let's appoint you my lawyer to plead my case, and let me beg a just trial with folded hands."

"Can you joke even in the middle of such suffering, Didi? The devil himself must have possessed you. Can you accept such falsehood without protest?"

"What's true or false is often hard to judge with one's mind, Mejobou! What I had taken for the supreme truth, I now realize was a great a falsehood. So if a falsehood is established as the truth today, what's the harm?"

"Harm! I swear, Himu's mother, Will you accept this insult when you are blameless?"

"An insult once inflicted can't be undone, Bijoli. What can I explain to them? If they say 'Now you are concocting a story to save yourself from a difficult situation,' I will not be able to bear that insult either."

Bijoli was simple, Bijoli was naïve. Her tears came easily.

"Is that possible?" she said.

But why should it not be possible? For those who had no difficulty believing such a thing about Mamata after she had lived with them for eighteen years – would such a small thing have been too much for them to imagine?

Unlike Bijoli, Mamata could not be angry with the wretched young man who had destroyed her permanent shelter by seeking shelter with her for a couple of hours.

Mamata no longer felt any mamata, any tender love, for the fragile home that had crumbled to dust at a single puff of misfortune.

As she was departing, Sudhangshu had said: "Do you realize what will happen to our honour, our social prestige, if you walk out on us like this ?"

"I do, but I also cannot forget that the thing called honour does not belong to you alone."

"Do you realize that getting our daughters married will prove to be an impossible burden now?"

"Perhaps it will, but the burden will not be mine. I shall have no more burdens to bear for this household."

The human heart, even when it hardens itself, remains weak! Why did tears spring to Sudhangshu's eyes?

"Where have you decided to go, Mamata?"

Mamata did not meet his gaze.

"I have decided nothing at all," she had replied, face averted. "I will have to see whether a woman can find a place for herself in this big, wide world."

Vermillion Clouds

SULEKHA SANYAL

THIS room of hers! Quite well furnished, with a large wardrobe and dressing table. Items of luxury arranged close at hand. A household bearing the clear stamp of affluence. A safe haven indeed! Still she wasn't happy, hadn't been happy in all these years. What use was it going about here and there, all dressed up, travelling by car? How could she fill the emptiness in her life? It was like the gap separating river from sea, body from mind. Would she ever fathom this man? They had been married for so long, the two of them. From the depths of poverty, Ananta had raised her to a much higher status, but did his duty end there? Her heart burned, as if on fire. Couldn't the man bring himself to open his heart, unfold himself to her, ever? Why go about as if he were a culprit?

Or had he found out all about her? The thought made her heart go cold. He had come to know about her past, a chapter of her life that she had erased. Was that why he gazed sorrowfully at her, waking up at night and pacing about, repenting what he had done? Perhaps that was not it either, perhaps he just didn't fancy her. Had he been looking for someone resembling the one he had lost? Was that why he still had such an aversion to her?

Every now and then, as she went about her business, her eyes would be drawn to the oil painting that covered half the bedroom wall. The first day, when she came to her new home after the wedding, she had stopped short in amazement. There before her was the shoulder length image of an exquisite woman.

"Bow before her, Malati," her mother-in-law had urged

her, "greet her with a pranam. This is Lalita, Ananta's first wife." With these words she suppressed a sigh; that, too, had not escaped Malati's notice. But she hadn't bowed her head. Neck arched like a headstrong horse she remained standing beneath the portrait. But seeing her mother-in-law suppress that sigh she felt quite disheartened.

At night it was the same. She burned with rage at the sight of Ananta gazing unblinkingly at the portrait from his chair. He, too, sighed as he turned his eyes away.

"If this is how you feel, why did you marry again?" she demanded in exasperation.

"Are you referring to Lalita?" A faint smile played on her husband's lips. "One day I'll tell you the whole story and you, too, will sigh."

After that on so many nights, she saw her husband rise from the bed, heard him sigh many times, watched him resting his head below the picture.

From that time on, the emptiness set in. She spent her days burdened with an extraordinary vacuum. How often she had shed secret tears. There they were, sighing heavily at the sight of a picture, and here she was, a living human being, … Erasing her past, she had stolen here like a fugitive in order to survive, concealing her name, suppressing her history. Had Ananta ever called her close and asked her about these things? Had the two of them ever opened their hearts to each other in confidence? The things she repeated in silence to herself, alone in a dark room, talking to the walls – was Ananta so heartless that he hadn't the slightest desire to hear what she had to say?

Sometimes she felt her heart would break with weeping at the thought of this wounded and broken body of hers, at the desperate urgency of somehow clambering out of this abyss of despair. At feeling bone-tired. How often had she thought of telling Ananta everything, of feeling unburdened after telling him, taking refuge in a corner of someone else's heart. Sharing her worries and anxieties with someone else, dividing her anguish and sorrow. But that didn't happen. Whenever she thought of them, she still had to hide her face in the dark. It had all happened so long ago, but was impossible to forget! Even now her mind shuddered at the terror of it at the occasional flashes of news she received.

Ma was chopping pui stalks. Resting the blade of her bonti on its side, she rose to her feet when her daughter did not respond to her repeated calls. Lying on the torn mat on one side of the veranda, the girl was heaving with unspent tears. Patting her, Ma couldn't help smiling.

"Come now, bapu! I won't hang myself. Go and take up that job, then. I can't accept the fact, that's why I said that. I hear all sorts of things, things that are not good. That's why I said it."

Since evening, the girl had been behaving like this. Some friend of hers who worked in Supplies had apparently promised her a job.

That something like this would happen, Manoda had guessed the very day she saw Binoy return home at an unaccustomed hour. Even the sight of his fever-hot face had not aroused her tenderness.

She spoke rather sharply: "In these days of war so many idle men are finding jobs. Even girls of a tender age are bringing home a hundred rupees, or a hundred and fifty. For you, a working man, to have lost your job – what is this?"

He hadn't responded then, but Manoda got her answer a few days later when, having coughed up blood, Binoy glanced at his wide-eyed wife and smiled: "That's why. Do you understand now why I lost my job?"

A few days later, giving up her studies in college, Malati

returned home with news of a job. Binoy had moved into a free-bed hospital. When she told him about the job, he smiled his approval.

"Khuki, my little girl, you must give me five rupees so that I can have some fruit. I'll get well," And he placed his hand on her head in blessing.

But Malati's mother kicked up a fuss: "What's all this about taking up a job! Should I hang myself then? Like father, like daughter! Do you think you can do whatever you please?"

Her face flushed, the girl fumed for a while then burst into a flood of tears: "How will we manage then, tell me? Baba doesn't get a proper diet, Montu's studies have come to a standstill. That pui-chorchori and rice you cook in the courtyard every day – I can't take it anymore. Never again!"

Listening to her petulant cry, Manoda felt like smiling, even in the middle of so much sorrow. This daughter of hers, so beautiful, yet so childish! God knows what fate has in store for her! Receiving no response to her repeated calls, it was the mother who finally got up to say: "Go, take up that job then."

Looking beyond the north-eastern corner of the house, one could faintly make out Esplanade East, that dead city. Long ago, when she was still in school, Malati, dressed in her frock and holding Binoy's hand, had wandered down that road. Pointing, Binoy would say: "Can you tell me what that is, Khuki? Do you recognize it? Silly girl! It's the Imperial Library. Tell me now, what does 'library' mean?"

Today, going inside, the fancy office décor aroused a strange feeling within her. Her entire body broke out in a sweat.

A very simple test, as if everything had been prearranged for her, so it only remained for her to accept the job. She would earn a salary of a hundred and fifty rupees, as much as her friend, Shefali. So much money! She could hardly take it in.

Had she ever seen such a large amount, at one time? And all of it would come into her hands at the end of the month, apparently.

But travelling back in the bus, Shefali made her feel rather disheartened. "It's hardly a large sum, a hundred and fifty! Do you think you can run your household on that? That's what many girls imagine at first, but you'd barely know where the money goes by the end of the month. It won't do for you to go to work in that torn sari, with a dry, cracked face -- you may as well give up hope of climbing up the ladder. You'll see how much you end up spending just on saris and face powder in a month. Set aside a hundred for those expenses alone."

"Wah, how will I feed Ma and Montu then?" she protested, her throat turning dry. "And I have to pay for Baba."

"Well, you'll have to get it somehow. Don't you have some claims over and above what's due to you? Haven't you seen Rekha who was in class with us? She gets three or four hundred a month because she's friendly with every senior officer." Tapping her on the cheek, she smiled: "You're very foolish. Now that you're in, you'll get to know what it's all about. Just keep them happy. With your looks, they'll seek you out, just wait and see."

All the way home, Malati thought about what Shefali had said. The untidiest, silliest girl in class Shefali used to be, but her transformation had been extraordinary. She was the first to take up a job under the pressure of circumstances, so she had the right to offer advice by way of explanation! But what sort of advice was this, what sort of guidance? As if her words were not fully understood, as if their meaning was strangely veiled. Malati's heart refused to be pacified; it trembled with uneasiness.

But diffidence, timidity, respect – these lasted only a couple of days. When someone entered the giant gates of Esplanade East, all these vanished in no time. But for some strange reason they weren't willing to abandon Malati!

Beautiful large eyes, complexion like buttermilk, this girl

had been attracting Sushanto Sen's attention too often as she passed from room to room. He recalled Drinkwater Saheb's order: a nice girl, a companion, someone he only had to look at to be reminded of that companion left at home. A girl who would stay close all the time. He had also indirectly hinted that in return Sushanto Sen would ascend to a higher grade.

"Will you take it on? he had asked, sending for her through a bearer. "It's a part-time job. No labour, but the money's good. I have heard about your situation at home – what can you accomplish with a hundred-and-fifty rupees?"

The girl said nothing.

"I know, you're a Bengali girl after all!" he guffawed. "You shrink at the very thought of being called the saheb's personal secretary. Will he eat you up? Please think about it."

That day Malati had gone home with the firm resolve to never accept such an offer! She would give up her job if need be, but she wouldn't take anything from the saheb!

But as soon as she entered her house, she saw Binoy. The hospital had been closed down, converted into military barracks, and the patients had been thrown out.

"Do you realize, Khuki" he said, trying to smile, "it's only a hundred rupees. If I could somehow get a hundred rupees a month, I'd get well. If I can stay at a sanatorium, I'd be cured in six months, just wait and see."

The effort to survive seemed to have unhinged him. Only his eyes blazed fiercely.

Manoda had gone out, but when she returned and saw Binoy she stopped short, then advanced, smiling: "Are you cured then? Did they discharge you? But you mustn't go to work tomorrow," she continued, looking happily at Malati and without waiting for an answer. "They're coming to see you and give their final word on the marriage proposal, Khuki. It's the same boy,"she continued, glancing in her husband's direction, "the boy from the Majumdar family who has passed his M.A. They're very keen on the match, they want the wedding in the month of Boshekh itself." Manoda prattled on.

"But who will support the household?" was all Binoy said, just once.

"Let the household go to hell!" she cried, bursting into tears of rage. "If it's beyond you, I'll take my son's hand and go begging in the streets. But is that a reason to leave our daughter unmarried? Don't I see, all around me, what's happening to all the girls? That we should live in times like these! If I could only see my daughter remain pure and good."

Biting her lips, tears in her eyes, Malati sat in her darkened room. Ma hadn't seen Curzon Park, hadn't watched the dogs near the dustbin fight with human beings over a fragment of meat and bone. These days, the screams of those who were starving in the streets brought tears to Manoda's eyes; while feeding them strained rice starch, she would add a few grains of cooked rice as well. If she had not yet become inhuman, it was because she got a few mouthfuls of gravel-mixed rice twice a day. That was why she had developed a perverse desire to eat her fill. She wanted to see vermillion in her daughter's hair-parting. Just as the rich had their whims, this obsessive fancy had her in its grip.

Wiping her eyes, Malati emerged from the darkness to face Binoy.

"Please proceed to Madras tomorrow itself, Baba. I shall send you a hundred rupees every month."

Manoda stared wide-eyed at Malati. Like a beast of prey, she raked her daughter's face, her eyes, her body, looking for something. Malati glanced once in her direction, throwing her a mocking smile:

"I'm giving up my present job, I've been offered a much higher-paid one. I will certainly send you the money."

Sushanto was pleased. "That's what I want," he said, breaking into a smile. "But you must keep up appearances for my sake. I mean, you must become a little smarter. He's a saheb, after all, and moody to boot. Who knows what he might fancy! All you have to do is take it in your stride. If you can keep him happy, all your domestic worries will vanish, I promise you. Just wait and see."

Malati's eyes were swollen from weeping. She had cried all night, gone personally to see Binoy off when he boarded the train. As soon as the image of a new bride with vermillion in her hair floated up before her mind's eye, she had strangled the thought, killed it. She must save her father, mother, younger brother.

As long as she could, she would keep all of them alive – she alone would cease to live. Could Sushanto Sen with his smiles and sweet words, make her forget the depths of disaster into which she was falling?

Not even a few days had passed when Malati came to Sushanto and burst into tears.

"Save me, please, from that drunken saheb! Let me return to my old job, Sushantobabu."

"What's all this!" He couldn't help laughing. Are you quite out of your mind? He's a saheb after all! Won't he drink a little, now and then? He's bound to behave like that, sometimes. For shame, Malati Debi. Don't forget, your father is in a sanatorium. Someone else has already taken your job. Please don't be childish." Seeing the girl's swollen eyes and face, his mind wavered for an instant. But the mind was a bucking horse after all! If you didn't use the whip, you couldn't bring it under control.

What use calming her down and sending her back, though? She came rushing back to him soon enough.

"Please transfer me to some lower position, then. I won't

ask for much money. Or else ..." Meeting Sushanto's gaze with her, desperate, anguished eyes, Malati proposed: "Please marry me yourself. That will save my mother, my brother. I cannot manage without money. You have a lot of money, after all. If I could get just a small share, that would be enough."

"You can't behave like this Malati!" Sushanto almost whispered, close to her ear. For shame, don't forget your younger brother, your parents. And besides ..." he continued, as if confiding a secret, "the war is almost over. The last Japanese troops have retreated from Imphal, and Berlin has fallen – can't you see how desperate the English sahebs have become? How much longer do you think this will continue? Our good old days will be back soon."

Malati felt like dying of humiliation and shame. How easily the man had laughed away her words, abandoning her, pushing her to the brink of disaster.

Whenever she tried to leave, tried to move on, she was reminded of Binoy's eyes, blazing with the desire to live. Malati felt like tearing out fistfuls of her hair. It seemed that there was no escaping these bonds that coiled around her like a snake.

Along with news of the war's end there came news about Binoy as well. Manoda remained frozen and silent, not weeping at all. It was Malati who had wailed, banging her head like a lunatic. A fire seemed to rage within her; she might have found solace in tearing her hair out with both hands. If Binoy was not going to live, why had he left, plunging Khuki, his little girl, into such self-degradation! What was she to do now? True, the villages had surrendered themselves to city streets, had died in order to survive. The girls who had gone with the soldiers had been discarded like torn shoes, the paint on their lips blurring with the tears in their eyes. The future of those girls, school dropouts, lost souls, was now fated to lie in those secret alleys. What was Malati to do now! Departing, Drinkwater had offered her his thanks for her companionship. The young Malati of those days, when she emerged from her immersion in a sea of bitterness and degradation, felt as if she could no longer face herself. Her body was aflame.

Manoda was gazing at Malati. Unable to shed tears, her heart was inwardly on fire. Reaching out with both arms, she called out: "Just stroke my breast, Khuki, it's burning so." Rushing to her mother, Malati clasped her in her arms, silently hiding her head in her bosom.

"You have such a good nature, just like goddess Lakshmi," her mother whispered. "I will not let your life go waste. This war does not have the power to thwart us."

Manoda played an active role in the history of the two years that followed. Like a bird of prey, eyes blazing, wings outspread, she shielded her daughter, kept her protected within her brother's household. Her son and daughter must survive in exchange for her part-time work as maidservant, two shifts a day. That was enough to keep Manoda happy. Procuring a minor teaching job, Malati would hand over the few rupees she earned every month to Mamima, her maternal aunt. But her uncle and aunt were none too pleased – theirs, too, was a humble household where meeting expenses was a struggle. Manoda ignored their annoyance, hunted frantically for a prospective bridegroom.

When the match was fixed, Malati objected: "No, Ma, let it be."

Glaring at her, eyes like a tigress, the mother caught her daughter's hand in a tight grip. 'Why not? I didn't hang myself then, but now I will."

"You, Montu, who will look after everyone?" her daughter demanded, bursting into tears.

"Last time you brought disaster upon yourself worrying about all that. Don't you remember?"

No argument worked after that. It had all happened so long ago, but why was it still impossible to wipe out the past! She must heal her heart that bled inwardly day and night, or what would she live for!

But again her eyes returned to the portrait, the picture that had proved to be the real obstacle. It would not allow the void in her heart to be filled, would not allow her to open her mind. Just those few lifeless, soulless brush strokes.

It had to be removed from this room, from Ananta's gaze. Reaching out, Malati struggled to pull it down, then gave up in annoyance and sat down. What singular beauty in the eyes of that woman! Who could ever call them lifeless!

Rising she picked up a vase from the table and took aim. If nothing else, she could smash the picture couldn't she? Disfigure that beautiful face. And then there would be nothing left.

The sound of shoes outside, and Ananta entered the room. With a start, she put down the object in her hand.

"Why are you standing there looking so disturbed? What's the matter, Malati?"

Forced to summon up a wan smile she replied, "Why, nothing at all – you're home late."

"I can't help it" Ananta cried agitatedly. "I'm going crazy with so many things on my mind. Tomorrow is the first of the month. As soon as the night's over, I must shell out an enormous amount of money to pay for all the rites of a yajna."

Seeing him collapse into a chair, his wife asked quietly: "Won't you have something to eat?"

"Later. Come, sit down – take that chair." Taking her hand, Ananta forced his wife into the chair facing him. "Listen, let me tell you about it. So many things piled up in my heart. I wonder I haven't lost my sanity."

At her husband's words, a world of pain seemed to fall away. Malati felt her heart hammering. For the first time, husband and wife sat face to face. He was opening his heart to her and she strained to catch every word.

"The crockery business has failed dismally, Malati. Nabin came by to inform me. At first we two were together, we brothers. I used to live on the ground floor, in a room with a low rent. I didn't possess any of the things that you see here. I ran a small business, but even that didn't do too well. Ma did all the cooking herself, her sons would sit down to a meal, their wives would serve them food. All we ever had was charchari made of saag and greens, but there was so much nourishment in it. There were none of these cooks and servants, drivers and chefs of today ... Then came the war. I was fortunate enough to land a military contract and the money flowed in. I grew and expanded. We bought two cars. Drivers, bearers, servants, cooks, the house seemed to be teeming with them. Nabin's son went off to study English at a school run by sahebs in Darjeeling. We were spending two hundred and fifty rupees a month, but even that was not enough. Nabin began to complain, and so did his wife. Ultimately, he constructed a house in Ballygunj and moved there with his wife. Since then, I have tried so many ventures, giving up one for another, but nothing has brought me satisfaction. Nothing did well. This was my latest effort and it too has failed. That's why I said I'm going crazy. As soon as I wake up in the morning, I must pay the cook and servants, deal with the demands of my office workers – just think! Thanks to the war, it is only our lifestyle that has grown more affluent. The money has all gone. I feel now that we were better off earlier."

Impossible to resist the temptation of making a slightly pointed remark!

"Indeed you were better off," said Malati, suppressing a smile. "After all you had Lalita then."

If only she could provoke some turmoil in the man's heart

with this remark, extract a confession from him! That Ananta loved Malati even more – was it still necessary to spell that out? But the admission would make her so confident, enable her to approach him easily, to slowly open her heart to him. But seeing her husband's countenance, she was rendered speechless. The blood had drained from his face, leaving it deathly white. Ananta seemed to be writhing inwardly like a wordless, wounded animal. Some fierce current seemed to be rising up in his throat like a flood …

Looking at him, Malati shuddered, her heart shivering with inexplicable terror. Perhaps Ananta would sit up now and tell her the sorrowful story of his past life. For an instant, she too fixed her frightened gaze upon her husband's face, then with a sudden sob, hid her face in his lap and remained still.

How late it was. The moon's pale light had fallen across the veranda outside. Rows of electric lights lining the wide stretch of Central Avenue … it was hard to notice the moonlight. The road was silent – no traffic, the occasional shouts of a couple of drunks, and far away, somebody's pet dog apparently barking at the sound of the street dogs' snarls.

"Get up, Malati," Ananta said. "Listen, let me tell you. You don't know the whole story after all." With these words he took her hand and forced her to sit up. "I made money in the war, but do you know whom I sacrificed to do so?" he asked, looking her straight in the eye. Smiling wanly, he pointed at the picture. "It was her. We hadn't been married long. She was an educated, beautiful girl. My business was floundering, sometimes we didn't even have one square meal a day, but I never saw her complain. Then the war broke out and Lalita took up a job. Somehow she would help me advance, that was her firm resolve. She developed contacts with senior officers, introduced me to them. They in turn led us to their seniors. In ones and twos, I got several good military contracts. The more

I earned, the greedier I became. Finally, I had set my sights on a big contract, but it was about to elude me by a hair's breadth. There was this military officer, notorious for being a bad character. The conditions he laid down were minor: he had seen Lalita, and would simply like to meet her once, get to know her. She wouldn't agree. 'No more!' she pleaded. 'Don't make me go any further.' But I was intoxicated by the lure of money. I walked out of the house leaving the saheb with Lalita. I returned to find the saheb gone. The door to my room was closed. I thought Lalita was sulking. On my way home, I had bought her a necklace set with precious stones, an expensive sari and blouse. I was convinced Lalita's anger would dissolve upon receiving these gifts. After banging on the door, calling out to her, when I received no response, I began to feel afraid." Ananta's hands were trembling, his face had broken out in a sweat. He was desperately trying to control his overflowing emotions. "Pulling out my revolver from the drawer, I rushed to the saheb's office and from there, having found out his address, to his home. He was sitting there drinking. He vowed he had not touched Lalita. There was fire in her eyes, he said, he had left in fear. His words revived me and I rushed home. The door was still closed. I summoned help to break down the door, and when I entered the room, I saw Lalita hanging from a rope." Wiping the sweat from his forehead, he pointed. "There, in that space occupied by the picture you see. I realized she had left me, her heart filled with contempt and reproach towards me." Ananta's lips trembled uncontrollably. Grown man that he was, his tears brimmed over and poured from his eyes. Ashamed, he quickly wiped them with a handkerchief and smiled dully. "As you know, I don't sleep at night. How can I? I can find no peace. I hear so many fragments of news all day, some rumoured, some true; slander and calumny. I feel so scared. I stay awake to guard you. I have lost Lalita, but I must not lose you as well. It's because the tree has blown away that I must keep the sapling well protected. Let the storm not injure its body."

"You don't know my story either, do you?" Malati asked, gazing at her husband, her eyes full of tears.

"I know everything Malati," her husband replied, taking her tearful, intense face in his hands. "Both of us are once bitten twice shy, like cows that dread vermillion storm clouds because they have seen a fire once before." He tried to summon up a smile, but the tears flowed freely. Malati wept as well, thinking about Lalita.

As with human beings who are healthy and whole, the anguish in their hearts streamed from their eyes in a torrent of tears, closing the gap that had kept them apart for so long.

The Shadow

LILA MAJUMDAR

"YOU can't say that, Gopen Babu," said Doctor Babu, stuffing the double pack of cards into their case. "Everything can't be explained by logical argument. All these people who have seen the apparition – they couldn't all be lying, could they?"

"No, that's not quite what I meant," replied Gopen Babu gently. "But the thing is, if the soul is infinite by nature, how can it assume a finite form?"

"Finite form, what's that?" demanded Chaudhuri Moshai. "The soul is not only infinite in extent, it's also limitless in capacity. It's no difficult task for the soul to assume a finite form."

"And in this case it doesn't even materialize as a form. It appears as a mere shadow: you can neither catch it nor touch it. You can look right through it, to the trees across the Ganga; you can even walk right through it if you wish."

Shuddering, Chaudhuri Moshai wrapped his shawl more closely round himself.

"Actually, Gopen Babu, because you never married and settled down, you want rational explanations for everything. There are many situations in this world where reason and logic don't work, but you have no experience of them, have you?"

Doctor Babu rose to his feet.

"I'll take your leave, Gopen Babu. In my house, too, nobody is willing to accept rational explanations if I get home late. I can't quite dismiss what you said about the infinite, though. But you know, even a six-foot-tall person's photograph can fit into a four-inch-square piece of paper. Of course, that photograph is not the person himself; it's no more than a shadowy image that resembles him exactly. Similarly perhaps, in special situations, certain events and characters leave their imprint on the screen of Time, and if those special situations recur, the imprints become visible, like photographic images. Who knows what really happens? Come, Danu, let's be off."

Danu was wrapping a scarf round his neck. Known in the locality as a talented singer, he had a singing role in the amateur play scheduled for the Durga Puja, so there was no end to the precautions he took. Besides, all this talk was already beginning to give him the shivers.

"Why worry any more about ghosts, Gopen Babu?" said Danu with a forced smile. "Rather, you should watch out for smugglers. You've seen what the papers say, haven't you? Apparently the smugglers have started deploying women, and their den is somewhere in this area. All they have to do is drop anchor in the middle of the Ganga and immerse all the gold. Late at night, their accomplices row there by boat, lift the stuff out of the water, and pass it on. What could be simpler!"

Chaudhuri Moshai guffawed loudly. "Arre, they don't even immerse it in the water. With the winter winds expected soon, are they likely to dive into the water now? Trust you to say that! I have heard from reliable sources that they tie the stuff to the chains beneath the buoy. All they have to do is to untie the knots and take the goods away. But the police have also sniffed out the truth, at last. They are lying in wait here and there. If they can only catch one of the miscreants, they'd extract all the information through interrogation."

"What's all this you're talking about!" protested Doctor Babu. "You should be a little careful, Gopen Babu. No one can say what criminals might do. Engaged in illegal activities for so long, they develop a mindset where the idea of committing the odd murder doesn't daunt them at all. And then you're living all alone. Moshai, can't you employ an old retainer or two? I must admit, the local people would die rather than spend a night here in this house."

"I did bring an old retainer with me," said Gopen Babu slowly, "but he simply refused to stay so close to the Ganga. Apparently the river-smells aggravated his asthma. He lasted just one night."

"It wasn't the smell of the Ganga or anything like that," said Chaudhuri Moshai, "those gardeners and workmen of yours scared him away with talk of ghosts, that's all. And they were wise to do so, too. You won't listen to advice, will you? I urge you to move into my smaller house. The same cook will prepare your food, you'll avoid the damp air of the riverside, and if you wish, even your old retainer might come back. The rent is only thirty rupees. But who ever listens to advice?"

After they had all departed, Gopen Babu locked the smaller gate and the veranda enclosed in thick American wire mesh, and moved to the side that overlooked the Ganga shore. It was just one veranda actually, encircling the entire house, wrapped in wire mesh all the way around. Apparently, this arrangement had been made in earlier days, because man-eating crocodiles had been spotted on a couple of occasions, when they came right up to the house at high tide. It was said that before Gopen Babu bought the property, in the last thirty or forty years, nobody had spent much time in the house. Not more than a night or two, at the most.

Just outside the veranda was a terrace paved with colourful fragments of ceramic pottery. A fountain used to play there, once. It had a stone basin, and there were a couple of stone benches near it.

From the veranda, it appeared to Gopen Babu in the faint starlight that someone was sitting in a corner of one of the benches. As if a frail, slim young woman, her whole body wrapped in folds of green fabric, was sitting there, facing the Ganga.

For the first time in his fifty-six years, Gopen Babu felt goose pimples all over his body. The woman seemed to have a mass of wet hair piled on top of her head, ornaments glinting at her earlobes and neck, her skin the colour of raw turmeric. He himself could not fathom how much of what he saw in the starlight was real, and how much was imagined. He also noticed the black box, about nine inches long, that lay on the bench, beside the woman.

At last, Gopen Babu came to his senses. Indeed, it was such beautiful women who were deployed by the smugglers. He was not unaware of the fact, after all. Truly, no one could ever suspect this woman, looking at the way she reclined her light body upon the bench, like a tender green vine. Even from so far away, Gopen Babu could sense her loveliness. A faint fragrance wafted to his nostrils.

Without a gun, without a stick, Gopen Babu unlocked the small door in the wire mesh surrounding the veranda and stepped out, unarmed as he was. A plump, fair man, with thinning hair, thick black-framed glasses perched upon his nose, his eyesight seeming to decline by the day. Who knows, when he got close to her, perhaps he would find that he was totally mistaken; that what he saw was quite different from what his imagination had conjured up after hearing all those tales. It was really unlikely that anyone could be there; after all, the only approach was from the Ganga, or over the two-foot-high wall. Besides, nobody from this locality would visit this house at eleven p.m., that was certain. But then, the local residents were mundane folk, all of them. How could such a woman belong here?

Descending the four steps from the veranda, crossing the

row of man-size red-rose shrubs lining the terrace, he came to the edge of the dried-up fountain to find, exactly as he had expected, that the bench was empty.

A strange sigh escaped him. Had Gopen Babu privately wanted, then, that such a woman should have indeed been there, in that place? Could such a woman exist? After all, she was a figment of the imagination, created from descriptions of all the beautiful women he had read about in verse, through all these forty years. What was it Danu had said? You could even walk through her if you so desired.

But then, why was the air heavy with an unfamiliar fragrance? Glancing all round him, Gopen Babu saw something pale green detach itself and emerge from the deep green shade of the gardenia shrub. Seeing her suddenly so close, Gopen Babu seemed to lose his wits.

"I am in grave danger," the woman said to him, with a wan smile. "Please help me. Hide this." So saying, with supreme calm, she offered Gopen Babu the black box she had been clutching to her bosom. Gopen Babu seemed to have lost his tongue.

"What … what's in there?" he asked, in an unnaturally hoarse voice.

She burst into peals of laughter. Her laughter bounced off the trees and spread its echo across the bosom of the Ganga. Didn't the woman have any sense at all? Who could say where the police were lying in wait for her? Gopen Babu had never seen a smuggler before, so he took a good look at her. Ah, were they so beautiful, then? Could it be possible? His eyes were dazzled. Her forehead was framed in short, damp tendrils of curly hair, the green stones at her earlobes glinting in the starlight, eyebrows like birdwings, so smooth and delicate that one felt afraid to raise one's voice. And yet, somewhere in the folds of her half-damp clothing, a blunt-nosed weapon with a sawn-off nose lay concealed. Apparently, these female smugglers were ace shots too; so Danu had read in a newspaper. Her fingers were truly like buds of champa blossom, an enormous emerald ring on one of them.

Why people happily committed sins, why it seemed worthwhile even to be condemned to hell – the answer to this mystery suddenly became clear to Gopen Babu. He reached out to take the box. It was so heavy, he almost dropped it. The woman came up very close, and smiled.

"It's very heavy, isn't it?" she asked. "Why don't you open it, to see why it's so heavy?"

With these words, she opened the lid herself. The box was full of gold coins.

"You must hide this in a proper place, okay?" she said, and for a single second, rested her soft, tender fingers on Gopen Babu's wrist.

Gopen Babu felt a strange ringing in his ears. This was what a blissful death might be like, he thought. The very next moment, the girl moved a long distance away.

"Those don't belong to me," she told him. "Later, when all the hubbub has subsided, send them to Banani Devi in Bonhooghli, okay?"

Gopen Babu was totally tongue-tied. He gazed fixedly at her. Little by little, she began to drift farther and farther away. Soon she had moved so far away that her green sari seemed to merge momentarily with the row of trees, then emerge, glinting, the very next moment. Then she vanished completely into the green, grassy Ganga verge, and it became impossible to distinguish her form.

Gopen Babu returned to his room with the box. His mind was crystal clear. There was no need to tell him where to hide the box. Shifting the croton that grew in a ceramic pot beside the steps leading to the terrace, he used a small spade to dig a deep hole. Placing the box inside the cavity, he carefully covered it with soil, and replaced the flowerpot above it. Then he lay in bed, calmly waiting for the policemen to arrive.

Sure enough they came, a couple of hours later, with Chaudhuri Moshai, who, as a leader of the village panchayat, could never be left out of such matters. They rang the bell at the main gate, and came in, looking rather embarrassed, just to ask a couple of routine questions.

"We ask because we have to, sir, for we know only too well that nobody can approach this place from the river. After all, our own people are posted on the river as well. But nothing is beyond these women, so we came here to ask after them. You can go back to sleep now, in peace. You keep the mesh door locked, I hope? The smugglers have secret links with some people in this village, there's no doubt about that. The way gold and valuables are passed on, it's beyond anyone's power to declare it illegal. We'll take your leave, sir."

After they had gone, Gopen Babu locked the door. He fell asleep as soon as he lay on his bed. A faint smile lingered on the corner of his lips.

The next morning, Radheyshyam, who had the key to the back door, came in with tea and toast to awaken Gopen Babu. There were dark circles under his eyes.

"What's the matter, Radheyshyam?"

"Nobody slept in the village last night, Babu, for the police conducted a search, all night long. The woman was captured from the house where Amin and his family live. They found gold under the wooden bed. I went to see. My word, how beautiful she was! I felt like weeping when I saw her."

Gopen Babu's hand was shaking. Putting down the cup with great care, he said: "Maybe someone else brought in the gold? Why would that woman have carried it?"

"That's what she says. Claims she knows nothing about it,

that she had just dropped by, that Amin's grandmother was her foster mother, and so on. She was crying a lot, that girl. There, do you see that lorry drive up? They're taking her to the thana. Why, Babu, what's the matter?"

Dropping the cup, Gopen Babu rushed out like a madman. Crying, was she? Perhaps she thought it was Gopen Babu who had told on her. Somehow the thought was unbearable. Approaching the lorry, he saw them hoist up a tall, hefty woman dressed in a red-and-blue sari, her whole body covered in gold jewellery, her lips and cheeks painted red. Some woman he didn't know. Ah, what a relief!

Smothering a smile behind his handkerchief, Gopen Babu went back to his room and ordered Radheyshyam to make him a fresh cup of tea. Almost at once, Chaudhuri Moshai arrived on the scene, hair dishevelled, bursting with excitement, with Danu in tow.

"So, she got caught out finally, didn't she?" said Danu, as soon as he had taken a chair. "If you're born a woman, why get involved in such rackets? Let's have some tea, Gopenda."

Chaudhuri Moshai sat down and stretched out his legs.

"Anyway, you're relieved of one threat now," said Danu. "The smuggler-woman has been captured. But now, watch out for ghosts."

"No, this is no joke," insisted Chaudhuri Moshai. "As it is one feels uneasy at night; that's why, last evening, I didn't say any more. Do you think this house has a bad reputation for no reason at all? Are you aware that this used to be Jagu Bose's garden estate, once? Jagu Bose died insolvent, and his mistress, a beautiful dancing girl, vanished with a boxful of gold coins – that was thirty or forty years ago. Jagu Bose's wife Banani Devi is still alive. Apparently, in her old age, she is living from hand to mouth in Bonhooghli, simply waiting to die."

Gopen Babu's blood seemed to freeze. Weren't those figures

supposed to be mere images, simply shadows, so you could walk right through them?

In the still, quiet afternoon, after shifting the flowerpot from its place at the edge of the terrace, he lifted out the box, wrapped it in cottonwool, packed it in a jute cover, and sewed up the seams. Gopen Babu went to Kolkata and dispatched a registered parcel to Bonhooghli in his own name, from the main post office. On his return journey, he took three unemployed, feckless nephews along with him. If they didn't learn to do some work, how would they survive?

Besides, he knew, didn't he, that the woman would never come back?

Kindred Souls

JYOTIRMOYEE DEVI

NEITHER of them knew each other. They were not neighbours. Nor were they from the same village. They didn't even know if they were of the same caste or creed.

But yes, they were one of a kind! Womankind. On their journey they got to know each other as women, that eternally fearful, fugitive form of existence. Both were dressed in saris. Aanchal tucked around the waist, country-style. Their saris were muddy, snagged in places, at the knee and at the back. Both were walking fast. Not running, but stealthily.

I say "both" but they were not walking together. There was a gap of almost twenty or thirty yards between them. It was quite dark. Behind the trees, in the bushes and thickets. They moved furtively, concealing themselves. And from time to time they would stop abruptly in their tracks at the sound of leaves falling, or of their own footsteps. Looking now ahead, now back, as if scared of something.

Dusk had deepened. Where they were going, they themselves did not know.

Suddenly, footsteps seemed to approach very close to Menaka. Startled, she turned to look back. About seven yards away, she saw a figure. A female form. Minu shrank back in terror and moved aside. Here's someone else, she thought, let her overtake me if she wants. Who knows which side she belongs to, whether she is spying for somebody. But the other person also stopped in her tracks. Her face was not visible. Neither of them could see the other clearly.

Gradually, the woman at the back came much closer. But

she did not overtake her. Silently, she too halted in her steps. Suddenly, from somewhere, they heard male voices, footsteps. In the dark it was hard to tell which direction the sounds came from. Ahead, behind, or from one side? How many were they, these people? Were there very many?

Like a pair of frightened creatures, the women instinctively closed ranks. Who were they, those who could be heard approaching? Enemies? Freedom fighters – the Muktibahini? Khansena, the Pakistan army? Whoever, whatever they might be, they were men … Were they good men? They didn't kill women after all … but … How terrifying that might be, but … Where could they escape? Suddenly, in an instant, two women, strangers to each other, knew themselves as kindred souls. Both were women, there was just one community to which they could belong: the community of those who fear men.

The footsteps, the voices, came closer. They flung themselves to the ground behind an unknown bush, the two of them. A dense bush it was. Very dark. Near their feet, their bodies, some creature slithered away. Was it a snake? A frog? A scorpion? What could it be? At least it was not a man. Whatever it was, it must be a fugitive like themselves. Not fearing the loss of honour-prestige-respect, but a living being, fearing for its life …

"Didn't you see a couple of women?" asked one of the approaching voices. "I thought I spotted them somewhere in this direction."

"Two of them? I thought I saw one."

"Not even one," a third voice intervened. "Just shadows cast by trees. If they were women, where could they have gone?"

"This is not the time to hunt women. Come on, let's go. Khan Saheb will be angry, he asked us to hurry."

The women wore saris in faded colours, not white. In the dark, the colours were invisible. Silently, holding their breath, they lay side by side, without a word. Not one word did they utter. What if they were heard? The jungle path was utterly silent. Whether they were close to a village, who could tell? They didn't even know the location of villages or neighbourhoods.

Where they had come from, how far they had travelled, for how long, from yesterday or the day before, what they had eaten, who else was with them? ... in their state of fearful anxiety they could no longer think of these things or understand them.

There was just a sense of terror, of fear, fear of mankind – today, who could seem more terrible, more fearsome, than a man? They had seen it, before they left. That horrific, demoniac, terrible aspect that men had assumed – they could not describe it in words. Could not speak of it to anyone, ever.

But now the two of them seemed to have grown very close, as if they were related. The same fear haunted both of them. The same anxiety. Did they belong to the same creed then? To which creed did anyone belong? Nobody remembered caste and creed anymore. They were of the same kind. Womankind. Silently, without introduction, they had become kindred spirits.

2

The travellers were gone.

They sat up slowly. The leaves rustled, as if they were human. Even that sound startled them. Was it a snake? Or a man? Could it be the wind? Or just the sound of leaves?

Stealthily they sat up, without speaking. Who were they afraid of? Of snakes, or foxes, or humans? They had no idea.

Soundlessly they rose to their feet. Wrapped their sari ends firmly round their waists, tucking the pleats so they hung knee-high. Just so their saris didn't trip them up.

Soundlessly they began to walk. In which direction? Who could tell? They may as well move ahead. They didn't run. What if the leaves crackled underfoot? What if the birds called out? Or flew off? Or if from somewhere, those humans, those people, those men, arrived on the scene?

They walked abreast, both of them. Identity, name, community, place of origin – it did not occur to them to ask or to learn such details. If only they could glimpse a group of men and women, a group of fugitive travellers, that was all they wanted. A group with many women. Ah! Then, joining the group, they could reach the edge of the forest, eventually reach some border, somewhere. They moved on in silence. Treading soundlessly. Was it light that dawned at one end of the sky? Was daylight to be trusted or feared? In daylight they would be able to see their way. Villages would become visible. But people on the road would also be able to see them. What if those people were evil folk? They didn't know whether daylight was to be trusted or feared. Were humans to be trusted or feared? Was staying alive to be trusted or feared? But how could they die? What form of death did people choose when in danger? How did women die? By setting themselves on fire, or drowning themselves? How?

3

Suddenly they arrived at the edge of a pond that resembled a small muddy pool.

And with joyous anticipation saw ten or twelve women, a few children, and ten to fifteen men, some elderly, some young, silently washing themselves in the pond. Washing the young ones' faces.

At the water's edge, the women were opening a few bundles containing chire-muri-khoi – flattened rice, puffed rice, rice fluffed and roasted. And in some bundles, salt, sugar and jaggery. Some of them carried small water pots, tiny bowls, and metal dishes. Others had dry, dark, ripe bananas. Or arum and unripe banana, boiled and mashed.

They settled down to feed the youngsters. They said not a word, as if performing their chores silently in a haunted house.

These two came down to the water's edge as well. Then Minu produced a bundle of chire from the corner of her sari tucked pouch-like into her waist.

The other girl produced some bread from inside her blouse.

In the early light of dawn Minu looked a little older than the other.

"Come," she invited, "put away the bread. Let's wash the chire in its cloth and eat it. If we don't find water anywhere else, you can have the bread."

They soaked a couple of handfuls of chire in their sari aanchals.

Dawn was breaking. Suddenly, Minu glanced at her companion's face.

"I don't know your name," she said. "My name is Menaka. Menaka Batabyal."

The other girl gave a start and moved away a little.

"My name is Rahima, didibhai," she responded. "I'm a Muslim, didibhai."

"Never mind," declared Minu after a short silence. "Come, have some chire."

"Will you accept bread that I have touched, didi?" asked the girl with some hesitation.

"Indeed I will if the need arises, bhai," replied Minu with a faint smile. "Come along now; after our small snack we'll walk along with these people. It's a large group."

Having eaten the aanchal-soaked chire along with a bit of gur, the two of them washed and tucked their aanchals around their waists. Meanwhile, the young ones in the other group had also been fed.

"Where have you come from?" an elderly housewife asked, at last. "Where are you going?"

"We have come from very far away," answered Minu after a short silence. "From a village in Khulna. If we accompany you, we may find the right direction. May we come along?"

"Who's that?" asked another elderly woman. "Your sister? Is there no-one else with you? What's your caste? Come along. Walk with us."

Minu glanced briefly at Rahima.

"Yes, she is related to my pishi, my father's sister," she replied. "She's my sister."

Before they could reveal who they were; the men rounded them up. "There's no time left for gossip now. We must hurry, there's no saying who might arrive, and from which direction."

Now, plucking up courage, Rahima gripped Minu's hand firmly. She was probably not more than sixteen or seventeen. Minu was a little older. Looked bigger, too. Besides she was the daughter of a Hindu, and accustomed to walking the streets that connected the village to her home. Gently, she too grasped the other girl's hand firmly.

Wordlessly, soundlessly, the group began to move.

As they wound their way along the turning, twisting path, their company gradually began to grow in size, as people emerged, from a corner of some street in some neighbourhood in some village. Nobody asked for introductions, for name, caste or religion. Step by step they were driven, propelled by their feet, their minds. Women fearing for their honour, everyone fearing for their lives, fearing for their faith, they were driven, no other thought in their minds.

They were kindred souls all of them today: they belonged

to just one community. A community of fugitives, a migrant community fleeing their land. The women were just women. Women fleeing for fear of being assaulted by men, men fleeing their land: Flight. That was their creed. Terrified of losing their lives, their faith, and their women's honour. All of them equal in terror.

4

How many days, how many nights had passed, who could tell? The sun in the sky was now cradled in the moon's lap. They arrived at the border.

There were no check-posts at the border. People came and went unhindered. Voluntary police, guarding the border, all helped them. Escorted them to the office. Through kindly investigation, officers were assigning the locations and addresses to which they were to be directed.

Those who had relatives and friends here could easily find a refuge, a place for themselves.

But what about those who had nobody? They hung about here and there, silent. Lingered beneath trees. Hovered near the voluntary workers who served the officers. Asked them for advice.

Menaka and Rahima belonged to this lot. Exhausted, the two of them collapsed beneath a tree. Now Minu asked: "Which village are you from?" Rahima named an outlying village in Khulna district.

"My didi and I and my Mama's daughters, my maternal cousins, used to study at a school in Khulna. We were boarders there. Our parents and younger siblings live in the village. If they are still alive, that is." She wiped her eyes.

"When this commotion began, everyone in town was frightened. The teachers at our school asked all of us to return to our villages. Some people did leave, but before the school was emptied out, the Khansena pounced on it one night.

Tears streamed from her eyes.

"After that, I never saw my sisters and my teachers; they were older than me, you see. Perhaps they were captured. Before they left, Didi and Hamidabano, Teacherdidi hid us in a tiny room. The four of us – Mahruma, Fatima, another girl and myself – we remained hidden in the coal cellar downstairs. Handing four or five pieces of bread and some gur to each of us, they promised to let us out once those people went away and the commotion had died down. Keep quiet until then, all of you. If you're hungry, eat this. After that – fire, screams, wailing, gunshots – we heard all the sounds." Rahima began to sob.

"Through a crack in the door I saw Teacherdidi and the others being dragged away. I couldn't tell where my didis were. I thought I heard one of them cry out loudly, once.

Then it was morning. They hadn't had time to approach this coal cellar. Their military van had arrived.

We heard afterwards that they had captured many girls and taken them away in that van.

Late in the day, we emerged. Some people from the village came to us and said, come, we must run away from here now. Join us, all of you, lucky they didn't lay hands on you.

We took to the road along with them, the four of us. Then we sighted the army and soldiers again, and scattered here and there. We were separated, somehow and suddenly I was alone. In the daytime I would creep along, hiding myself in hollows and crevices. Only at night could I walk a little. How many nights, how many days went by, I can't remember. Then the other night, I saw you."

Minu had been clutching her hand as if she were her little sister.

5

One by one all of them advanced towards the officers' room. Volunteers would call out and escort them in. Hindu and Muslim officers met them together.

It was late afternoon. Somebody had given them a handful of muri, chire and gur. They were handing it out to many people, to those who would accept it.

Now they were summoned to the officers' room.

"Where are you from? Your village? Are you sisters, the two of you?"

Gripping Minu's hand, Rahima remained silent.

"From Khulna," Minu responded. "Just one of us."

"Just one?" came the surprised query. "Then who is she? Not your sister? What's your name?"

"She is a fellow traveller," Menaka clarified. "Not my sister. My name is Menaka Batabyal."

"What's your name?" (To Rahima) "Which village are you from? Who else is with you?"

"My name is Rahima Sheikh. I used to study at the school in Khulna town. My parents live in the village. Or they used to. There's no-one with me. I met this didi on the way. I am a Muslim."

"Where will you go?" wondered the officer. "Have you an address to which you can go? Or shall we arrange to send you to a camp? You seem like sisters, the two of you."

"I have the address of my father's maternal cousin," Menaka told him. "Their house is in Baagbazar, in Ramkanto Bose Lane. But they don't know me. I have never seen them either. I can't recall the house number."

"Then how will you go there? Do you know the names of the people who live in that house?"

"That I know. Umeshchandra Roy."

"Well, we could try and locate them. They would accept you, wouldn't they?"

Menaka remained silent. She didn't know the answer to that.

"Do you know anyone's address here?" he asked Rahima. "Have you ever visited this country?"

"No, I have never been to this country," replied Rahima, terror-stricken. "The address I have is in Dock Road, somewhere in Khidirpur, the marital home of my father's sister. They know my father's name. But they have never seen me. My phupha's name is Rahamat Ali. He writes to my father at Eid; I have met him sometimes. He works in the docks."

"Where should I send the two of you then?" said their interrogator, nonplussed. "These addresses will take a long time to locate. If we had the numbers it would be quicker."

Minu and Rahima stood hand in hand as before, together, as if they were close kin.

"Then Menaka Batabyal, let me arrange to send you to the camp at Nabadwip, and Rahima Sheikh, should I send you to the Muslim camp at Murshidabad?"

"Please send both of us to the same place babu," pleaded Rahima, clinging to Minu. "Send us to Nabadwip."

"Yes, babu," begged Minu as well, drawing Rahima close. "That would be best."

The officers smiled. Some of them were Hindu, and some were Muslim.

"They wouldn't want a Muslim girl at the Hindu camp," the Muslim officer pointed out.

"Then please find places for both of us at Murshidabad," cried Menaka in agitation.

Again the officers smiled, Hindus and Muslims alike.

"Daughter of a Hindu, how will you live in that camp?

What will you eat, and how? All those things, all the things they eat!"

They clung to each other, the two girls, and wiped their eyes. But at the Hindu camp the people were very conscious of purity and pollution; they would never want to keep a Muslim girl. And a Hindu girl could not live on the food served at a Muslim camp. This was something all the officers knew.

"Look, little ones, you simply met on the way," they said, looking at the girls with great compassion. "Yours is just a travelling acquaintanceship. At the camps, you will find people who will be much closer to you, like your own relatives."

"Don't cry. Why are you afraid? Go where we send you."

Rahima burst into a flood of tears, clasping Menaka in both arms. Menaka was weeping too.

"We shall never meet again," they said. "Please send us to the same place, babu, please!"

"I will stay in a corner of didi's room," sobbed Rahima.

"Assign me to the Muslim camp," cried Menaka. "I shall organize my own cooking separately. Otherwise I will never set eyes on her again, she has nobody to call her own."

The officers smiled in perplexity.

"No, no," they assured the girls, "you will certainly meet again. Each of you will have the other's address after all."

What address?

Which place? Ramkanto Bose Lane? The Khidirpur Dock ...?

So many camps ... So many places ... Such a vast country!

Tears streamed from the eyes of both women.

Face Up

KABITA SINHA

STANDING at the main entrance, Putul was watching Tani milk the goat. And lolling on the ropestring cot that belonged to Tani's family, the neighbourhood gang of growing boys, the gang of gossiping idlers, was eyeing Putul.

At that very moment, Pulin entered the alley. It was hardly an alley – a yard and a half wide, slimy with mud, a blind crack that had sliced its way through the midriff of a large building, dividing it in two. The tiny shack in which Tani and her family lived leaned against the wall where the alley ended. Tani lived there, with her mother the cowdung seller, and her father the porter. And the goat. A few people leaned out of crooked windows on both sides, and from the terrace above. They were sipping tea, gossiping. Watching the kites in the sky. Those who were waiting for their kilo or half-kilo of milk, were gazing at the foaming liquid in the tiny pail clutched between Tani's thighs.

And sure enough, they were turning around to gaze at Putul, too.

Who could have predicted such a transformation? Was this Putul the same skinny Putul of yore? The spindly little girl that she was when Haran got married? Putul had come here along with Haran's bride, to spend a few days with her didi. That was when Pulin had taught her the game you played with potsherds. Really, what wonderful games one could play all by oneself, with these potsherds! You think of something and fling it up in the air, then catch it as it falls. If it lands face up, your wish comes true and face down, it means failure! And as they played, how their little dreams began to take shape, and how, digging tunnels of fiction, they began to travel inwards!

To get to this house, you had to take exactly five turns from the main road.

Yet, what a difference that small distance made.

On the main road, such bright lights, so much noise, garment shops, swimming in the waters of Goldighi, sports commentaries relayed on the transistor.

And here? In this alley?

The houses all falling apart, wobbling like a row of decayed teeth. It was doubtful if they could withstand the onslaught of the approaching rains.

But still, Pulin felt distressed at the rare sight, still to be seen in these charmless buildings, of the odd porcelain tile from British times, segments of parquet flooring, or a fragment of stained glass on a window-pane. Such sights pierced Pulin's heart. As did Putul.

There was too much of the flesh in Putul's body. It was too overwhelming. Earlier, when Putul came near, Pulin's nostrils could sense the faint fragrance of lemon-flavoured oil, from her body the scent of damp earth from the countryside. Now it felt as if Putul's heavy tresses carried only the sweat of a rain-damp body and the odour of washing dishes. Still, sometimes, on very rare occasions, in Putul's glance, her smile, Pulin would detect traces of a fine parquet design, or the shape of a cornice. Today he received another such glimpse.

In front of the common entrance, insects hovered on a puddle of stagnant water. Stepping on the bricks placed in the puddle Pulin went in, brushing past Putul, and from her sari he caught the whiff of a lighted stove.

Stepping in through the dark cavernous entrance, one couldn't see anything at first. The damp darkness brushed against one's body like a fringe. Gradually, as the eyes grew accustomed to the dark, Pulin could climb up along the passage at one side, circling the courtyard and arriving at his own refuge at the far end of the building.

What had this building been, once upon a time? The small, even niches lining the space beside the courtyard may have been the stables where horses were tied. Now, in every niche, lived a family. As for the courtyard in the middle, it no longer existed. Dividing up this space, adjoining the niches, low walls had been raised. For each home, this became the cooking area, the space for washing dishes.

Whenever he returned home at this time, Pulin saw women scrubbing dishes or washing clothes, each in front of her own little cell. The smell of dirty dishes pervaded the air, and smoke gushed up from their respective cooking stoves. Looking sideways, one glimpsed the dim, high beds inside the niches, boxes and trunks, bedding rolls, or sometimes an infant struck dumb. So many outsiders came in and went through the passage across the courtyard from the cells, that the women did not even raise their heads to give them a passing glance. Or perhaps they no longer had the desire to see anything any more.

To Pulin they all seemed the same. Clothes hitched up to their knees. A bunch of broken women in faded colourless saris. Putul's didi, her elder sister Nirmala, was among them, too.

In each, Pulin could see shades of his own mother. Even in Putul. What shades? Who could tell? Pulin hadn't yet figured it out.

Walking along the passage, he crossed the length of the courtyard and came to an enormous room. Perhaps the walls separating one row of rooms had been broken down. Here, there was a noisy clanging all day long. It was a small printing press. On one side were compositors' cubicles, on the other, the machines. And at the back, walled by leaning piles of paper and high stacks of galley proofs, was a space like a narrow alley, about four feet across, perhaps. That strip of space was Pulin's. Though quite long, it was narrow. Along one side of this space that belonged to Pulin rose a wall of paper, and on the other, a salt-encrusted uneven wall. So unstable was the wall that nobody wanted to live there, fearing it might collapse any time. Indeed, there was cause for fear. For it was just during the last rains that that disastrous event had occurred. The building's ceiling was so high that one got a crick in the neck just trying to peer up at it. Above, it was sootblack. Along the salt-eroded wall, a narrow brick staircase rose step by step to end abruptly at a blank wall. Why should there be this unexpected, peculiar staircase, resembling a series of crudely hacked ledges, and why should it suddenly vanish when it came up against a wall? Pulin sometimes wondered. Suddenly one day, during a torrential downpour, a portion of that blank wall, a portion shaped exactly like a door, collapsed. Thank heavens Pulin was at the neighbouring press then, drinking tea, or he would have copped it that very day!

Anyway, a large chunk of the upper portion of Pulin's refuge was now open to the sky. That hadn't hampered Pulin at all. If it rained he let down a rolled up curtain-like length of tarpaulin. In fact, he thought it was great fun to go up the carved-out staircase to stand at the broken gap. People at the press had told him there had probably been a secret chamber on the other side of the wall in the olden days, a concealed hideout, perhaps. After all the house was so ancient. But what was there now? Going up, Pulin had seen merely an uneven stretch of terrace that clung to the wall. There ... no, let it be. That was Pulin's private business. In that place, Pulin was his own sole companion.

"Will you be going to the market?" Haran called out, sticking his head out of the printing press when he saw Pulin approaching.

"I will," Pulin replied as he advanced towards his shelter. "Get ready, I'll join you soon." Crossing the lighted room of the printing press, when he arrived at the entrance to his own living area, Pulin scrubbed his feet, washing them with water from the bucket beside the drain. Then wiping his feet on the folded sack placed there, he entered his secluded space. The entire area was covered with a reed mat. Beneath the soles of his feet he felt the delicate texture of the matting. He had beaten off the cockroaches, rats and mosquitoes, using incense and Flit. The only thing he had failed to banish was the smell of salt-eroded brick and old newspapers … The moment he reached his hideout, his heart would fill with satisfaction. Pulin was orderly. There were his clothes, hung neatly on a rope. His tin box was compact. The bedding rolled up. And there were the objects required for an office-boy's job. Also the cooking stove and some utensils. From the dark well of that small strip of space he called his own, Pulin glanced up at the brightly lit opening above. Before his eyes rose the late-afternoon sky, the colour of aubergine-blossoms, filling the broken oblong space left by the door that had vanished. What a feast for the eyes! Pulin's eyes drank deep of its wonder.

Carrying water in a tiny pot, Pulin slowly mounted the wobbly staircase, stepping gingerly on its ledges. As if he was climbing up to a temple!

Rising above the odours, the constrictions of the human world, above the clanging of the machine, the bleating of Tani's goat wafted towards him like the sound of a tinkling bell. The higher he climbed, the more violently did the wind lash his face and eyes.

When he was a child, in the area adjacent to Pulin's slum

lived Dadiburi, the washerwomen's old grandmother. Dadiburi would stretch out her swollen legs and tell stories, only about her village. About the Parvati temple in their village. A whitewashed temple. Anyone who visited the riverbank would ring the enormous bell once before going on their way. Wheat fields all around. Golden yellow. Grasshoppers hovering, with their brown glassy wings.

Against the aubergine-blossom-coloured backdrop, in a red flowerpot, swayed the plant. How beautiful and succulent its body! Pulin kept count. He knew every leaf by heart. On all four sides towered highrise buildings. Perhaps the plant felt lonely. When he went to the market this time, he would ask the old plant-seller where, in which forest, which garden, he had found the plant. With supreme tenderness Pulin wiped each individual leaf with water from his pot. Then he said: here, let me shower rain directly upon your head, just for you. As it was bathed, the plant glistened and grew dazzlingly bright. Swaying, it revealed to Pulin graceful leafbuds sprouting from the space between its twin branches. Shy buds from which new branches would grow. On every branch, in every leaf-cluster, bunched flowerbuds, swelling in readiness to bloom. Fragrant nectar surging within the buds.

When they blossomed tonight, Pulin would be intoxicated by their fragrance.

Thinking about it, Pulin felt goose-pimples all over his body. The aubergine-blossom sky would be even rosier then.

"Where are you?"

Putul's voice spiralled up from down below. Pulin started. And at that very moment, a few leaves fell off at his touch. Bending to pick them up, he noticed that the leaves were a pale yellow. Pulin stopped short, and his face grew pale as well. This was the rainy season, wasn't it? Not the season for falling leaves, surely.

"Aren't you going to the market?" Jamaibabu was calling! Down below, everything was suffused in darkness. From above, you couldn't see Putul's form distinctly.

"Tell him I'm coming!" replied Pulin, addressing that unseen voice.

Feeling the wall, Pulin descended with practised steps. He switched on the light.

Putul was still standing there. Glancing once at Pulin, once at the crudely hacked-out steps, she remarked: "Very brave of you, I must say! Did you actually come down those very narrow steps?"

They were indeed extraordinarily narrow, dangerous too. Virtually blending with the wall. You could hardly make them out. Casting her eyes about Pulin's chamber, Putul now glanced up at the rectangular opening. Just then, a lifeless leaf floated down from above.

"Isn't that hasnuhana?"

Putul took the leaf from her hand. In a melancholy tone she predicted: "It won't live!"

Pulin looked at Putul as if she was a murderer. Then he picked up his shopping bag.

As they approached the bazaar, Pulin asked: "What arrangements have you made for Putul?"

"I'm taking her to the hospital tomorrow!" Haran informed him.

"The sooner the better!" Pulin declared.

"I had to introduce her as my own wife! Had to say we have three children."

"Once it's done, send her packing!"

Haran nodded. He knew why Pulin had said this. In fact, Haran's own wife was at her wits' end regarding Putul's voluptuous youth. Ever since she had arrived, it felt as if meat was constantly cooking in this alley, this neighbourhood. Yet, where else could she go? Haran told Pulin everything. If confiding all made one a friend, then Haran was indeed Pulin's friend. His wife Pushi's natal home was in a suburban area close to Kolkata. About three months ago, some people had picked up Putul on her return from the weekly market. Afterwards they had abandoned her next to the railway tracks. Now there was no choice but to bring her to Kolkata. Haran, Pulin and Pushi had thought nobody would get to know. If they handled things wisely, Putul could return with her virginity restored. But ever since she had come here, the atmosphere seemed charged. Everybody's mind, their eyes, their thoughts, seemed to be directed at her navel. Even Putul's.

In fact, even Haran's.

The moment he approached the bazaar, Pulin felt as if he was listening to a jatra concert. So many people. So many items on sale. Such artfulness in the way the items were displayed! He was reminded of his mother. In winter, wrapping his mother's sari around him, holding on to her little finger, he came to scavenge the market. For discarded cauliflower leaves, rotten tomatoes, soggy potatoes.

"What are you thinking, Pulin?"

"I'm thinking, if all these fancy things had existed then, maybe my mother might not have brought me here ..."

Privately, Pulin told himself the truth.

"Sometimes I suspect my mother was the daughter of an eminent family. I now understand some of the things she said, some odd details of her conduct."

"All the better," Haran affirmed. "Then we would never have been born. Nor would we have suffered so much."

"No, no, this birth is very auspicious. It has great rewards." No, no, Ma wanted him, had allowed him to be born. Pulin understood this in his very bones. Otherwise, his life could not have been so full of joy. Such joy!

At the entrance to the market Pulin saw the old man, the plant-seller, leaning against a wall in a trancelike state. Beside him were a few plants stuffed into fistlike lumps of soil.

For a moment Pulin felt the urge to bend down and tell the old fellow: "O buro! Old man! Your daughter the hasnuhana is well."

But by then Haran had moved ahead, and Pulin had also remembered Putul's words: "It won't live!"

Suddenly leaning forward, Pulin asked the old man: "O buro, where do you get your plants from?"

"From Kakdwip!"

Having uttered the words, he dozed off at once. Pulin tried to recall the number of the Kakdwip-bound bus, on which his friend Raghunath worked as a cleaner.

The bazaar was only too attractive to Pulin. All these fruits and figs that had forced their way out of the earth's bosom. The very sight of farm produce pleased him no end. The sight of anything that had come to fruition. Those succulent pomegranates arranged on the flat basketware mat. How lovely the grace that seemed to flow from their bodies! As if someone had pumped the elixir of youth into them. Mustard greens like green lace. Ridged textures – bitter gourd, pale yellow lemons. After seeing all the greens and vegetables, Ma would boil sweet potato with urad dal. Sometimes, shredded cauliflower leaf with rice.

That tiny niche in the slum. Lighting the coal-stove, Ma would make hot rotis. In the glow of the firelight, her angular face would glisten. Deep hollows beneath her eyes. Now Pulin realized how young his mother had been then. How beautiful. In that tiny chamber, Ma would lie on the high wooden bed with all sorts of people. Hide Pulin under the bed. Mother and son, they played a strange, secret game. Unknown to others,

Ma would sometimes lower her arm, letting it dangle close to Pulin, who would take her hand and stroke his own eyes and cheeks with it. The man with her would never realize that although he had paid the full price, he was being deprived of one arm.

At such times Pulin would understand that Ma had descended to Pulin through her arm and cuddled up close to him. He knew that his mother had detached herself from her corpselike body. From then on, he had learnt how to separate the mind from the body. That was why he had never been able to despise his mother. He knew that she was just not involved in any of these things. That slum, the dirty waterlogged toilet, men's needs and desires, sweat, flies and mosquitos, torn clothing, maggot-infested rice – his Ma could dismiss all such things at will.

How?

Take for instance the way the two of them, mother and son, having washed their hands and feet just before going to bed, in summer having fetched water from the roadside tap to wipe clean their bodies and limbs, would lie down. They would then enter the world of stories. Stories of long, long ago. Of olden times. Times of joy. That was why Pulin hadn't been able to roam the streets like other boys, playing, having fun. He used to study at the corporation school. A clean, tidy boy, hair well combed. That he was different, everybody realized. That was why when he once developed fever and high delirium, his teachers had personally carried him to the slum. Speaking to Ma, they had called her "apni," using the respectful mode of address. Pulin had noticed it at once. One of the mastermoshais was saying: "Why not send him to night school in the evening? After all, that is when you ..."

"But it is my profession," Ma protested. "There is no shame in it, babu! Let him know all about it. So what?"

"Do you belong here?" one of them had asked. "I mean, were you born here?"

"No, I belong to a far-off place," Ma had told them. "To Rangpur."

That was when Pulin got to know. His mother was from Rangpur.

"So? Aren't you buying anything?" Haran urged him.

"Oh? Yes, I will," Pulin assured him. "I'll buy some cheap vegetables from outside. Tell me, Haran, have you tasted alur dal, made with potatoes?"

"How can you have dal made of potatoes?"

"My mother used to make it! Cooking potatoes until they dissolve, blending them with water, adding a lot of peas. Rangpur cuisine, our very own."

Pulin said the words "our Rangpur" with great pride.

"Wah, very nice," said Haran.

Actually, Pulin had never been to Rangpur. And actually, Pulin's mother had never cooked alur dal.

All this was part of the game they played, he and his mother. Towards the end, when she started going from house to house washing dishes, she would come back home and go for a bath. By then, Pulin would have dusted and swept their room and laid out the bed. Flinging some coal into the washerwoman's stove next door, Ma would make some hot khichdi. Or she would buy some muri, puffed rice. Having made a meal of that, they would call it a day. Then Ma would say: "Now, Pulin?"

"Yes Ma!"

"What did you buy in the bazaar, tell me?"

Every day Pulin went to scour the bazaar. From a distance he eyed the vegetables, fish and meat of the finest quality. Like a parrot he would recite the names of all those vegetables, and all the varieties of fish and meat.

"Good! You have done a fine job of shopping," his mother would approve. "How succulent is the cabbage! How perfectly shaped the tomatoes! Aha! You have bought the best peas in the market. How wonderful – how many cooking stoves should I light? May as well light all three . . . By the way, have you brought some juicy lemons? Imagine, he's forgotten the lemons! Hurry up now, go and pluck some from the Raja's orchard. There's plenty there."

Then, lying in bed, the two of them would indulge in make-believe cooking. Their meal over, they would board the train. The little chamber would become a railway compartment, and their wooden bed the bunk. At every station they would have hot tea, and for Pulin, extra milk, warmed up. Most days they went to Puri, and would collect countless invisible seashells on the sandy shore of an unseen ocean.

The rain came down in a short, sharp shower. Opening his umbrella, Haran said, "I remember, it rained like this on my wedding day. You and I had come to the market to shop for the wedding."

"Indeed it did," recalled Pulin. It was only a couple of years ago that Haran had got married. On just such a rainy, overcast day. Suddenly that day, walking past that old plant-seller, Pulin had plucked up the courage to buy a tiny hasnuhana seedling from him.

"A plant!" Haran had protested loudly. "Where will you keep it? Where is the space for a plant? It will die!"

Pulin had privately said to himself: if you can maintain a wife, no less, can't I look after a plant! So now, Pulin would compare Haran's wife and his own plant.

But outwardly he said nothing.

At the time of her marriage, Pushi's appearance had been as dazzling as Putul's.

Initially, in the damp, sunless corridor, the hasnuhana

plant had indeed begun to droop. If the wall had not collapsed to reveal the open terrace, the plant could have actually died.

But today Putul had driven an enormous nail right through his heart. The plant wouldn't live, she had said!

Suddenly Pulin remembered, remembered which Kakdwip-bound bus his friend, the cleaner Raghunath, serviced.

At night, before retiring, Haran and Pulin were standing at the main entrance, smoking bidis. Haran seemed to be fidgeting for no apparent reason. Inside, everyone had fallen asleep. The press had just been shut down. Only Pushi was needlessly prolonging her household chores. And in the passage beside the courtyard, Putul was intently playing with potsherds.

As soon as Pulin went in, Putul informed him: "I went and saw your plant from up close."

"You climbed up that staircase?"

"Yes. The plant is swimming in the moonlight now, but it won't live. It's just a bunch of roots. All roots. It might die today, or tomorrow. But it will die."

When Pushi's little boy started crying, she at once stopped arranging the coal in her stove and rose to her feet. In the yellow light of the low-powered lightbulb, all Pulin could see of her at a sidelong glance were roots, roots, only roots. Arms, neck, bosom, collarbones, sagging breasts – just roots everywhere.

"Yes, if there are really more roots than soil, plants won't survive," agreed Pushi, as she offered her son some milk.

Crossing Putul, Pulin crept to his own shelter after washing his hands and face. Barebodied, clad in a clean dhoti folded double, he laid out his bed directly facing the rectangular opening right overhead. Even now, he spread the kantha embroidered by Ma on top of it, although the soft fabric of the kantha's uppermost layer was now tattered. After a little while, the rectangle of moonlight shifted, falling upon his bed. Pulin stretched out his arm. The long shadow of the hasnuhana reclined on his arm. Pulin's tiny alcove was redolent with the intoxicating fragrance of the hasnuhana. Lying there, with the shadow of a sweet-smelling, beautiful young girl resting on his breast, his eyelids drooped in blissful satisfaction.

At midnight Pulin awoke all of a sudden; the shadow of the hasnuhana was sobbing, face down, at his feet. Drowsy as he was, he climbed up the steps, went and stood on the terrace, alone.

The moon at that hour was directly overhead. The night was far advanced, deathly still. The hasnuhana plant glittered like dazzling green silverfoil. As if its entire body was draped in a green Banarasi sari embroidered with paisleys in gold zari. The moon like a bridal ornament adorning its forehead. Laughing with gay abandon, with all the fragrance and simplicity of a sixteen-year-old girl, unaware of what the future held in store.

"I shall never let you die," vowed Pulin in a suppressed voice. "You will live, you will remain alive!"

But after a few days?

Pulin shuddered. He saw the vision of a drooping, yellowish, sad looking plant. Just roots, only roots! Rushing down the stairs, he came out into the passage to splash water on his eyes and face, and found Putul by herself, playing with potsherds in the soiled moonlight of the passage. As soon as Pulin came and stood close to her, she shrank from him.

"Will you also bother me like Jamaibabu?" she asked. "Tomorrow it will be time to leave. Why carry on, anymore?"

Stunned, Pulin realized Haran must have … with Putul … could it be …?

"Do you play with potsherds a lot, Putul?" he asked, changing the subject.

"Yes, a lot! Just as you taught me to imagine things, remember?

Just like that! For instance:

Face up, a prince will come your way,
Face down, you'll have nothing!
Face up, a golden household is yours
Face down, your luck is hollow!
Face up, you'll have a rosy baby boy
Face down …

Suddenly, Putul burst into wild sobs.

Face down it's all over!

In the dark, Pulin laughed out loud. He remembered his mother. His Ma had survived after all, just because …

Because his Ma could make up whole worlds.

Putul too had learned how to invent make-believe worlds.

Slowly, Pulin drew her up. From the way he held her, Putul felt no fear. Leaning on his shoulder, she went to his living area. Laying Putul down on the bed upon which the moonlight had descended, Pulin asked her: "Where are we going tomorrow, can you tell me?"

"To the hospital!"

"No! We'll go to Kakdwip! By bus! You, me and she –" as he spoke, Pulin pointed at the hasnuhana.

"And then?" asked Putul, brightening.

Pulin realized that Putul, forgetting everything else, was listening intently to his made-up story.

"Then, in Kakdwip, we'll find a nice place where the soil is good, and leave her there, okay?"

"I'll find the place!" declared Putul, her eyes glittering. "I can recognize good soil! And then?"

"Then we will leave our mark there and come away!"

"Yes, that will be wonderful. Sometimes, we'll go and pay her a visit. There's a lot of soil there. Spreading her roots, she will grow, produce fresh new plants!"

Touching Putul's tiny forehead as she stood enveloped in moonlight, Pulin asked her: "Now tell me truly, did the potsherd fall face up? Or face down?"

"When?"

"When you wished for a rosy baby boy?"

"Shall I tell you the truth?" Putul asked, resting her cheek against Pulin's chest.

"Yes!"

"Face up!"

Giribala

MAHASWETA DEVI

GIRIBALA hails from Talsana village in Kandi subdivision. It had never struck anyone that she might have a heart and mind of her own. Our Giri is neither beautiful nor ugly, just ordinary. But her eyes are full of life. She'd catch your eye because of those eyes.

In their community, even now, it is customary to pay for the bride's hand in marriage. Aullchand had handed over Rs 80, heifers, calves, so much stuff, to Giri's father. After that he had married Giri. Truth be told, Giri's father had also presented his daughter with four bharis of silver, pots and pans, floor mats and a cartload of bamboo. And why not? Giri's father owns several bamboo groves. Aullchand said, "It's only because the hut's burned down that I'm leaving your daughter behind. Give me some bamboo, I'll build a home, then come to fetch my wife."

Aullchand left and wasn't seen again. After a few days Bangshi Dhamali, the ED peon, came to Giri's house. Bangshi Dhamali is ED peon at the Nishinda sub-post office. Because he can't support his household on Rs 145, Bangshi spends his evenings helping the doctor at Nishinda treat his patients. The doctor is attached to a hospital, and so of course he lures patients away for his own private practice. As a result, Bangshi too has plenty of clout over the neighbouring villagers. They know it's only via him that anyone can get to the doctor.

Having watched the doctor at work, Bangshi has himself begun to spout words of medical wisdom. As a result, he is now held in even greater esteem.

Bangshi addresses Giri's father as Mama. Nobody can remember exactly how this came to be. Bangshi Dhamali said, "I've been to Bethuadahari. A couple of other places as well. What do I hear? You've gone and married your daughter off to Aullchand?"

"He came along and I agreed."

"Indeed! And how much has he paid you?"

"Eighty-one rupees, and a few things."

"Can you handle the risk?"

"What risk?"

"What can I say! I'm a government servant, the doctor's right-hand man as well, couldn't you have asked me just once? Aullchand's not a bad sort. Smoked a lot of ganja with him, that can't be denied. But that money and that calf – it all belongs to Chan'an. Chan'an's marriage was fixed for Kalhat. So Aullchand, being Chan'an's paternal uncle, went to pay the bride price."

"What!"

"Well, Chan'an's mother was in tears. She'd begged and borrowed to get her son married. What kind of man is this fellow, tell me? Neither land nor property, loitering about Chan'an's house all the time …"

"No land or property?"

"No, no."

"He took a cartload of bamboo to build a hut …"

"That's what I'm trying to tell you. After selling the bamboo to Chan'an's pishi for a hundred rupees, he's gone off to the Banpur fair."

Giri's father sinks to the floor in despair. Bangshi Dhamali continues to list Aullchand's exploits. Finally he leaves, saying, "The boy isn't bad. But just like I told you, no land or property. Roams about from fairground to fairground, singing. Otherwise, he's not bad."

"But Mohan never told us any of this. It was he who proposed the match, after all. He never breathed a word."

"Why should he? They're best friends."

Giri's mother says, "I'll get my daughter married all over again. Cheat, scoundrel! I'm not sending my daughter to him."

But when Aullchand turns up a year or so later, he doesn't give them a chance to refuse. He brings an enormous sweet tuber, new clothes for his bride, a stool made of jackfruit-wood for his mother-in-law, four new jute sacks for his father-in-law. Of course, Giri's mother repeats all the things Bangshi told them. Aullchand merely beams magnanimously and says, "Can't live in this world by Bangshi-dada's words, Ma. Your daughter's going to live in a new hut now. And that's no lie."

Giri's mother braids her daughter's hair, dresses her. Then she says, weeping, "This man, my child, is like the tree with a thousand roots. Growing right in the heart of the house. Every time you uproot it, it grows back again. Every word he speaks is a lie but oh, how cleverly he plays with those words!"

Giri says nothing. The groom is supposed to first pay bride price to the bride's father. All this is true. But still, she's a girl. A girl's discarded by fate, lost if she's dead, lost if she's wed. Giri senses that hard times lie ahead. She sobs silently, alone. Then she sniffs, wipes her eyes and says, "Bring me home when the deity is worshipped. You will, won't you? Feed the brown cow. I've chopped the straw. Don't forget to water the hibiscus."

And so, at the age of fourteen, Giri goes to keep house for her husband. Her mother packs pots and pans for her new home. Aullchand says, "Just add a bit of rice and dal, Ma. Got a job with the babus. Have to report for duty as soon as I get back. Won't have time to go to the market."

Giri takes rice, dal and salt. Then leaves home. Aullchand walks at a rapid pace. Says, "Now let's see you move those legs of yours."

Aullchand takes her to a hut made of brick, once they enter the village of Talsana. Mango, jamun, guava, all kinds of trees in the babus' orchard. In one corner is a ramshackle hut meant for the keeper. Aullchand says, "I'll build us a place to live in, for sure. Ever seen anything like this? There's the pond, over on that side. Let's see you nip down to fetch some kindling, and put some rice on the boil."

"But it's getting dark! Isn't there an oil lamp?"

"Lamp? Now where would I find a lamp?"

The babus' maidservant, arriving suddenly, comes to Giri's rescue. The woman swears at Aullchand, gets an oil lamp. Takes Giri to the pond. Says, "Do your parents have hearts of stone? Leaving a tender little girl in the hands of that ganja fiend? What's he got to feed you? Grazes the babus' cows, works as a day-labourer, hardly earns a pittance every month. Works sometimes, sometimes goes off, god knows where. Girl, if you've got even a grain of good sense, then listen to me, go to your parents' tomorrow itself, leave those bits and pieces of silver there."

Even then Giri doesn't run back home the next day to deposit her jewellery. Instead, she is seen lovingly plastering clay on the ramshackle hut, its frame protruding, at the corner of the orchard. From the babus, Aullchand gets hold of a piece of tin sheeting. Fashioned with a bamboo frame, that becomes the door of the hut. Very soon, Giri gets to work in the babus' household for a meal wage. After a few months, Aullchand says, "Wife, made a householder out of me, you have. No parents, never known a home and family, drifted from one place to another."

"Get help from the babus to build your own hut, get hold of some land."

"You think they'll part with it?"

"Why not? A newcomer's expected. Will he be born in

another's home? Even the wretched boshtoms have dwellings of their own."

"You're right. My heart aches for a home of my own too. Never felt this way before, though."

A home, how they yearn for a home of their own. But their first daughter, Belarani, is born right here, in this very hut. The girl is barely a month old when Giri returns to the pond to wash the babus' mosquito-nets, sheets, rugs. The mistress of the babu household can't help commenting, "That girl's crazy about her work, I must say. Works well, too."

Overcome by an immense magnanimity, she gives her boys' old clothes to Giri's daughter. She tells Giri, "Leave your work. Let the child have your milk or how will you cope?" Belarani, Paribala, Rajiv, are born to Giri at intervals of one-and-a-half to two years. And when the youngest daughter, Maruni, is born, Giri has an operation to prevent future childbirths.

Meanwhile Aullchand has prodded and pleaded with the babus and acquired two kathas of land. Even built a hut of sorts.

Now he wanders from place to place, working as a day-labourer. He is enraged. "Had an operation, did you? That's a sin. Why did you do it? Go on, tell me!"

Giri remains silent. Aullchand grabs her by the hair, hits her a couple of times with his fists. Giri suffers the beating silently. Then she says, "They said for you to go to the panchayat. They're building a road, men are needed. They'll give grain."

"Why don't you go to your father, tell him to give us some bamboo."

"What for?"

"Dying for a home, weren't you, and look at the mansion you live in! Some bamboo would give us a house to speak of."

"We'll work hard, make our home."

"How?"

"We'll have to try."

"The silver, if we were to pawn it, or sell …"

Giribala stares, unblinking, at Aullchand. Aullchand lowers his head before her gaze. Giri has placed her few bharis of silver in the hollow of a piece of bamboo, entrusted it to the mistress of the house. Even now, she works at that house. From the age of eight, Belarani has been running a thousand errands at the same house for a meal wage. Even she is ten years old now. Fed on the rice of the babus' house, the girl grows rapidly, flourishing like a weed in the rains. That bit of silver will be required to get the girl married. That bit of silver, and Rs 22 earned through hours of bone-wearying toil.

Giri says, "I won't sell the silver to build a house. Baba gave all he could, provided a cartload of bamboo for the hut. The price of that bamboo, even in Nishinda, was then a thousand rupees. One hundred and sixty-two bamboos."

"The same old story."

"Won't you get our daughter married?"

"A daughter means a female slave for someone else's house, after all. When he read my palm, Mohan said that the fifth time onwards there'd be only boys. You've gone and turned barren because you want to wander."

Giri gripped the bonti tightly. She said, "Speak such evil and I'll slash the children's throats and then my own."

"No, no … I won't say such things …" Aullchand quelled his tongue. He spent the next few days worried and anxious. Perhaps it was then that he began hatching his plan.

The root cause of this was Mohan.

Mohan appeared out of the blue one day. Lots of work in every village with the bus route from Krishnachowk to Nishinda now being made an asphalt road. Both Giri and Aullchand have been going to work. They earn grain, mouths are fed.

Mohan has also been working. Still the same vagabond, hasn't married, hasn't settled down. He sells the wheat and buys rice, pumpkin, fish. At night, he sprawls out on Giri's veranda. Wandering through cities, drifting through villages, a complete bohemian in speech and manner. Looks at Aullchand and clucks sympathetically, "Stuck in the mud, are you, pal? Clean forgotten the life you had?"

Giri says, "Stop your churlish nonsense."

"My friend had such a great singing voice."

"That he did. Brought money, too. But that money never got home. Wouldn't buy food for the children."

It was Mohan who said one day, "No girls at all in the land of Bihar. Yet the bride price's very high there. So, those folks are coming here, taking our girls away. Paying so much! Sahadev Bauri got five hundred rupees for his daughter."

"Where is that?"

"Would you know if I told you, pal? Very far away, indeed. And they don't speak Bangla."

Aullchand said, "They paid five hundred rupees?"

"You bet."

The conversation ends there for the moment, because just then a fire breaks out in Kali-babu of the panchayat's cowshed, sparked off from a pile of smouldering hay, the smoke from which acted as a mosquito repellent. A huge uproar. Everybody rushes towards it.

Giri forgets the conversation, Aullchand does not. Who knows what Giri was thinking, for her husband's words caused her no alarm. Because one day, Aullchand said, "Who wants your jewellery? We'll get Bela married, then fix our house with brick and mortar. Fed and fattened in the babus' house, how attractive my daughter looks!"

Even then, no warning bells rang in Giri's mind. She said, "Found a boy?"

"Just see how it all takes care of itself."

Giri said, "The hut's sagging to one side. Need to prop it up a bit. How else will it stay up?"

It was with this idea in mind that Giri went to visit her father for a few days. Carrying Maruni in her arms, holding Pari and Rajiv by the hand. Bela wept a lot. Because she was leaving her behind, Giri had pressed eight annas into her hands. "Buy yourself some sweets, girl. You want to visit your grandparents, you can go another time. Now work hard. We're gone four days at most."

How could Giri know that she would never see Bela again? If so she'd have taken her along. If so she'd have clasped her close. Making the girl slog at the babus' since she was seven, was that mere fancy? Couldn't feed her, couldn't clothe her. A kiss on Bela's forehead and Giri left for her parents'.

A girl's discarded by fate, lost if she's dead, lost if she's wed. Still, their daughter, after all! The father has bought three bighas of land with his profits from the bamboo trade, been apportioned another two bighas as his share of property. The father says, 'Couldn't bring you home, khuki, but stay a few days now that you're here.' The mother says, "Let me fry some muri, pick some arum. What kind of a marriage is this, child? How your skin used to glow! And now, turned soot black! Your lovely hair gone, your bones sticking out! Spend a few days looking after yourself, let your health improve." The brother says, "Why not stay, didi. For a month, I'll make sure there's enough to eat."

Lots of pampering, lots of loving care. The father says, "Bamboo? Of course. You're here for a bit, take some when you go. How can you have good in-laws without a good home? They'll see the house, know they've married into a good family."

Giri could have got more out of her father if she had wept and pleaded. The mother said, "Girl, just ask for a maund of rice." But Giri didn't. Why should she? Give, if you've a mind to. Why should I ask? Giri walked slowly over to the hibiscus bush. See, so many flowers. She had planted that bush. How nice the courtyard looked, freshly plastered with cow-dung, the roof newly thatched. If her mother agreed, Giri would leave Rajiv here so that he could go to school. She bathed her children, scrubbing them with lots of soap. She bathed too, washed her hair clean. Then she went for a walk in the neighbourhood. This little respite, unimaginable bliss. The mother had sent her brother to the canal to catch fish. A single irrigation canal had transformed the area. Raise two crops a year, catch fish all the year round. Giri was content. Her mind at rest, at peace.

Bangshi Dhamali came round. "Poor, poor Giri! How you suffer at the hands of that Aullchand! Doctor-babu's built a house in Baharampur. The sons study there, the wife lives there, too. Had Aullchand been a man, he'd have looked after his children. You could have worked there, kept your youngest with you. A part-time job in the neighbourhood too, after your work at the babu's. Could have set up house with your children. All of them could've worked for a meal-wage. Can city ways be village ways?"

Giri smiled a little, "Dada, let that be. Now tell me, all the riff-raff are getting land, so can't your Rajiv's father get some too?"

"Has he tried? Come to me? Said anything about it? I work for the government, I'm the doctor's right-hand man, sure enough I could have done something."

"I'll send him to you."

To Giri it all seemed like a dream, unreal. They could have a house, perhaps some land, as well. She knew only too well that her husband was an absolute vagabond. Yet her heart filled with pity as she thought of him. No home, no land, how can such a man be a householder? How can he settle down? "Tell me, dada, should I send him to you?"

"Can't you see your father? As good as in the panchayat. And Mama, what about you? Surely you should arrange for Aullchand to get a bit of land, first of all?"

"I tried, but he insulted me in public and stalked off. Said he could get it on his own."

Giri knows nothing of all this. "Oh, Bangshi-dada! I beg you, please tell me what needs to be done. He knows no better. There's a roof over our heads, true, but the moon shines through it at night and the sun mocks us in the daytime. No leaves to thatch it with, no straw. Bela's to be married, but where will the groom's folks sit? Find us a match for her."

"There is a boy, haven't you noticed? My own paternal cousin. What a nice shop the boy's set up! Sells groceries."

Giri was relieved at this news. Rajiv said, "I can go everyday to Jamai-dada's shop then, get oil and salt on credit, right, Ma?"

Giri rapped him sharply on the head. "Growing to be your father's son. Eat on credit and twiddle your thumbs."

The two days stretched into six. As they depart from her father's home, Giri dressed in a new sari, the children clad in new clothes of the Bangladeshi brand "Nilam! Nilam", stamped with the deadsahib symbol, a bundle of rice on Giri's head, Bangshi Dhamali wafts in like a straw in the wind, breaks the bad news. "Disaster or blessing, call it what you will. Tremendous news, oh Mama! Aullchand said, 'Come, Bela, let's go to your Mama's.' Took her to Kandi on that pretext, with Mohan's connivance. Married off that mother's pet, that timid twelve-year-old girl, to a stranger from another land. They're strange folks, live in Bihar. Five of them have married five such Belaranis and gone back to their land. It's all part of the girl-trafficking business, oh Mama! All the addresses they've left are fake. It's a common racket nowadays. Aullchand's got four crisp hundred rupee notes. Now Mohan and he are sitting at home, getting drunk. Aullchand is weeping 'Bela! Bela!' and Kali-babu from the panchayat is swearing at him, calling him names."

Giri's world falls apart. She bursts into wails of despair. Her father says, "Let's go, I'll take some men with me. We'll find the girl, thrash that father of hers. Cripple him for life. And we'll fix that Mohan for good as well."

Mohan is nowhere to be found. Aullchand strikes his own ears in remorse and laments loudly, occasionally blustering, "It's my daughter I've married off, so what's it to any of you?"

They search high and low. Giri goes crying to the babus with her silver necklace. "Please speak to the police, oh babu! Announce it on the radio. My Bela knows nothing beyond Talsana. You also know that my man's a monster. Why did you entrust my daughter to him?"

The babu explains to Giri's father, "Thana-police means lots of trouble, very expensive, too. The damage is done. This is a new racket that's begun. All this talk of marriage is just a front for girl-trafficking. The racket's in full swing all over Murshidabad. They come, give a few hundred rupees. A few crisp notes are enough to make the beggars lose their heads. The police won't touch a case that's full of holes. They'll tell you, if the father gets his daughter married, what can the thana do? Poor Bela, curse her fate!"

Father, neighbours, the babu's wife, everyone offers the same explanation to Giri. "Fate rules over everyone. What can you do? It would have been good had you been fated to keep her with you. She's a girl, not a boy. A girl's discarded by fate, lost if she's dead, lost if she's wed."

Her father sighs, says, "Your daughter's sacrificed her own life, as if she's given her father the money for the house."

Crazed with grief, Giri sighs, "Don't you send any more bamboo, Baba. Let the devil do what he can."

"No use going to thana-police, child."

Giri leans against the wall and sinks to the floor, silent. Closes her eyes. Amidst this numbing grief, the truth suddenly flashes across her mind. Nobody is willing to give much thought to a girl-child. She, too, shouldn't worry. She, too, is female. Her father, too, had surrendered her to a monster without making any enquiries first.

Aullchand senses the change in the air. So he tells the father, "Your daughter's not all that innocent either. To hunt for the girl, the necklace is produced. If she'd given her jewellery earlier, the house would have been built, daughters would not have to be sold. And look, what a shameful thing to have done. She has an operation, comes back barren. Says, 'You can't even feed us, what would you do with a son?' Well, I've shown what I could do. Even daughters can yield profit, see how much money I got."

Giri beats her head against the wall overwhelmed by rage, by grief. Everyone rushes to stop her.

Over time the uproar dies down. The babu's aunt is a wise lady. She says, "An adolescent girl is her father's property. What use is it for you to shed tears?"

Giri doesn't sob anymore. Grim-faced, she leaves Pari at the babu's house. Says, "If your father comes to get you, I'll chop you to pieces if you go with him."

And if Aullchand tries to speak to her, she doesn't answer him at all. Just stares unblinkingly at her husband. Aullchand is scared. He says, "It's a-l-l for the house. So we can build a house, right?"

"Right. Tell Mohan to find out where they eat human beings. Why not sell off these three too? Enough money then for a fine house. Can't Mohan find out?"

Aullchand says, "Never met anyone as heartless as you, wife. Asking me to sell the children! No wonder you made yourself barren. How else could you speak this way? And your father was willing, so why didn't you take the bamboo?"

Giri leaves the room, sleeps on the veranda. Aullchand whines for a bit, then falls asleep.

But time's a great healer after all. Over the years Giri accepts everything. Aullchand buys bamboo matting and makes a hut. The roof is thatched with palm leaves. Rajiv becomes Kali babu's apprentice and Maruni grows up playing in the courtyard. Looking at Pari, Giri cannot smother the fire that rages in her heart. The same smile, the same gaze, the same tilt of the head. The mistress says, "What a good girl she is. Loves her work."

Because she loves her work, Pari sweeps the babus' huge rooms and verandas ten times over, carries the paddy-sacks to the pond for washing, plasters the courtyard, so huge, like a field, with cowdung. Giri feeds Pari some muri, fried chickpeas or sweetened chickpea balls, then roams around in the babus' orchard collecting leaves and branches. In the middle of the afternoon, she is surrounded by rustling leaves, scurrying squirrels, a gentle breeze ruffling her unkempt hair. She remembers then, the plaintive note in Bela's voice, "But Ma, you're frying muri today! When they call from the babus' house, will you tell them that Bela will go to work tomorrow? Today she'll stay home?"

Such a big girl, and she still liked to sleep with her face pressed into her mother's bosom. The low wooden stool on which the babu's aunt used to sit for her oil-massage had fallen on Bela's foot, grazed it. In the end, warmed-up oil from the lamp had been used to soothe the pain. If Giri had fever, Bela would ask for time off from the babus' house to run home and cook the rice before going back again.

Bela, Belarani, Beli
Not discarded, our dear Beli
Beli's her name, I said
Lost if she's dead,
Lost if she's wed.

Gone, gone where? How far? Remembering, wondering, Giri would whisper in memory of her lost daughter, "There, there! Wherever you may be, stay well, stay safe, my girl. If I knew where you were, I'd fly to you like a bird. But I don't know, little one! I took the address and had Babu write a letter. That address was fake, my dear!"

Back home, Giri cooks rice. Eats with Maruni. Aullchand's rice stays in the pot. The days he doesn't go to work, he lies stretched out on the veranda. The days he does, it's mostly on small-time jobs. Buses now ply on the Krishnachowk-Nishinda bus route they had built. Get onto the bus and you'll reach Kandi in an hour-and-a-half. Now there's work going on, digging a drainage outlet from the irrigation canal. The babu's son now throws his weight around there. Working as an overseer, he has managed to extract a bus-permit as well.

It's there that Giri catches sight of Bangshi Dhamali. With quite genuine concern, Bangshi exclaims, "Oh dear, Giri. I didn't recognize you. You look such a wreck! Pining for that daughter of yours, I suppose … well, what can you do about it, after all?"

"That's not it, dada. It's because Pari is ten years old now."

"Ten?"

"Why, the time your doctor-babu built a brick-and-mortar building, the time *electiri* came to Nishinda, that's the time Pari was born."

"True enough."

"If only we'd listened to you then, moved away, all of us! Even the boy's working as an assistant. If we'd moved then, they could have gone to school."

"Don't know about school. But the town is like an ocean, your children would have been working by now."

Giri understands that Bangshi is angry at the suggestion that her children could go to school.

"Let it be, dada. They'll have to earn by the sweat of their brows. What's the use of some two-bit reading and writing? So why don't you find a match for Pari?"

"I'll let you know, let Aullchand know."

"No, let *me* know."

"This is an empty grudge you bear, my dear. He did something foolish once, can there be no forgiveness for that? Can wedding arrangements be discussed with a woman? The other party will wonder if there's something wrong with your family. When you arrange a match for your son, his prospective in-laws will listen to you. But will they listen when your daughter's marriage is in question?"

"I should know what happens."

"Let's see. There's one fellow, plies a rickshaw at Keshtochowk. Quite old, though. About twenty-five."

"That's okay."

"The girl will live in Keshtochowk itself. No land or property, but the rickshaw's an asset that brings in money for four or five days. In the evening, the chap rolls bidis. But she'd have to keep house. Got no one to cook and clean for him so he wants a wife."

"Let's see. If it works out, we'll fix the wedding for this Magh itself."

The heart that had broken over Bela's loss now sees a ray of light. A glimmer of hope. Giri says, "Whatever I've got, I'll give it all. No point keeping it. I'll worry about Maruni later. My own daughter, how I can sing her praises! She slogs at the babus' house for a meal a day, and see how pretty she's grown. Who'd take her for a ten-year-old? Come dada, have some tea."

Sipping tea, it's Bangshi who says, "So Mama's got two more bits of land, two more granaries. Really, he's done well for himself. A feast for the eyes. But they never come here, never bother to find out how you are. It's a painful thing for you to hear, sister, but even your own folks aren't always your own. Mama mixes with his equals now, not with someone in your station in life."

Giri sighs. Undoes the knotted corner of her sari tucked at her waist, takes out some money to pay for the tea. Says, "Oh dada, remember Pari."

"I'll remember."

Aullchand meets Bangshi, they speak about the rickshaw-puller. Aullchand is delighted. He says, "Dada, it's a rickshaw-puller that I've in mind as well. He plies a rickshaw at Baharampur. Headful of hair, complete with beard and bristling moustache, all dressed up in coat-pant stamped with the dead-sahib brand! Don't you worry about this any more."

Later, when Bangshi meets Giri, he says, "I've spoken to Aullchand. You don't have to worry any more."

Aullchand goes in search of Mohan. Mohan's is the brain that guides him. Lalbagh, Dhuliyan, Jangipur, Ziaganj, Farakka, is there any place he hasn't been to? In Delhi, Meerut, Dhanbad and Tatanagar, the flesh trade is rampant, flourishing. A great demand for nubile young girls from West Bengal. The rich clients, the traders, are fond of tender flesh. Fed and fattened, a girl can be used to recover all costs within a few years.

Mind you, sir, the wedding game needs to be played. If you offer money outright the village folk will mob you. So it needs to be said, "Girls are scarce in Bihar …"

The wedding ceremony is performed, priest and all. Then you must say, "I'll complete the remaining rites and rituals back home, and then we'll have ... what's called conjugal relations. With your kind permission, let me take away the bride."

There have been several instances when girls have been taken away with the excuse of, "I've come from Bihar to get married." Now a new ruse is required. The local tout can locate the girls.

Even he doesn't get to know the full story, although he senses there's something fishy afoot. But he'd rather not know what exactly the fraud is. He's been asked to supply brides and that's all he does.

The parents-brothers-uncles of the girls don't suspect a thing. All they know is they're giving the girl, they're getting the bride price. The groom's a foreigner so you need to keep it secret. People are no longer well-wishers – if they know how much money we're getting, they'll throw a spanner in the works. A foreign groom is best for us. Bengali grooms still pay the bride price, in communities where it's the custom, but they ask for a watch, a bicycle, a radio, five-seven thousand rupees gone before you know it.

Aullchand goes looking for Mohan. After the Belarani debacle, Kali-babu had said, "No more odd jobs for you. You won't find work at the panchayat."

Armed with his education (up to fourth grade), Mohan has now set up operations around the Nishinda Block Office. Selling fertilizer as soon as the farmers acquire some, grabbing a share in the agricultural debts – he has a lot to do now.

Aullchand's proposal has him shaking his head in vigorous denial. "No, thank you. Mohan Mandai wants nothing more to do with your affairs. Done with charity, enough's enough. Getting a girl married is a virtuous business. You got the money, what did I get? Those folks gave me forty rupees. And you? Took the money and built a house of bamboo-lath. I'm scared of your wife, mister."

"Don't worry, she's the one who suggested this."

"Is that so?"

"Just you listen," Aullchand says, "Why the rickshaw-puller from Keshtochowk? You stick to the background. Send out feelers. Aren't there rickshaw-pullers in the city? Wished for the longest time to have in-laws in Baharampur town. Increases my esteem in the village, also gives me a toehold in the town."

"A rickshaw-puller from the town?"

"Yes, mister. Give it a try. But make sure you look in Baharampur. No more folks from that Bihar place. Must be a rickshaw-puller from town, my daughter will stay in town. We'll come and go, bring her home sometimes. Bela's mother is still upset with me. Now her doubts will finally vanish."

"You want to get friendly with your woman?"

"It's better that way. The bitch doesn't think I'm human. I want to prove that I can get a daughter properly married, too. But I can't manage that without your help."

Mohan laughs. He says, "Go on, then. But I won't be seen anywhere. I'll just provide the contacts. You're asking for a son-in-law from town – what if he hands you a list of demands?"

"I'll have to borrow money."

"Got it. Now go."

Mohan realizes that this time he'll have to tread very carefully. The "just-arrived-from-Bihar" party will remain backstage. In the forefront will be the rickshaw-puller. He will be the groom at the wedding. And a good thing, too. This time, five girls must be procured. Rickshaw-puller … rickshaw-puller … now, who can do the job? A visit to town is on the cards.

The business of Pari's marriage brings Giri and Aullchand a little closer once again. Finally Mohan tells Aullchand, "I've found a groom."

"What's the deal?"

"Has a watch. Owns a radio. Plies a rickshaw, so he doesn't want a bicycle. Groom's clothes, bridal wear, mat-umbrella-shoes, not very much."

"Will he pay bride price?"

"A hundred rupees."

"A place to live in?"

"A rented room. But the rickshaw is his own."

Aullchand and Giri are delighted. When the boy comes to see the girl, Giri stays out of sight but looks him up and down carefully from her hidden vantage point. The boy's name is Manohar Dhamali. Sturdy of build, bearded, moustache, too. There really is a rickshaw-puller called Manohar Dhamali in Baharampur. This boy is actually Panu, just acquitted for lack of evidence in a robbery case. Even Aullchand doesn't know this. After coming out of jail, Panu has married two Paribalas, one in Farakka the other in Jalangi, and handed them over to his new masters, the "we-are-from-Bihar" gang. For five weddings he is owed five hundred rupees, not bad at all. Panu's next stop is Siliguri.

Last time, for Bela's wedding, they couldn't invite the relatives. This time Giri's parents come. Conch shells are blown, the women ullulate. Giri, oily and sweating, cooks rice and meat in the kitchen. She's dressed Pari in the jewellery she'd kept safe with the babus. Her mother has given her new clothes to wear. The babus have offered fifty rupees by way of help. Her father has brought rice. The groom arrives at the wedding in a bus, with five companions. Smeared with turmeric and alta, Pari looks very much like Bela.

The next day they hail a bus from the main road and leave.

That's the last time they see Pari. The next day, Aullchand goes with Rajiv and Giri's brother to town, to see his daughter. They're gone for the longest time. Afternoon turns into evening.

Then night. The hours roll by. Giri hears the scrunch of shoes in her courtyard. At once, warning bells ring in her mind. She opens the door to see Bangshi Dhamali. Bangshi's clutching Rajiv. He sobs, "Ma!" And Giri knows at once that disaster has struck again. She looks at him, silent. Her brother says, "Didi! I'll explain."

There's not much to tell. The Manohar Dhamali who lives in town is a middle-aged man. They'd tried asking around. "Didn't find your man at his address? How will you? Sounds like Panu. Yes, yes, he's been going around, getting married quite a few times these last few days. Seems to have joined some kind of racket."

Giri interrupts, asks, "Isn't Mohan involved in this?"

"He's the ringleader."

"And Rajiv's father?"

She runs to find Mohan. Everyone says Mohan's made five to seven hundred rupees out of Pari's wedding. Needs girls, wants money, he's lost his head as well!

A big crowd collects in Giri's courtyard. "Get hold of Mohan, thrash him" "Get the thana-police involved" "What about the law of the land, after all?" Many words, much noise.

Aullchand returns in the wee hours of the morning. Overwhelmed by the gravity of the situation, he has come back roaring drunk. Where did he get the money? "Yes yes, my name is Aullchand Sardar, sir! Could Mohan give me the slip? I wrung his neck and squeezed the money out of him. And why shouldn't I, tell me? Isn't the girl my own daughter? Didn't you go and sell her off under false pretences? Now you want to take the money! Why should I let you? Where is Pari's mother? Why did you have that operation, wife, the more daughters you produce, the more money you acquire. If I don't build a thatched house for you … Pari my child!" Aullchand bursts into loud sobs, then lies down on the veranda and is asleep in an instant. Her mouth dry, Giri forces out the words, "Please go back to your own homes."

Everyone moves away, goes home. They wonder what Giri will do. Maybe she'll die, maybe she'll drown herself. Everyone says, "Maruni will meet the same fate. What a scandal over a girl's wedding. Go, Giri, plead with the babus, tell the thana-police."

Giri stares at them, eyes wide in surprise. Shakes her head, no. No, she won't do anything.

Aullchand's made money, let him do something. Giri shakes her head, disagreeing, "No, no."

Bangshi Dhamali says, "Who knows what God had in mind. One daughter got them walls of bamboo and the other, a thatched roof."

Giri stares at him.

Aullchand thatches the roof even as he weeps for his daughter. The more his eyes fill with tears, the more Giri's eyes stay dry.

The babu's pishi says, "She's the mother of a girl-child, after all! They say, a girl's discarded by fate, lost if she is dead, lost if she is wed. And your fate is no different. Don't I know why you shed no tears? Small sorrows make you weep but great grief turns you to stone. Let's see you get to work. You'll get used to it, my girl, but you've got to feed that mouth at the end of the day."

Giri stares at her as well. Then says, "Speak to the mistress. Give me my dues."

Giri takes the money and knots it into the corner of her sari. Returning home, she stands in the courtyard. Not a bad house. Walls made of bamboo plastered over with clay, a thatched roof. Not a bad home. Just the kind of house she'd wanted, after all. Perhaps she had wanted too much. That's why Beli and Pari had to be handed over to the pimps. To be prostitutes, to those men. Pimps. Were any of those girls bought to play wife? Never.

What a house! Aullchand glances at Maruni furtively, then carries on with his work. Giri stares at him, unblinking. Aullchand thinks to himself, no matter how sad she is, she must love the way the house is now.

When they get up in the morning, everyone is dumbfounded. How extraordinary, how very extraordinary. Giribala has gone to town, boarded the bus from the main road in the early hours of the morning. Maruni in her arms, Rajiv's hand clasped in her own. Later they come to know that getting off at Nishinda she'd told Bangshi Dhamali, "Tell Pari's father he can rot for all eternity in his house." Giri will work in the town as a maidservant, bring up her children. If Aullchand tries to look for her, she will lay her body across the railway tracks.

The news amazes everyone, sets their heads shaking in disapproval. What happened to Bela and Pari is common practice. But why leave your husband and go away? What kind of woman is that?

Everyone is convinced that it's not Aullchand but Giribala who's at fault. An indescribable relief fills them, all of them, when they reach this conclusion.

Walking through the streets in town, Maruni clasped to her bosom, Giri thinks to herself, "If the heart had mustered up courage earlier, I'd have left then, long ago. Would Pari have been lost to us then, or Bela?"

Tears stream down her face as she remembers. But she walks on.

Translator's Note: *ED peon:* an Extra Departmental postal peon, a casual, not permanent government post. *Boshtoms:* colloquial reference to devotees of the Vaishnava sect of Hindusm. *Alta*: red lac dye applied on women's feet on auspicious occasions.

From Kailash to Kolkata

BANI BASU

THERE was consternation on Mount Kailash, the celestial abode of the deities Shiva and Durga. The ceremony to consecrate the idol was over, but Ma Durga had still not finished packing for her annual visit to her parental home on earth.

"What's all this packing for?" Shiva demanded. "The floods have swept away everything, I'm told. As if they'll want to worship you now. They'll be praying with a vengeance, they will!"

"Was it I who sent the floods?" fumed Ma. "All the rivers and waterways are choked up within. There's no proper planning. If they suffer the consequences of their own misdeeds, how can that be helped? I go home just once a year, baba, I'm not willing to give it up."

Saraswati was standing before the mirror, Lakshmi's red Banarasi sari draped across her shoulders.

"Have you taken leave of your senses, Chhoto?" Ma scolded her younger daughter. "Why this silly craving for that red sari?"

"Red is very much in vogue these days in your paternal home," pouted Saraswati. "Why can't I wear it this once?"

"Wear it if you wish," said Lakshmi tartly, throwing her a sidelong glance, "but don't say I didn't warn you. That bright red will set off your dead white complexion and you'll look like you have leucoderma."

Saraswati rushed out in fury. "Why do you say such wounding things, Boro?" Ma complained to her elder daughter. "You seem to be growing more perverse by the day."

"Look, Ma, you've duped me for a long time, calling me Lakshmi, the docile, good-natured one. It's always don't do this, don't do that – my whole being, repressed for so long, is now threatening to erupt like a volcano. These days, your angelic Lakshmis receive no respect at all. Besides, I'm no longer willing to put up with everything in silence. Here, you can keep your wooden money-casket. And here's your owl. I can't stand its wordy preaching any more." Lakshmi flounced off.

Ma collapsed in despair. How could they say such things? Lakshmi not carry her money-casket? Saraswati don a red sari! No, this wouldn't do. She was utterly confused.

The distant cry of a peacock brought Ma back to her senses. Kartika was approaching. Perhaps her son would be able to find a solution. But when told of Ma's worries, Kartika exclaimed:

"Forget all that girlish nonsense! Whether to wear red or blue, whether to carry a money-box or a cosmetic-box – these aren't real problems, are they? I on the other hand have a genuine need, Ma. Do you want to hear about it?"

"If I refused to listen, I'd never hear the end of it, would I?" said Ma testily.

"It's nothing much Ma, all I need is a temporary 'Mumbai bride'," Kartika confessed sheepishly.

"What? You know your public image is that of a bachelor god! It would be disastrous!"

"I'm not discarding my bachelor identity," sulked Kartika. "I only want to live with a woman for a few days. Not one of your celestial women, the kind that Indra and Brihaspati cohabited with, but just living together with an earthly woman. Like Zeus did. You people are so straitlaced about everything, baba."

"An earthly woman when there are so many apsaras in

heaven?" demanded Ma severely. "Why would an earthly woman agree to live with you? Speaking of the Greeks, have you forgotten the Apollo-Daphne episode? Daphne ended up as a laurel tree after all, just to elude Apollo."

"Don't worry on that score Ma," Kartika replied. "There is nothing women of the world won't do these days for publicity and money. If someone can claim to be Kartika's girlfriend, can you imagine the publicity she'd get? And speaking of apsaras, those old-fashioned wiles aren't popular any more, okay? All the Rambha-Menaka-Ghritachis, those old-time apsaras of yours – do they keep abreast of recent advances in the sixty-four arts?"

"But Women's Lib has arrived on earth, I hear," said Ma. "Apparently women have now developed a new sense of self-esteem. They no longer want to be treated as commodities, so I'm told."

"Forget it," Kartika retorted, "all that Women's Lib stuff is for those who are that way inclined. Not everyone is … I mean, not so extremely … you know?"

"Leave me alone now, Kartika," sighed Ma, "let me think a little."

"Think fast, Ma. Sashthi, the beginning of Durga Puja, is almost here." Whistling the popular tune *tututu tutu tara*, Kartika sauntered away. And almost immediately, Ganesha the pot-bellied one appeared on the scene.

"Ma-go," he said as soon as he arrived, dipping to touch her feet respectfully. Ma was deeply attached to this elephant-headed son of hers. He was as obedient as he was deferential. And diligent, too – he had transcribed the entire text of the *Mahabharata*!

"What was that fop doing here, Ma?" Ganesha demanded.

"You'd best not know about that, bachha." Ma knew Ganesha was too simple, his nature too pure and unsullied, for such depravity. It wouldn't be right to tell him about Kartika's request.

"I have a favour to beg, Ma," said Ganesha, lowering his trunk.

Ma's face fell. "What is it you want, bachha?" she asked.

"I want a divorce."

"What vorce?"

"Divorce, divorce. When a marriage breaks down. I can't pull along with Kala my banana bride any more. If you permit, I'll draw up the papers."

"But Kala is needed to start off the Saptami puja, re!" Ma was flabbergasted.

"I knew it, I knew it! The moment I ask for anything, you act thunderstruck. I don't matter, after all, I'm only there to do all the dirty work. You found an elephant-head somewhere and promptly stuck it on my torso; that wretched rat squeaking away below ground – you wasted no time in deploying it as my carrier. Kala, that limp, stupidly inactive banana plant – you quickly got her married to me. You think it's an amusing game, don't you? As if I don't understand. You allow a snow-white swan for someone, a rosy owl for someone else, a fantailed peacock for another, and a huge lion for yourself; but to me you assign a black, hideous, filthy, rat ..."

Ganesha's elephant-trunk began to hiss like a hooded serpent. His eyes flashed fire. Exuding fury like a shower of sparks, he stormed out.

For a long time, Ma lay frozen, as if in a faint. Then she felt someone stroking her hair. Was it Shiva? Looking up, Ma beheld the divine bull, Nandi.

"Ma, you lost consciousness," he said. "Please forgive me for touching you without permission."

"What is there to forgive?" said Ma faintly. "You did the right thing. I don't feel too well."

After a small dose of the legendary celestial drug Bishalyakarani, Ma's spirits lifted. When she sat up, Nandi said: "I have a humble request, Ma."

"What might your request be?" Ma was now feeling really apprehensive.

"Well, I hear the number of asuras, those terrible demons, has gone up considerably this time, Ma."

"What? More asuras? Asuras are constantly being born, they are all over the place, but when did they acquire the audacity to encroach upon my pedestal?"

"If you permit me to say so, this has been going on for quite some time. Slowly and imperceptibly, the trend has grown. There's no help for it now but to destroy them. The human race is in grave danger."

"Which asuras are these, Nandi?"

"The Drugs-Asura, Ma, the Aids-Asura, the Politics-Asura and the Corruption-Asura."

"What!"

"Yes, Ma, ten weapons will no longer suffice. If you agree, I'll give you the Brahmastra, Shiva's ultimate weapon of destruction."

"Give it to me," said Ma, and went into a meditative trance.

Pal Moshai found himself in great difficulty for this year's Puja. Sector 50 had ordered five asuras with their idol. In five different colours. Sector 60 had left a film star's picture with him – their idol must have a face that was the spitting image of the star. Lakshmi-Saraswati must be attired in ghagra-choli. Sector 70 wanted a play of psychedelic lights. All the images had to be stark white, but presented in break-dance postures. And Sector 80's demand … oh, it was too much to bear!

He couldn't take it any more. All these years, he had believed that image worship and idolatry were not the same thing. It is not easy to apprehend an abstract divinity without attributes. So, during the first stage of meditation, the forms of gods and goddesses have to be imagined into being. As the Sanskrit saying goes, a divinity with physical attributes must be invented to serve the worshipper's purpose. In the idols he created, he wanted to represent attributes that were superhuman, yet desired by human beings. But today, there was a clash between the clients' order-forms and the artist's creative norms. What was he to do? After all, there was a lot of money at stake! All he had to do was to create a bunch of dolls. What a dilemma! At midnight, Pal Moshai sprang out of bed. If he must make statues without following the rules of the shastras, then he would invent a new scripture. New idols, envisioned through the artist's eye.

When the people from Sector 50 arrived to collect their idol, they almost came to blows with him. "What is this? Where are Lakshmi and Saraswati? And Kartika-Ganesha? Have they vanished into the furnace?" Pal Moshai's artisans stood around, looking crestfallen. Pal Moshai emerged from his room like an angry lion, its mane flaring.

"With five indomitable asuras closing in on Ma, there's no place on this battlefield for anyone else," he declared. "There's only Shakti, the female principle of power. And Prajna, supreme wisdom. I have used up all the clay required for Lakshmi-Saraswati-Kartika-Ganesha to augment the power-packed contours of Ma's body. Ten arms will no longer suffice, so I've given her twelve. I've created new weapons. Take it or leave it. Otherwise, you can have the advance you paid back."

"I must say it's a regular Mumbai-sized image though Ghontna," observed Pantu, joint secretary of the Puja Committee. "Besides, where will we find a proper idol now?

Pal Dadu, the old men of our locality won't attack us for this, will they? And what about the priest? Will he agree to worship such an idol?"

"If you can't find a priest, let me know," Pal Moshai assured them.

All Ma's offspring were now ready in their respective odd attire. Kala went whining to her dip in the Ganga. Casting a sidelong glance at her, Ma saw that behind her veil of unbleached fabric, Kala looked quite unhappy. Ganesh the pot-bellied one was secretly making faces at her from beneath his elephant trunk. Meanwhile, Kartika's roving eye followed all the girls who came and went in the prayer-mandap, dressed to the nines. He was looking for a suitable girlfriend.

"Disgusting!" exclaimed Ma. "This is no Saptami puja! Nandi, I can see that this will be the last of my home visits."

The evening arati had barely begun when the Pushpak chariot left the scene and whizzed away, high up in the air. It flew past all the the puja pavilions, one by one.

Suddenly, Nandi cried out: "Stop, stop a moment, Bhringi. Ma, just look at this."

Pushpak was hovering just above the Sector 50 mandap. Durga's third eye pierced the pavilion's ornate fabric roof and beheld a glorious image there. All by herself, a lone, single deity. "This is where I belong," she murmured to herself. Heaving a sigh of relief, Nandi and Bhringi dropped her off. What a disaster it would have been, had they been forced to take her back to Kailash! So what if Ma was full of Shakti, she would still have created a scene, shedding a flood of tears.

The sandhi-puja ritual was performed with great fanfare, to the drumbeats of the ceremonial dhak. Sector 50 had apparently won the prize for the year's best Durga idol, so the celebrations were phenomenal. Smoke from the incense burners made Ma's eyes stream with tears, and the din was enough to deafen her. All the same, her countenance bore a gentle, encouraging smile. Let them, let them; let them have their way. Once they came to their senses, they wouldn't remain so besotted.

Having swilled raw liquor, the bigwigs of the area were dancing with dhunuchis, brandishing the incense holders. It was the night of Nabami, the ninth and last evening of the Puja. Suddenly, Ghontna demanded: "Why are twenty-five thousand rupees unaccounted for, Pantu? The receipt has been issued, but the money's not there! It's the money collected from the ads you brought in, you sonofabitch!"

"Dare you question the Secretary!" cried Pantu. "And in the midst of all this merrymaking? Do you know I can fling you into a dhunuchi and reduce you to ashes as I dance?"

"Would you pick a fight with me, you thief! Either you've made off with that money or you've donated it to Akhil-da's party fund. I've often seen you hobnobbing with Akhil Biswas of late."

"Watch out, Ghontna!" With these words, Pantu swung his arms and sprang upon Ghontna. At first, nobody realized what was happening. As soon as it dawned on them that Secretary and Treasurer were fighting over money, the crowd split into two. Some supported one, some the other. Ultimately, in the brawl that broke out, it became impossible to tell who was beating whom, who was wrestling whom to the ground, or who was smashing whose head against the wall. It was like a scene from Kurukshetra. A swarm of people appeared, seemingly from nowhere, to join the fray. To make matters worse, many people began to loudly accuse the neighbouring sector of having engineered the whole thing, hired goondas to ruin the puja in this sector. Armed with lathis, rods and knives, another crowd charged threateningly towards the neighbouring sector.

Ma was in a trance induced by the Nabami puja rituals. When she came out of it, she saw policemen everywhere. Teargas, lathi charge, bricks thrown in retaliation, bombs, soda bottles, bullets. Corpses littered the place. But the police were attacking human targets. It was beyond their power, after all, to destroy the asuras who threatened human beings. So Ma unsheathed her eleventh weapon.

Wasn't that a beeping signal from above? Ma realized that a higher authority was taking charge of the situation. Was the apocalypse imminent then? Was all this a rehearsal for the final great flood that would destroy the world? Would the human race be wiped out now, through their mutual destructiveness?

Long before the idol was deconsecrated and the mirror ritually immersed to signal the end of Durga Puja, Ma abandoned the desolate mandap and mounted her elephant. Departing, she left some tears in the idol's glassy eyes. She was a mother, after all, and a daughter, too.

Playing with Dolls and a New Love Story

AHANA BISWAS

WATER belongs in the canal, not in the river. It will rise and swell just once, during the rains, and that will be enough to fill the canal. Actually, the canal is a dead tributary of the Kunur river. Once upon a time, a knee-deep current flowed in it all year round. It would feed the cows and oxen, the lowcaste Bauri and Bagdi boys would catch fish there, laughing and chattering, but now it's full of coarse sand. For two or three months in the year it is brimful of water, hence the long bridge. Because buses headed for the main road ply on the bridge, the space beneath is where people play games.

"Games, indeed, playing with dolls, more like!" Borobou, the eldest daughter-in-law of the house, pulled a face as she seasoned the dal with spices spluttered in hot oil. At her words, Chhobi burst out laughing, covering her mouth with the end of her sari.

"You're so right, Didi," she said. "The grown men of this village never seem to lose their fondness for dolls – all their childhood games didn't satisfy them. Look at Sidhu's house in our neighbourhood – their entire household is involved! This whole village is remarkable."

The mention of Sidhu made Borobou cautious. She didn't say much these days. She kept her distance even from the other daughters-in-law of the house. It was only with Chhobi that she indulged in casual chit-chat, because she was a girl from her own paternal village. Ever since their young days, she had been like a sister, a friend. But how tales carried, who could tell! Who would want private confidences to reach the ears of all and sundry? If there were rumours about Sidhu's family, her own family wouldn't be spared, either. Money always attracts envy.

"Unless the Moiras are shifted out of this neighbourhood nothing will change Chhobi, let me tell you," she declared. "The boys, the men, why are they to blame? Have you seen the Moira women's clothes? A hundred washes, and they don't even die. There has to be some limit to their disgusting behaviour – chhi!" Borobou cleared her throat noisily in order to change the subject, and to indicate to Chhobi that she didn't fancy discussing it any more. Getting up from the ledge outside the cooking area, she stepped into the courtyard. These days, she had to step up and down with care, her body had grown so heavy. It wasn't as if all the people of the world would look after her if she fell!

Descending the steps, Borobou was taken by surprise. Spitting, she took some time to express her amazement. There was Dhyangabou, Mathur Master's lanky wife! A very arrogant woman she was, never came here, except for some holy ritual. Must be something urgent. Borobou was desperate to find out why. Everyone in the household, young and old, was dying of curiosity too.

"So, baba, at last you have come to pay us a visit!" Borobou greeted her, forcing a smile.

"As if she would come on her own, Ma!" her daughter Beli called out from within. "I have dragged her here to collect some sewing from me." Borobou's eyes couldn't be relied upon. If she started sewing from one end, the stitching veered off in the opposite direction. Beli too couldn't handle needlework. It was Dhyangabou who helped her with all her sewing assignments for school. Beli sought her out very often.

Dhyangabou's appearance was rather odd. Not only was she thin, she was also taller than most men. Thick, reddish tresses and large tawny eyes with long lashes. A relative, she lived in a house that shared a wall with theirs, but she had never come across for a chat, not even once. Nor would she stir out of the house. She sat inside all the time, eyes fixed on the window, gazing out. From there she saw everything, and would call out to Beli. Sometimes, Borobou would get angry with her daughter. Don't go to such women, they bring bad luck. Beli would praise Dhyangabou night and day. She worked such wonders with wool, with crochet. Beli even stood up for Dhyangabou in arguments. These days, she went to her for help with her studies too. She'd say, Ma, Dhyangabou has passed just one assignment of mine, and Mathur Master has passed three. What they teach us in school is so poor, Dhyangabou is much, much better! History, geography ... the way she teaches, Ma, it's like enjoying a story.

2

As afternoon passed and dusk descended, it was time for the teatime gossip assembly in the house. The four brothers came home from work, and there was chit-chat, consultation, criticism, and so on. The eldest of the four, touching fifty, travelled to town every day. He traded paddy and coal. Mejobhai and Sejobhai, the second and third, looked after some other affairs. Sudha Video Hall was flourishing too. It was the village cinema hall. Thatched roof, viewers crowded on the floor. Countless bugs in the floor mats. Still, people from all the neighbouring villages thronged the hall. Sometimes, along with *Love Story* and *Khalnayak*, blue films were also screened, disguised in *Ramayana* cassette-covers. The higher the ticket price, the larger the crowd. All you needed to know was the art of making money. Chhoto, the youngest brother, observed all this, which was exactly what the eldest, Boro wanted. Chhoto was quite smart. Friendly with some of the layabouts in the neighbourhood. That helped, but could also be a hindrance. It was something Boro preferred to ignore; or perhaps he thought a few habits like this would at least keep the boy from breaking up the family (out of love for his wife), and the property wouldn't get divided. Yet that very matter had begun tormenting Boro of late. After all, things don't always work according to one's calculations. Still, one must wait. Chhoto was not interested in money. He lounged on the front veranda all day, gossiping with passersby on the street. His attention was actually fixed on the Moiras' tin door. Sometimes he would aim small brick pellets at the door. Dark-skinned girls would emerge to swear at him, and Chhoto would make placatory gestures at them. All the villagers saw this as they went on their way. They were not aware, these people, that trade survives on a good reputation; nor did they understand discretion. These days, Chhoto was very friendly with Sejo. Boro knew the source of this intimacy. Muttering and whispering to each other, all the time. He really couldn't stand it. He hadn't realized earlier that his brothers would prove to be so witless. But times were bad, it wasn't possible to reprimand anybody. And even if one did, would they listen? He spent very little time at home. When he came, he would somehow cross the street, closing his eyes and ears to everything. One or the other was bound to be loitering at the alley's entrance. Just as Hindus who are new converts to Islam consume more than the usual quantity of beef, so when girls of a respectable bhadra family enter the trade, they abandon all pretence at outward appearances. Yet Boro in his childhood had seen their old, bent father, so polite and deferential, working in the sweetshop at the bus stand. Must one take to this trade as soon as money becomes scarce? Boro really didn't want to set eyes on them any more. He was growing old, these things didn't please him. Sometimes they even swore at him as they passed. But what could he do? He had thought of buying their house but not only had his brothers objected, once word got out, the Moira women had released a flood of unspeakable curses from their door. Although everyone was aware that all sorts of shenanigans went on in this brick-built town house, these whores made the whole business publicly known. Boro had no idea how terrible some things sounded when put into words. They had grown up in the same neighbourhood since childhood, had come to each other's aid as companions in distress on so many occasions. He had left nothing owing, repaid everything down to the last measure. They had not been so hard up then. On many occasions they had even refused to accept payment. What had come over them now? The real cause of their anger was not *his* desire to buy up their house, but their desire to know why they hadn't been kept in town. As if they were like heavenly apsaras, all of them! Even in daylight, you needed a hurricane lantern to make out their features. Greed is a terrible thing. Greed for money has brought them to this, Boro thought, they don't know how to live up to the prestige of an honourable man.

These days, they go and complain at the Party office at the slightest pretext. The village folk gather around to watch the fun. Then they corner him, all of them together. That's where the problem lies. For the Party to turn hostile is like overturning the auspicious Ganesha idol. The Party applies pressure. It is necessary for members to be of good character, they say, so people may see and learn by example. Otherwise the Party's image will suffer. Boro laughs to himself. After listening to all this, he had once asked the village headman:

"Dada, surely these leaders are men?"

"Men indeed, but extraordinary men," the pradhan had assured him gravely. "Don't you breed ducks in your backyard? They go into the water, but when they return is there any water on their bodies?"

He said nothing to his brothers nowadays. It was good for business for them to remain together. It was possible to extend their land, their trade, on the strength of their reputation. He had married off two of them. For Sejo, he had found a girl after hunting high and low. Daughter of a friend, this was one occasion when he hadn't taken a single paisa. That had earned him a very good name, as well. There wasn't such a beautiful girl to be found in any of the villages nearby. So many girls and married women, some known to them, some not, had come by to look at the bride.

Even Mathur Master's Dhyangabou who never visited, had come to see her. Borobou would say she was too arrogant to walk on ordinary soil. She urged them to raise a high wall alongside Dhyangabou's. To block her window. Which was indeed illegal. But why were the wives so angry because she looked out? She was only looking, after all. But one day he too had glanced at the window. Eyes like burnished copper, that seemed to devour all that went on inside their house. What was there in those eyes? They were quite large and beautiful. What was there in some people's eyes? Boro didn't want to upset Dhyangabou, nor Mathur Master. Of course, that's what he used to think earlier, when he hadn't realized how spineless Mathur was. Playing cards all day. Hadn't acquired much style or reputation as an educated young man. Had gone to the city to study but hadn't returned with any skill besides drinking. Normally it was the masters who ruled the roost in every village. Panchayat upwards, all the authorities were teachers, each with his cane to flog people with. But Mathur could neither teach, nor use his cane. His home remained peaceful, apparently they never quarrelled. Mathur had no bad habits either. What did he see, this young man, in such an angular woman?

At home, whenever they all got together, there was talk of Dhyangabou. First criticism, now laughter. Earlier, Mathur was seen as master operator, for he had taken forty thousand as his marital due. A year before his marriage, offering up that forty thousand, he had obtained his job by grovelling at the secretary's feet. But now Mathur was his wife's bonded slave. Apparently he handed over his entire monthly income to her. He'd play cards with the Mallik boys, then go home in time for dinner. Why he remained with that skinny, hoarse-voiced wife was hard to understand. After all, she was no woman, she was a witch.

Sejobhai the third brother mimicked Dhyangabou's walk very well. Watching his exaggerated postures the other brothers, their wives, sons and daughters, would roll about in mirth. He would even mimic the way Dhyangabou called out "Beli! Beli!" from her window.

Although Sejo's act had won him applause in many quarters, in his own home, Beli (his elder brother's daughter) would always spring to Dhyangabou's defence. Grimacing, twisting his arms in many telling gestures, Sejo would demonstrate how Dhyangabou made love with Mathur Master. If she happened to be present during this obscene mimicry, Borobou would collapse laughing, clutching her abdomen.

"Thakurpo," she would gasp, "had you joined the jatra party, you would have gone very far."

The eldest brother, rocking in his chair, looking as calm and grave as possible, absorbed everything, wanting to say: dear brother, all this strikes you as so entertaining but such things are common in this world. I have seen so much of them.

"Boudi, you were there when Mathur got married," Mejo said to Boroboudi, his elder sister-in-law. "Such a lanky girl, did you check her out properly?" Mejo and Chhoto would egg Sejo on. A shower of sparklers seemed to fly from Sejo's lips. As long as he was there, he would keep them entertained. That was why Sejo was popular with everybody.

Mejobou relished Sejo's remarks greatly, but upon hearing them, would go and hide in her room. All things should not be heard in everyone's presence. Listening to him, her body felt a strange yearning. It became hard to contain. She couldn't control the urge to see Sejo, her younger brother-in-law somehow, somewhere. There was temptation in Sejo's words.

But Sejobou – or Notunbou, the new bride – was nowhere to be seen. After completing her household chores she would enter the house. If someone asked her a question she'd answer, but otherwise it was impossible to extract a single word from her. People eulogized such behaviour as a sign of bashfulness and modesty. Her husband's piercing wit entered her ears as well, but she showed no change of expression. Carried on with her chores, slowly, very skillfully, with her tiny hands.

Beli alone raised her voice. In the general hubbub, only her father heard her, noticed that Dhyanga tutored Beli. Beli passed her exams every time, was the only one in the house to achieve good results. Following her example, her two brothers would also learn. It was Boro's great desire to make masters of the two boys. If they somehow cleared three examinations, the rest could be taken care of. A lumpsum at the end of the month was not to be scoffed at. Borobhai would console Beli. Then, silencing all the others, he would listen to what she had to say.

Beli, who was in seventh grade and mature beyond her years, was eager to prove that Dhyangabou's husband was a man.

"Mathur Master slapped her in my presence, once," she declared. "Dhyangabou merely said she couldn't get up so late every night to open the door. Dhyangabou cries, too. Because she doesn't shriek when she cries, you don't get to know. She sheds lots of tears. She said, 'Beli, you must study hard and stand on your own feet. I had wanted to study, but my Baba got me married. That explains my predicament.' Mathur Master doesn't really love her, Baba."

3

The word "love" on Beli's lips made Sejo laugh. Love. What was love, damn it? Was one supposed to cavort with one's wedded wife like they did in films? Who loved whom in this village, who languished at the feet of the Moira or Bagdi whores – such things were common knowledge. But they were sugar-coated pills all of them, bitter inside, polished on the outside. Sejo couldn't stand his own wife. So what if her body was white and soft like kneaded flour, and so what if she was built like the goddess Lakshmi? She expressed herself neither in words, nor in blood. One had to shake her to see if she was human, or a doll.

But the quarrel with Saki of the Moira family reduced his reputation to mud. They had been arguing over rates, but on that day Sejo was in fine fettle.

"Hiking up your rates every month, do you take this for a lawless land where anything goes?" he demanded. "We're kind enough to let you live across the road from us, remember."

But Saki was not to be cowed. On the contrary, she claimed, that the place belonged to her forefathers. Besides, but for the Moira women, how would the four brothers have survived in such good shape? Then she compared him unfavourably with Sidhu Ghosh of the neighbouring area. Sidhu had bought her a rubia blouse to match her sari. Because they lived across the road from her, she was kind enough to meet them under the bridge for such a low rate, otherwise, even if the girls starved, these men couldn't care less. Boro, the eldest, spent lavishly in the city, but these other two were evil and miserly.

Saki began to weep, making a terrible racket. Their parents didn't get the girls married, after all it was because they were dark and ugly that their daughters looked like this. How unfortunate they were!

Sejo Master suppressed his rage at the comparison with Sidhu Ghosh. Below the bridge it was lonely and desolate. Few people wandered the street, after dusk. Sejo Master decided to teach Saki a lesson. She didn't know him! Ruthlessly, Sejo Master performed the deed with which a thickheaded man proves his virility, thinking he was the world's most successful hero. He felt like tearing her from limb to limb, but realized he no longer had the strength. He felt like kicking her one more time but his legs refused, even feet have a sense of disgust, after all! Sejo thought – she won't get up till tomorrow. In the morning everyone will see her, a free show. Groping in the dark, he picked up the rubia blouse and put it in his pocket. When Saki came home, he would burn it on the veranda, in full public view. For someone who earned a living from taking off her clothes, to fancy a rubia blouse! Chhi. He spat on Saki's body.

But by morning, trouble broke out. By then the workers had arrived at the house. Borobabu was giving them instructions. Everyone had already been served tea and snacks. The three wives were completing their chores outside the kitchen. Spreading a reed chatai on the ground, Beli settled down to study along with her two brothers. The pressure of housework was high – Borobabu had to set out by ten, after his meal of rice. But just then, Saki's didi, her elder sister, came rushing through the entrance straight into the courtyard, setting up a real commotion.

"Your deor stole a blouse last night!" she screamed, going directly to Borobou. "Tell him to give it back! Refuses to pay up, and then steals, as well!"

Borobou, Borobabu, Sejo, Mejo, Chhoto, all began to shout. Not to be outdone, Saki and Saki's didi let loose a stream of foul curses, their voices rising to a crescendo. In front of so many people, Saki began to scream, so everyone could hear:

"These men, they rob the Moiras' blouses for their own wives. See, all of you, what things have come to now!"

By then, a crowd of people, young and old, had swarmed in. Dhyangabou's face appeared at the window above. Sejo couldn't fathom how Saki had come there so early. They just wouldn't die, these whores. It seemed to Sejo his blood wouldn't cool until he had thrashed Saki in front of everyone. Borobabu had the same thought. He ordered the workers to lift the two filthy women and fling them out over the fence. Putting their heads inside the tiger's cage, these women didn't know the consequences. But the workers wouldn't budge.

"Babu, they are contemptible, let them go," one of them said in a low voice.

Sejo fetched an iron rod from somewhere, rusty from long disuse. The matter must be settled somehow today, he must kill somebody.

"Come on, let's see what you can do," Saki taunted him. "I went to the Party office before coming here. The Party leaders are on their way. Just try raising your hand on me!"

Sejo stopped in his tracks. Pushing through the crowd the area pradhan, Habul Master, Surojitkaka and other major Party leaders made their way in. Greeting them with a namaskar, Borobabu led them into the house.

"Just look at their contemptible behaviour!" he complained. "What sort of neigbourhood do we live in, dada? No respectable bhadralok can live here. Please do something about it. Your presence is a great reassurance to all the bhadralok."

Habul Master and the other Panchayat members pacified

Saki and her sister and sent them home. Asked them to drop by at the office later.

"You are rich folks, all of you," the women screamed on their way out, "but we warn you we'll take the skin off every man in this village and hang it out in public. Before the elections we'll show you how fair and spotless each man's complexion really is."

The pradhan's fair complexioned face was turning red. These women had to be taught a lesson somehow but it was a difficult task. It was the Party that had given them so much power. A terrible truth dawned on the pradhan: if the Party were destroyed, it would be at the hands of these women.

Eventually things subsided. The crowd dispersed. Then they discussed things over tea and pappad. The pradhan, Habul Master, Surojitkaka – were not always available, after all. Borobhai grabbed the opportunity to raise a lot of urgent matters, including the possibility of buying up the Moiras' house opposite. It had become so calm that everyone forgot the shameless interchange that had taken place only moments earlier. It was already so late that Borobabu decided not to go to work that morning.

Just then they heard an agonized scream from the kitchen. They spilled out of their rooms, all of them, and rushed into the courtyard. It was Mejobou who had screamed, she who had been chopping vegetables in the kitchen. Descending into the courtyard, everyone saw with stunned disbelief that on the ground beside the cooking stove, lay burning red-hot coals. Standing bolt upright, upon them, holding on to the post was Sejobou. A brick-red glow seemed to radiate from the toes of her fair white feet.

"Hold her, catch hold of her!" cried Borobabu.

Mejobou was closest to her, yet she stood there, stupefied. She tried to grab Sejobou, but couldn't make her budge an inch. There was Sejobou, feet clenched, mouth clamped shut. Just then, in a flash, Dhyangabou appeared on the scene, rushing in from somewhere. Perhaps she had been watching from the window. Long legs, head uncovered, clothes flying.

"Hold her, hold her head!" she cried, and lifted up the foot that had burnt like brick. Fainting, Sejobou collapsed into Dhyangabou's lap.

4

Mathur Master's wife carried Sejobou away to her own home. Though she lived next door, though she was a blood relation, though Beli was constantly going across to that house to tend to Sejobou or inquire after her, even so the people of this house had not welcomed this move. But in the present situation, it had also been impossible to oppose Dhayangabou. Such things happened in every home. Eventually all wayward men settled down to family life. But that Sejobou, renowned for her bashfulness and docility would do something so theatrical, nobody had realized. Certainly not Sejobabu, not even Borobabu, who spent his days managing human beings. He too was now praying to goddess Durga for deliverance. What a mercy the woman hadn't set herself on fire, hadn't swallowed poison! Had she died, they would have been stuck with thana, police, lawyers, courthouses. A huge waste of money! They didn't lack for enemies in this village. Just imagining the possible hazards, Boro resumed chanting Durga's name.

But Sejo remained morose and taciturn. He hadn't stepped out even once since the morning. He spoke very little. Did his wife want to die? How could she have done such a thing? After all, most men in this village were of dubious moral character but their wives didn't act like this! Sejo had said to Boroboudi, "Let my wife spend the night at home, at least. She can go back there tomorrow morning. It doesn't look good for a married woman to spend the night in someone else's home." But Dhyangabou had not allowed his wife to return home.

"She is unwell," she had insisted. "I will look after her at night. Trying to move her will create problems. Besides, she is a daughter-in-law of your family, and it is to you she will return when she recovers."

Sejo was deeply disheartened, couldn't sleep at night. It was because of him that his wife had taken such an extreme step. The thought struck a chord somewhere in his heart, made him feel more important than everyone else. But surely his wife could have spoken to him before she acted? Sejo's anger was now directed at his Dada. Just because Dada fed, clothed and supported them, did he have the right to ask why Sejo's wife should return? Were good looks all that mattered? Sometimes, Sejo felt like leaving the village, going and living in the town house. People would gossip for a few days, but then everything would die down. Actually nothing really mattered to the people of this village. Some of them might go out of their way to spread a few rumours for a couple of days, but the next day onwards, everything would return to normal. Such was the character of this village.

But he hadn't realized how lethal was the whiplash that Saki had dealt to his honour. Sejobou had forced him to acknowledge it by demonstrating what it meant. He could have Saki expelled from the neighbourhood, from the village, but could he do the same to his wife? Where was the need for her to have acted so drastically! It was not a custom in this family to abandon one's wife. He would grow old, must spend the rest of his life with her. Sejo felt quite helpless, began to develop contempt for everybody, including his family and the entire village. Did this wife of his deliberately speak so little? Would she have been more talkative if she had married a different man? Did she dislike him so much then? She could have gone back to her parents' home, after all, who would hold her back if she wanted to leave? And yet it was because of him that she stepped on to those burning coals. Sejo seemed to feel the heat beneath his soles. He began to feel sorry for his wife, felt a strong desire to see her. She had remained standing for a long time, poor thing – must have been badly burnt. Dhyangabou had had her examined by a doctor, taken care of all the expenses. Sejo felt grateful, but couldn't restrain himself from wanting to see his wife. How to wake up people so late at night? Nor could he go across at the crack of dawn, people would laugh at him.

Sejo sat up. Then lay down again. Tried to summon sleep. Determined what he would say to people the following day. There was no one in the kitchen, he would say: she collapsed in a dizzy spell, her feet, struck the cooking stove. But no, Sejo couldn't stay in bed for long. Couldn't control himself. Whatever else he might be, he was not a man for self-control. He scaled Mathur Master's low fence. On the veranda downstairs, Master lay asleep in bed, his snores making a hissing sound. Slowly, Sejo tiptoed upstairs. He could hear subdued voices. Suppressed laughter. Taking cover in the dark, Sejo looked in through the window and witnessed an unprecedented love scene.

The kerosene lamp flickered dimly. A pillow was placed under his wife's knee. Her fair, exposed foot, smeared with ointment, seemed to float in the air, free of contact with the bed. There was no sign of agony on his wife's face. She was chatting cheerfully with Dhyangabou. Sejo had never seen such a heavenly smile on his wife's face. Beside her, Dhyangabou was saying something to her in an indistinct voice. He couldn't hear anything. Slowly, their lips met and merged. Never before had he seen such untroubled mutual desire, such a simple, exquisite dreamlike scene. He felt he was in a sort of trance. He couldn't believe his own existence. He and his younger brother had peeped into many windows as adolescents but they had never seen such a sight. It pained him that he was seeing it alone; it diluted his enjoyment and he longed for someone else to view it with him. Let there be someone to bear witness. If no one else, at least let Chhotobhai see it.

Without pausing to think, he rushed down the stairs. Two steps down, his heart began to tremble. He stopped. This was his wife after all, his wedded wife. He seemed to have forgotten this fact. What was it he wanted to show, and to whom? What he himself had never been fortunate enough to enjoy. Paralyzed, Sejo glanced back once. Hearing sounds, Dhyangabou had turned up the kerosene lamp and was standing at the window. In the light of the flame, her eyes could be seen clearly. They looked even more unnatural. Someone seemed to have robbed Sejo of all his strength, as if by magic. He couldn't move. But Dhyangabou's eyes bored into his body like the point of a sharp blade.

Proprietor

NABANEETA DEV SEN

STAGGERING unsteadily in the crowd, when she finds that tiny bit of standing room by the wall at the corner near the door, Mita feels as if she's attained salvation. She's no longer used to boarding a bus, and the very sight of these rickety private buses frightens her. Thank god she's at least grown partially accustomed to riding minibuses nowadays.

After fifteen years, Kolkata seems a different city. So crowded, so much dust, so much garbage and such roughness all around. The factory is located in an area where nothing is available, neither taxis nor minibuses. In the absence of a car, there's no option save this private bus.

She has boarded the bus by the front door; the long Ladies' Seat is full. The fat lady is a good soul, she stretches out a helping hand, and pulls Mita's bag onto her lap. Now Mita manages to lean against the wall, standing somewhat more comfortably. She must ask for the bag at some stage and take out her change for the bus fare. Catching a sudden glimpse of her own face in the mirror in front of her, Mita feels pleasantly surprised. She's not looking all that grimy and washed out, after all, is she? Considering how hard she's been working with artisans, all this time. They send fashion designs from abroad, and it's not easy trying to explain those designs to local workmen. Labour is cheap here, leather is cheap, too. If only one can get the work done with some care, the business is bound to flourish. Mita personally supervises the work, she supplies goods to a foreign company with a famous brand name. Until she met Krishnan, she had assumed that South Indians couldn't do business, they specialized in shooting up the corporate ladder. Krishnan destroyed this assumption. His export business is thriving. Mita works hard, shoulder-to-shoulder with him. Krishnan is amazingly calm and patient by nature; over the last fifteen years, there's been no particular quarrel that Mita can recall. Yet, they have had to go through all sorts of adjustments. From being a receptionist in a multinational company, Mita has become the director of so many companies today. She owns a spacious penthouse in a ten-storey building on Camac Street. No, there's no need for her to ride in buses. It's just that her car happens to be at the workshop, and her mother has borrowed the other car to visit Boromami. No, Krishnan has not left her in want of any comfort. Their daughter is studying at the convent school in Kurseong, and there's no end to her father's anxiety about this Gorkhaland affair. Krishnan rings up morning and evening saying, "You must go, go and bring Romi back!" But why? Isn't the school full of other girls? Why this fuss? Besides, Romi Krishnan is not even a Bengali name. What exactly is he afraid of? Taking a cue from their son-in-law, her parents, too, have started singing a similar tune. How will she explain to them that it does the kids great harm to disrupt their studies at this stage? To bring her back to Kolkata now and try to get her admitted into a different school would be nothing short of a nightmare. Romi is sweet enough as girls go, but she's grown up to be quite tough and self-reliant. This is the advantage of having lived by herself in a hostel right from childhood. The way Mita used to be shifted around along with her parents, constantly transferred elsewhere, studying in ten or twelve different schools had done her a great deal of damage. Who would she explain this to? She won't allow the same thing to happen with Romi.

Mulling over all this, Mita has been casually resting her gaze on the rows of garish yellow characters inscribed in English on the inner wall of the bus, directly in front of her eyes. Just as in Sukumar Ray's nonsense rhyme, the Raja eats a packetful of fried peanuts but doesn't swallow them, so Mita has been looking at the inscribed characters, but not reading them.

Suddenly from deep, deep within her body, arises a tremor. Her hair stands on end.

What's that?

What's that written there? On the inner wall of the bus?

Whose name is that?

In an instant, the characters dance away, float away, blurring and beginning to fade.

Steeling her mind, clearing her vision, Mita takes another look. She tries to read.

There it is, written quite clearly. Like a notice.

> PROPRIETOR:
>
> SHRI SHUBHASHIS MAZUMDAR, B.SC.
>
> 132/2 C GOBINDO GHOSHAL LANE
>
> BHABANIPUR, KOLKATA 26

First, the name.

Then, the address.

Yes, the very same address.

There may be many people by that name, after all.

But that address?

At that address, by that name, could live only one human being in the whole world. He who had been named Shubhashish, combining the Shubha from Shubhamita and the Ashish from Debashish.

Fifteen years ago, he had been nine years old. He would go hopping and skipping to school, dressed in a white shirt and khaki shorts. Returning home one day, he couldn't find his mother anywhere.

How is he? How much has he grown, the owner of this

bus? What does he look like now? A lump comes to Mita's throat, pain awakens gradually and wrenches her heart – who could have said that a wound suppressed for fifteen years would remain so raw? Who could have known that so much blood would still flow from it? Shubhashish Mazumdar.

Covering each new textbook with brown-paper, his mother would lovingly write his name on it.

"Your Shubha and my Ashish, with the combined auspiciousness of both, how blessed will the boy be – nothing will happen to him even if an atom bomb falls on his head," Debu had laughed out loudly. The joke about an atom bomb falling on the head of her newborn baby had not appealed to Shubhamita at all. "Be quiet, will you? You and your wicked talk!" she had rebuked.

The very same Shubhashish.

"Not Shubhasheesh, Shubhashish." Debu would teach everyone the correct spelling. Shubha could not stop laughing. When she returned, dog-tired, to the partial darkness of the house on Gobindo Ghoshal Lane, stepping like a stork to avoid the rotten fish-scales and dead kittens in the garbage heap, the child who came running to hug her, calling out "Ma" – a single word that instantly spread sunshine, brightening the world – that same Shubhashish.

She's not likely to make a mistake about that address.

The house built around a courtyard by Debu's paternal grandfather. Getting smaller and smaller, the divided portions now add up to just a few rooms, part of the veranda, and a bit of the courtyard. A jointly owned house. Debu's paternal grandfather had a passion for getting married. Three wives had he. Seventeen living male offspring. That's what Mita's parents had objected to. Who can say for sure that the grandson won't take after his grandfather? All the same, they had agreed. They had no option. They had to yield to their daughter's stubbornness. Disappointing many better suitors, it was the youngest clerk in a multinational company, the poet Debashish Mazumdar, whom Shubhamita Dasgupta had ended up marrying. No, Debu's parents had not been uncaring towards her. Debu's two younger sisters had been beside themselves with joy at having acquired such a beautiful sister-in-law. His elder brother and boudi remained somewhat distant, she was never particularly friendly with her sister-in-law; even after keeping house for ten years, the two sisters-in-law had not become two sisters.

Their share comprises just four rooms. The two brothers occupy the two larger rooms with their respective wives. At night, their father sleeps in the sitting room. Their mother, in the small room, with her two daughters. Her paraphernalia for her puja is also kept there. Yes, there is a common family prayer room in the attic, the marble room. But every wife has her own deity in her room, just as each of them has a separate cooking stove. As their kitchens have become "separate," so, too, their prayer rooms. Even the deities are separate, to each her own.

Shubhamita was a small-town girl. Thanks to her engineer father's transferable job, she had travelled all over India. She had no experience with a joint family. Her romantic notions were shattered every moment. The ultimate was the prayer room, kept under lock and key. On Thursdays, there was a family Lakshmi puja, with the blowing of conch shells and ringing of prayer bells. The hired priest came daily, unlocked the door, replaced the flowers and woodapple leaves, and left after offering the deity some water and sugar candy – little things that none of the daughters-in-law ever offered to do. How amazing! With so many daughters-in-law in the house! Shubhamita was a working wife, it's true; even if she had the will, she didn't have the time. But what about the others? Throughout the entire neighbourhood it seemed a register was maintained to record Mita's comings and goings, her movements, dress and appearance, everybody noted down everything and found her at fault. And in this enormous house, of course, every room contained a book of daily accounts for her. At first, she was terribly disgusted, crossing the dirty slum on her way in and out. While she was growing up, Mita had lived in small-town bungalows on open, spacious, tidy streets. Handkerchief pressed to her nose, the discomfort caused by her unfamiliarity would reveal itself in her gait. The neighbourhood did not view this with kindness.

Day after day, the sight of the new bride dressed in a printed silk sari, with painted nails and lips, short hair puffed up like a memsahib's, going off to work merrily with her husband by her side, was something the people on that street had never seen before. In middle-class homes, housewives would regularly raise their curtains to look out, old men on roadside ledges would stare at her; in front of the slum, at the public water tap, at the coal-shop, everywhere women and men would gape open-mouthed at this shameless bride.

In this way, seven years went by. During this period Shubhashish was born, he joined school, the sisters-in-law were married off and produced children, the father-in-law died, and Krishnan arrived as Debu's new boss. Debu may not have made great progress in his profession, but in his life, there has been a great change. Of late, he has been completely preoccupied with his poetry magazine and his writing. Heart and soul. Neither his office, nor his home interest him any more. He is hardly ever home, both Shubha and Shubhashish have become unimportant now, having lost out to the great claims of "Art." As for returning from work together, that stopped long ago. Apparently, his literary friends drink heavily, so in their company it becomes obligatory to drink a little bit as well. When Debu returns, he is unsteady on his feet. Mita feels disgusted, though she has seen plenty of drinking in her life. After all, her father used to host many parties in their own house. But nobody got drunk, did they? Nor did they vomit. At the end of a party, all of them would happily drive away, back to their own homes, only Debu would return tottering at midnight to drown the courtyard in his vomit.

Mita washes the courtyard by sloshing bucketsful of water on it so that their relatives won't see anything in the morning. The house has a water problem; you have to fetch it from the tubewell. The water in the reservoir is not enough for the entire household. Debu is becoming more inconsiderate by the day. Under the influence of alcohol he is shirking his work, getting reprimanded at the office for shirking, drinking even more after being reprimanded, shirking even more after getting drunk. All the writing about love – gradually, even that goes to the dogs. That beautiful quarterly, *Poetstory,* winds up in the end. Who is this Debashish? Shubha cannot recognize him any more. Far from resorting to sulks and tantrums, even when she tries to reason with him gently, he pays no attention – from the next day, he stops speaking to her. If his mother tries to talk to him, he yells at her. If his brother makes oblique remarks, he attacks him with objects close at hand. At first, Shubhashish would start wailing, Boudi would retaliate in her ringing, nasal tones, mother would run around trying to put a stop to the quarrelling. Gradually, things came to such a pass that little Shubhashish stopped crying, but would run away from the house instead. Mother would weep silently. Boudi would wrap her arms around her own husband, and drag him into their room. Mita would go out in search of Shubhashish. Debu would start shouting and continue to do so until he fell asleep.

One day, after this had become a nightly routine, Shubhamita went up to Krishnan and said "Sir! you are his boss, please forbid him. Let alone giving us money for housekeeping, Debu has even made it difficult for us to live in the house – have him examined by a doctor, please, do something, whatever need be. Please save us."

No, Shubhamita did not go to her father. Baba had not yet retired, he was in Durgapur, quite close to Kolkata. It was no use telling Baba and Ma. They would suffer, and Debu wouldn't listen to them. On the contrary, Ma would lash out at Mita – "I tried to stop you right from the beginning, Mita! I told you all those old aristocratic families are no good!" No, Mita didn't want to hear any of those things. Much better to approach that calm, courteous South Indian gentleman who happened to be Debashish's boss. Once pressure was applied from above, Debu was bound to restrain himself. In a private company, you had no choice but to obey your senior.

The history of what followed was somewhat different.

Within a couple of years, Shubhamita left that house to move into a spacious flat on Lake Road.

Krishnan had been able to make provision for Shubhamita but he couldn't alter Debashish's habits. Once the divorce was confirmed, Mita went through a registered marriage with Krishnan. But she couldn't take Shubhashish with her. He remained with his father, at Gobindo Ghoshal Lane. Once he's eight years old, according to the Hindu Marriage Act, a son is supposed to live with his father. The mother has no claims. When he failed after trying very hard to dispel Mita's grief for her son, Krishnan arranged for a transfer to Mumbai. Mumbai, Bangalore, Mumbai. For five years, Mita didn't return to Kolkata at all. She would write sparkling letters to Shubhashish from afar, parcel him new clothes on his birthday, and send money for the Pujas. It's true that none of these things was ever returned to her, but no letter acknowledging them had come, either.

It was in Mumbai that Paromita was born. Under pressure

of all kinds of work at home and in the office, one day her letters to Shubho ceased altogether. At some point she stopped sending him money as well. Debu had simply not allowed his son to maintain any contact with Mita. How long can one continue a one-sided effort to sustain a relationship?

Mumbai, Bangalore, Mumbai. Then, suddenly, Yemen. Taking early retirement, Krishnan left his job to go off to the Gulf where he took up a lavishly paid assignment, after getting his daughter admitted to the school in Kurseong, and leaving her under the guardianship of her maternal grandparents. He returned immensely wealthy, and an established businessman. Krishnan has to keep moving around all the time, attending to his many business concerns; Mumbai today, London tomorrow, Yemen the day after, and Singapore the day after that. But then, Shubhamita now lives in comfort, in peace even. She hasn't spared a thought for Gobindo Ghoshal Lane. After retirement, her father built a house in Salt Lake, but still likes to stay with his daughter occasionally, in this tenth floor flat of hers, on Camac Street. His daughter spends most of her time alone, after all. His son-in-law travels worldwide. The granddaughter lives in the mountains. No, he and his wife also have no contact with Shubhashish. Debu has completely eliminated Shubhamita's family from Shubhashish's life.

At the Mumbai office, Mita received word that after the divorce, Debashish had not become a "Devdas"; on the contrary, he had actually stopped drinking gradually. It is said that two books by the poet Debashish Mazumdar have now appeared in the market. Although she had spotted them in a stall at the book fair, Shubha hadn't bought them. She wouldn't buy them. She doesn't want to know what Debashish has been writing, what he has been thinking.

Not Shubha, just Mita. Baba's Mita had become Debu's Shubha. Now, for Krishnan, she is Mita again. Just Mita.

"Ticket?"

With a single jolt, the conductor's extended palm brings Shubhamita back into the present. Picking up her bag from the lady's lap, she looks once again, to see – Proprietor Shubhashish Mazumdar.

How much is fifteen plus nine? Twenty-four years! Dear God! No more letters, this time she will go herself, in person. She is not afraid of Gobindo Ghoshal Lane any more. Debashish can't keep Shubho away from her any longer. It is necessary to inform Shubhashish that apart from the bus he is also the proprietor of another important moving object, a living one.

Copper Goddess

JOYA MITRA

NOW the moon has set as well. Beneath the guava trees, on the pale earth, the moonlight had cast a web of shadows through the twigs and foliage, but even those have been erased by the darkness. Now that the patches of light have been eclipsed, everything has turned deep black. Way back, close to the beginning, I had heard that shadows weren't really black, they were deep purple, matted grey or even dark sepia, but not black. But now, in that place, what could shadows be except a deep, dark black! Darker, perhaps, than this body of mine, these two hands. How is that possible? I have volume after all, and mass, am bound to be darker than the darkness of empty space. Empty? Is that place empty then? Empty it was, indeed, when I saw it in the evening. An extensive swamp where the high grounds descend in a slope. Very suddenly. Meaning, from this end, you can't imagine there would be a swamp in that place. And just across, the land rises again. Like a continuation of this small hillock. The swamp like a – not quite like a bowl, but a wide plate – in the midst of high ground all around. You can tell from just looking at it that it is shallow. Created perhaps by the rainwater that runs down into it from all sides. In some places, clumps of arrowlike reeds, close to the water's edge. Dry, light brown now, at the end of winter. Skirting the swamp, walking randomly beyond the mounds of gravelly reddish soil, one can see the pumphouse a little way off and beside it, in the midst of this landscape ranging from yellow ochre to burnt sienna, a few sudden, incongruous patches of green. Fairly large patches. On the other side, some cultivated fields belonging to someone. And there, in that place, cucumber trailers on bamboo frames, and orchards of guava.

How odd the guava orchard had seemed at first. I have been seeing guava trees ever since I was a child, in the neighbourhood schoolfield, and besides, before the house came up on the land to our east, there was a guava tree in our very own house. Of course I was in quite a junior class at school then, but I do remember it. Smallish, the tree was, the fruits light, yellow, tiny and perfectly round. Then they cut it down. In its place, for some days, were brickstacks and some other odds and ends. And then, that three-storeyed house next door came up. Now we can't even remember that the sun shone into our rooms once, and on the small garden-like space in front. But this guava orchard is different. At first I didn't realize what was different about it. Overhead, something like a ceiling of leaves, and through it, even in the afternoon, the harsh sunlight could not penetrate; what filtered through was a pale green light. And beneath the trees, no undergrowth, only crumbly white earth. The soil here was not like the red land that surrounded it. Then suddenly I realized that there was no tree I could climb. There were trees alright, their trunks were visible, maybe ten or twelve of them, but there were no low branches. As if the bases of the trees were like pillars in a hall. Branches, twigs and leaves had mingled overhead to create a sort of awning. It was impossible to identify the trees to which the branches belonged. Guava trees, as far as I knew, were quite sturdy, with upright branches, so why were the trees in this orchard like this! Strangely similar to creepers. Who knows – these days, all sorts of things happen in agriculture, I hear, perhaps they are even growing guava creepers! You have to hand it to the human race. Yet, if they can change so many things, understand so much, then why can't they change their own ways! Why don't they understand each other! Rina didn't let me hold her baby in my arms that day, didn't even let me touch her. Said that my sleeves were stained with turpentine. Just an excuse. If I had washed my hands with soap, would she have allowed me? She wouldn't.

I know it.

When I say I know, I mean, she herself had declared:

"My daughter is mine alone. I shall bring her up as I like. Since you insist on living in the same place, and won't set up a decent household of your own, we, too, have no need of you. You must not come here again."

Why was Rina so different? She hadn't been like this before.

In the early days, when she saw my paintings, visited the Lalit Kala, how dreamy her eyes used to be! She didn't want to be introduced to anyone else, those days. She had no taste for my friends' crazy lifestyles, their appearance and dress. How often she had said to me:

"You are entirely different from them, so beautiful …"

Yes, this was something she said repeatedly. In her eyes, this kurta of mine, the colourful bag on my shoulder, were very attractive. Apparently she also liked this face of mine.

I used to laugh. "You like me because, next to my dark complexion, your fair skin stands out all the more clearly," I'd say.

But she would only laugh. All those things, how did they change so suddenly after marriage! She flung aside that very sling-bag, Bipinbaul's gift, declaring it "unfit for civilized society". Her general opinion of me too, as a person, had begun to express itself: "Unfit for civilized society. Not presentable."

For her, civilized society meant her household, the relatives within it, neighbours, and all her old friends. I knew it was the way she had been brought up, in that place; her tastes and preferences were bound to match theirs. But she had liked me, too, after all. I was the same then as I am now; I hadn't tried to beguile her with false pretences. To this day, I can't understand exactly when, at what point, Rina began to take a dislike to me. When things came to such a pass, so very quickly. Not just dislike, it seemed she had begun to hold me in contempt. I couldn't figure out how to handle her constant irritation at everything. Sometimes, she would quarrel with me for not having brought her anything, ever. Jasmine garlands or an entire cluster of nagkeshar blossoms I had once plucked from a great height with such difficulty never counted for "something" in her view. When I fell off the cart, trying to pluck the nagkeshar, it had been very painful, my ankle twisted and swollen, but she paid no attention. Because Ma had applied lime and turmeric, she called it "primitive medicine". The pain kept me awake all night. My eyes were burning, and I suffered, I don't know whether from the pain in my foot, or at Rina's turning away from me to fall asleep in peace. Yet, in our pre-marriage days, in the Eden Gardens, under the nagkeshar tree, while gathering the large petals from the grass, it was the same Rina who had said, with an expression of despair:

"I couldn't find a single flower intact."

That very day, I had decided that, come what may, I would pluck not just a whole flower but an entire bunch for her one day. I hadn't plucked the flowers immediately. It didn't come to me naturally to be in such a hurry about anything. I felt it smacked of a sort of showmanship: as if to say, look at me right now, praise me immediately. Forget it. Who knows, those who act in such a way, perhaps they're the ones who are in the right. Timing is all. Time moves at a different pace for each person: slowly and leisurely for some, in a great rush for others. And they keep forgetting what has taken place earlier, forget even about themselves. When I bought a sari for her one day, like everyone else, she was angry with me. Didn't even hold the sari and look at it properly. Maybe she had had a minor tiff with Ma on some matter. Ma thought Rina would take possession of me, change me. Rina felt I was too much under my mother's thumb. Ma would always blame my nature, saying I was lazy, rascally, whimsical. Rina, too, had the same complaint. And besides, minor tiffs take place between all of us every day, with someone or the other. But did that mean she would never be pleased, not even once? If not, then not. But she was sometimes pleased, sometimes not, the same thing sometimes pleasing her, at other times throwing her into a rage – why should that happen? At first I was afraid to touch Rina, lest I end up hurting her. Actually, with all things relating to women, I have this strange uneasiness, this fear, that they can't be treated casually. They are too delicate for that. Yet today, with this girl …!

Why was she sitting in such isolation in the light and shade of dusk, legs outstretched, next to the swamp, near the reeds? Why did I feel she didn't belong to this place, was not one of this entire swarming group of ours, but someone distant and peaceful? Like the swamp itself.

We have come here, all of us, to have a good time. Sketching and so on will happen, of course, but actually we all know that what we want is to emerge from our own respective shells. That explains the house, so large, the vast garden with its broken walls, arches, stained glass patterns, just for nine or ten people. On all sides, such a huge field extending across the entire universe. The house is an abandoned property belonging to one of Apareshda's wealthy friends. With the house comes the caretaker-cum-gardener. A special person he is, too. Comes and goes like an apparition. Mostly he is silent, but when he speaks the dialect is so strange, you can't understand half of what he says. Yesterday, he pointed to a tree in the garden, declaring it was sandal wood. But it had no fragrance, nothing. Nothing in common with the wood Ma used to grind to make sandal-paste for her deity. What nonsense! The man said it was not nonsense, it apparently took a hundred years for a sandal tree to acquire its fragrance. Just imagine! That means whoever plants the tree can never hope to smell its fragrance. Why plant it at all? So that others can enjoy the fragrance a long time afterwards? Or just for the pleasure of planting a sandal tree? A bit like the old masters and their paintings, like those legends, those pictures, a painter painting because he can't help it. Not caring what others might say, who will like it who won't. And the question of selling it wouldn't arise at all.

Rina thought my pictures, too, would sell for a hundred, a hundred thousand dollars! She thought being a painter meant enjoying that kind of international reputation. People would instantly recognize one's name the first time it was uttered, would stare in amazed admiration. When none of these things happened, when she saw that our faded household consisted of just two rooms with a strip of courtyard, the two nayantara plants so like our parents, water stains on the stairs to the terrace, she began to slowly grow infuriated with my painting. I removed all my art equipment from the bedroom and placed it in the attic above the stairs to the terrace. That was where I worked, day after day. In the intolerable heat. So often staying up all night before an exhibition. Still it infuriated her. Some nights, she would rise and come up, fling aside my brushes. Her lovely face, as if on fire, was beautiful and cruel. I would drop everything and come downstairs, lest my parents should awaken. Often, upon waking up in the morning, I would find that the brushes she had flung were lying here and there, hardened and stiff. Exactly as if they were dead. At such times, Rina would expect me to shower her with affection. Didn't I want that too? I wanted every moment to sweep her off her feet with my affection. But the way she seemed to close herself off, erasing everything that had happened that day, the previous day, the previous week, erasing everything, craving just the rapture of the moment – I couldn't accomplish that. The Rina of ten minutes ago, just descended from the attic, flaming face, clenched teeth, the words she said rang in my ears and distracted my attention, preventing me from immersing myself in her. Gradually I grew afraid of her, and then one day suddenly she threw me off balance and hissed those words at me through clenched teeth. A flash of fury set my head aflame. I could have struck her, or … or flung her down, to show her whether I was able or not, in exactly the same language, the same explicit gestures my friends would have used. But in reality, none of those things happened. I opened the door and stepped out onto the terrace. Setting out in the morning, I wandered here and there, visiting my friends, the Lalit Kala Akademi, returning home when my body was broken with fatigue. Her words and everything else remained embedded in my consciousness. I didn't feel like going back home. Rina had left, gone to her parents. I felt a tremendous sense of relief. But the house felt empty, her things scattered all over the room. Her smell. She had broken the mirror, struck it with some object. Broken images, reflected in the countless fragments of glass.

Then I went to her. Hearing about her condition from her mother, I went, flustered and agitated. Her parents and elder sister were very civil. Showed no emotion. Rina was sometimes in, sometimes not. None of them ever asked me to stay. My daughter had turned out like me! Dark. During that one year, I never held her in my arms. Once or twice I touched her.

"You can't hold her," Rina would say, her face hard as stone. "She will get hurt."

Rina's mother told me to sell the house and buy an apartment in a good area so that our daughter could grow up in a decent environment. There was no future in painting. Try to use your connections in Bombay-shombay to see if …

Ever since we were children, Ma would say that girls like art and music. Take Saraswati, for instance, the goddess of learning and art. Saraswati.

Yesterday they were calling that girl by the name "Swati." Today, as we rose to leave the edge of the swamp, why did she say her name was actually Saraswati? Did she change it to Swati because Saraswati was too old-fashioned? Then why, today, on that uneven open field, with the red glow of sunset to one side and the gold of the rising full moon on the other side, why in the midst of all that did she disclose her old-fashioned real name to me alone? Real name! Does anyone know what someone's real name might be? What was her connection with that swamp!

Just a little before midnight, when the flames of the fire under the open sky were soaring upwards, lost in their own thoughts, when the bottles passed around from hand to hand were empty and our bodies aflame, I left the group and went alone to the top of the hillock near the swamp to take a walk by myself. Should one remain alone in the moonlight? Didn't she know any better? When I gripped her hand, she rose to her feet in silence, as if she had been waiting there all along for me. When I was trying to fool around with Sudipta yesterday, she, too, was willing, but that wasn't the same thing. That was like deliberately playing a game. Ultimately, I didn't. I couldn't. As soon as I tried to pull Sudipta close, something within me was extinguished.

Is this girl actually the swamp itself on which the moon's image can be seen? Beside which is a forest of reeds? Who lay calm and still beneath me on the ground a little later, like the swamp itself, while feelings awakened in me which I didn't know the meaning of, as if from deep below the earth, like the vines of some primeval jungle rising up, twining about my legs? Did I run, hand in hand with her? How did I reach the guava orchard? I was on fire, full of intense heat. My jacket had caught fire, too. Flames were burning my face, chest, fingers. I hadn't looked at her face. Had flung her to the ground with great force. Her bosom was white as the pale earth. Her throat. Looking at it, I felt it was drenched in moonlight. I felt the moon's image floating upon her bosom. When I tried to draw my lips close, her arm embraced me. Ever so gently, as if her arm had not left the ground at all. As if she was an extraordinary plant under the filigree of moonlight. Spreading her branches, touching mine. I wanted to draw her close. Closer still, closest of all. There was no fire within me now. I was calm. From Saraswati's bosom I felt a breeze that was cool like a snowcapped peak. I raised my arms, clasped her very close. Placing my right hand on her throat, very slowly and firmly, I strangled her.

When I left, I didn't turn to see if her lowered head hung to one side. Colour of the moonlit earth, the colour white, there was no other colour but that.

Was anyone there then, at the swamp's edge? And in the guava orchard?

Mindscape

SUCHITRA BHATTACHARYA

THE car was cruising along the Jessore Road. Not too fast, nor too slowly, at a medium pace. Robin's middle-aged non-Bengali driver was cast in Robin's own mould: he rarely gathered speed. Even at this midnight hour, with very little traffic on the road, he was being habitually cautious.

Not that we wanted him to speed up. Robin believed in going slow, moving with circumspection, in every area of his life. Saurabh and I still succumb to the temptation of speed once in a while. But right now the situation was different. Just this evening, a tragic accident had taken place, due probably to that very element, speed. Apparently a truck had collided head-on with Tathagato's Maruti on the highway, near Krishnanagar. Bhaswati was also in the car and both had died on the spot. Having received such bad news, would anyone rushing to the spot from Kolkata have had the courage to drive fast?

It was a November night. A stealthy chill in the air wafted across our eyes and faces, yet we did not feel like rolling up the car windows. Thought we would suffocate without that little bit of air. Our eyes gazed vacantly at the scene outside, barely noticing anything. To our right was the airport runway. Even at this late hour a plane took off with a roar, but none of us paid it much attention. An empty lorry thundered past, but our heads didn't turn at all. The sudden death of two living, breathing human beings had numbed our senses. Or numbed mine, at least. It was impossible to believe that the Tathagato with whom I had had such a long adda just a couple of days ago, was no longer alive! Of late we hadn't met Bhaswati very often, but even she was a friend of twenty years, after all! For both of them to be gone forever in a single instant – was life so impermanent, then? Could death be so cruel?

Saurabh was sitting beside the driver, Robin and I were at the back. We could sense that all three of us wanted to speak but were unable to find the words. Silence was building up a suppressed tension inside the car. To shake off my uneasiness I took out my mobile phone from my pocket, and began fiddling with it.

"It makes no sense," muttered Robin suddenly.

It was as if we had been waiting for this cue. At once Saurabh turned around to look at us.

"What was that?"

"Nothing makes any sense at all. All of a sudden, on some strange whim, they set off on a jaunt midweek, the two of them … and then without warning, this double tragedy …"

"Where were they going?"

"Bethuadahari or some such place, I suppose. Every now and then he'd go off somewhere at random, taking Bhaswati with him. Did he ever tell us where he was going?"

"But how did the police get hold of your number?"

"From Tathagato's diary. They called up Tathagato's flat first, but who'd answer the phone there? The flat was empty. I believe my number was first overleaf …" Robin leaned back in his seat. "Just my bad luck, I was getting ready for my meal after helping Bultu with his homework, and at that very moment … Your dinner was ruined too, right?"

"Hmm. I had just swallowed my second morsel."

"Does it make sense? Any sense at all? The way we are rushing there after receiving the news, even this makes no sense. There's no telling when we'll receive the bodies! We'll just have to keep waiting like a bunch of starving crows …"

"True." Drawing out a packet of cigarettes, I offered one to

Saurabh. I seemed to feel a little lighter at being able to resume talking after a long silence. Cigarette clenched between my lips, I said: "The post-mortem will take at least until tomorrow afternoon. Only then can the question of handing over his body arise. If at all they release it to friends, that is!"

Saurabh lighted his cigarette, shielding it from the wind. Exhaling he said: "That we'll have to manage with a bit of persuasion. We'll tell them Tathagato has no-one in the world… He really doesn't in fact. A divorcee, not obliged to provide for his children, parents gone, elder sister in America, never heard of any relatives asking after him … So apart from us, who else does he have!"

"See if the police buy your argument!"

"They will, they will. Hanging on to the body will be a hassle for the police. I'm carrying my identity card, can even write a couple of lines if required …"

"And what about Bhaswati?"

"She doesn't concern us." Saurabh added, in English: "She's a married woman; it's her husband's problem." Turning back, he asked Robin: "You have informed Ashisbabu as well, haven't you?"

"Of course. I called him at once."

"How did he react?"

"At first he just couldn't believe it. Said Bhaswati had gone to see her sister. Kept muttering, how could she be in Krishnanagar … But when Tathagato's name came up, he paid attention. Fell silent for a couple of seconds, then burst into loud sobs."

"Oh no, that was no good!" I shook my head. "Why did you have to tell him about Tathagato?"

"What else could I have told him? Your wife died in an accident while driving about Krishnanagar all by herself? Just savouring the air? Is that believable?"

"Perhaps not. But still …"

"There's no room for "perhaps" and "but" here, Joy. Bhaswati was with Tathagato, so the news can't be suppressed. Besides, what Ashisbabu thought or not, what kind of shock he suffered at the news, these are irrelevant at this point."

Saurabh was of the same opinion.

"It is necessary to tell the gentleman the truth, after all," he said in a detached voice. "And it is also necessary for the gentleman to hear the truth. There is no middle path here. This middle class hypocrisy about covering things up, hushing up the murmuring, it doesn't work after the person's death."

From a rational point of view, Saurabh was right. But for some reason I felt uneasy. Had Ashisbabu known about Bhaswati's illicit affair? Surely he suspected something. Living under the same roof, could he have failed to sense something from his wife's activities, her general demeanour? Besides, it had been going on for several years. Unless one was utterly blind or stupid, one was bound to suspect something. He may not have known everything, or so it seemed from what Tathagato had said. Indeed there are many unpleasant truths in this world of which we are aware, yet as long as they remain concealed we learn to live with them. But when the veil is suddenly ripped off, doesn't the bare, unadorned truth seem intolerable? Take my eleven-year-old marriage to Sharmishtha: no children yet, but have we ever gone to a doctor to find out which of us is incapable? Why don't we? For fear that the truth will be discovered. Rather let the doubt linger: there is comfort in doubt, we survive on it. Ostrich-like, perhaps, but none of us is above that, after all! Not even Ashisbabu. If the papers were to publish names tomorrow, how would this bhadralok show his face to his circle of acquaintances? Did Ashisbabu deserve such dishonour in his middle-age? Bhaswati had also remained childless, that was the only saving grace. Three infants lost from the womb.

The car crossed Madhyagram, turned left off Jessore Road. The bustling settlements on both sides of the road were now extraordinarily quiet. Street lamps lined the desolate road like an array of feeble sentries. A short distance ahead, we arrived at the level crossing. The gate was open. The Ambassador lurched across the railway lines, bumping against the uneven surface. Suddenly a swarm of stray dogs began barking in unison. The silence of the night was shattered.

Robin cast a fleeting, irritable glance at the dogs. Then, turning away, he observed gloomily: "I think we should be worrying about the other problem."

"Which is?"

"What if Ashisbabu doesn't claim the body at all?"

"Nonsense, why should that be? Didn't you just say the gentleman was crying bitterly?"

"That was his immediate reaction. Once he gets somewhat used to the idea, he may not feel so sorrowful. What if he reacts differently then? After all, the scandal won't enhance his social prestige. Besides, there are also words like anger and wounded pride in the dictionary, right?"

"But that means deep trouble, I say! What will happen to Bhaswati's home?"

"Ah, why jump to negative conclusions at the very outset?" I blurted out, unable to contain myself. "Ashisbabu is a genuine gentleman. Whatever feelings he might harbour in his heart, he will certainly take care of his wife's last rites."

"Suppose he doesn't … what then?"

"Then somebody will show up from Bhaswati's parental home. Her dada, or else a younger brother … And if they don't, we are there after all." I added, after pausing for breath, "Bhaswati was our friend, too. Not as intimate as Tathagato, perhaps, but we've known her since our college days … We all attended Bhaswati's wedding, and we still meet on the odd occasion …

Can't we take on the minor responsibility of Bhaswati's cremation?"

"Stop being a wise owl. Yes, if such a situation arises, it's we who will take care of everything, I realize that. But …"

"But what? What buts can there be?"

"I'm just thinking about Tathagato's guts." Robin's voice suddenly became shrill. "He was so irresponsible, so irresponsible …!"

I gently pressed Robin's hand. "Let it be, Robin. Is anything to be gained from bringing up such matters now!"

"I know nothing of gain or loss. All these years, the bastard led his life exactly as he pleased. Even in death, he didn't conform … Must I hold my tongue even now?"

"Have we always held our tongues, Robin? Haven't we reasoned with him? Haven't we told him, again and again, that he must now change his life partner?"

"That's why it rankles even more. We couldn't bring about the slightest change in Tathagato. He accepted no rules at all, the bastard." Robin sighed loudly. "I have been observing him right from his college days, a slave to his passions. Not the slightest control over them. All of you remember his torrid affair with Bhaswati in college? Always clinging to her like sticking plaster. Corridors, library, cinema hall, coffee house, the Ganga shore, Victoria … Those days, I was closer to Tathagato than the rest of you. He used to recount every detail to me. When he kissed her, what else they did … And after graduation, the same fellow dumped Bhaswati and took off for Delhi! Returned to Kolkata after his M.A., but pretended he couldn't even recognize Bhaswati. We heard later that he had such a wild fling with some Poonam at JNU that Bhaswati seemed tame by comparison. Then, after he started working and fell in love with Joyita, Poonam also vanished from his mind. But he couldn't last out with Joyita either, could he?

Married her, within a year Toton was born, and that was that: all his love flew out of the window. We all know that Joyita was not a bad housewife at all. Organized, practical, with good taste. As a wife, good enough. A little too attached to her parental home, but was that such a crime? An only child if she happens to be a daughter, often performs a son's duties. Am I wrong? But how Tathagato tormented his Joyita! Leading an absolutely reckless life, returning home drunk every night, kicking up a row as soon as he entered the house ... You may not know this, but he also used to frequent a gambling den those days. His own pocket cleaned out in ten days, he tried dipping into Joyita's salary! How long could someone like Joyita put up with such a husband? Just three years and the relationship was in shreds. Joyita survived by escaping with her son. But even that didn't bring the bastard to his senses, did it? After one broken relationship, the second time at least he could choose carefully, marry again and mend his ways. Settle down! But was there any sign of that? His old love reared its head again, and the fellow invaded Bhaswati's household. Bhaswati was quite happy with her husband and her home, but he played upon her sentiments and messed her up completely. Bhaswati's equilibrium was utterly destroyed. If you're so in love, get Bhaswati to divorce her husband and marry her yourself!" Robin paused for a while. Then, with a sigh: "Ultimately, Tathagato was satisfied only when he had destroyed Bhaswati."

I was listening to him without comment. Not that I accepted everything he said. It seemed to me that Robin's perspective was biased. He had made a virtual villain out of Tathagato. Was he such a bad sort really? As for why Joyita and Tathagato didn't get along, could the reasons be quantified so easily? Can a third person ever completely understand why a husband-wife relationship breaks down? However much a person may confide in his buddies, something, somewhere, remains concealed. Something only the four walls of their room are privy to. Why Tathagato returned to Bhaswati or how their unstable relationship had evolved over the past five or six years, could Robin really comprehend? Why for that matter did Bhaswati encourage Tathagato when she already had a husband?

Saurabh was now looking ahead. Eyes on the windscreen, he suddenly blurted out:

"So you've decided Tathagato is the sole culprit, Robin?"

"I was just stating facts. Who am I to judge?"

"But I suspect that you are getting your own back."

"For what?"

"Because the two of you didn't see things the same way. Because although you said he was vain and conceited, he called you a domesticated pet."

"Is this what you make of my words! Wasn't Tathagato my friend? Isn't that the bond makes me rush there in the middle of the night?"

The car was moving a little faster now. Nothing of the road could be seen beyond the glare of the headlights. There was an eerie darkness on all sides. In fields and open spaces. In trees and thickets. Even in the irregular clusters of human habitation that seemed to rush upon us suddenly at intervals. A sliver of a moon had risen in the sky. But its beams couldn't pierce through the pre-winter fog to reach the earth. Looking out in the half-light and half-dark, Robin muttered to himself:

"Tathagato is like Tathagato, I am like myself. I concentrate on family life, love my wife and son, avoid wasting money, am not addicted to any form of intoxication … there is a certain discipline to my life. And this is the life I like. Tathagato's barbed comments, why should I take them to heart? But am I forbidden to say that I don't like Tathagato's lifestyle? There's no denying the fact that Bhaswati lost her life because she fell into Tathagato's clutches."

"I disagree!" Saurabh shook his head vehemently. "I strongly disagree."

"Didn't Bhaswati lose her life for no reason? Was Tathagato in no way responsible?"

"On the contrary. It was because he fell into Bhaswati's clutches that poor Tathagato ..." Saurabh had turned again to face us. He reached out to take a cigarette from me. Lighting it, he continued: "You narrated the story of Tathagato's life, but rearranged it to suit your point of view. I believe Bhaswati used Tathagato. As a student Tathagato was extremely brilliant and very handsome, so it was Bhaswati who went all out to befriend him. This great college romance was nothing but a pretence on Bhaswati's part. It was because she ditched him that Tathagato left for Delhi and turned to Poonam in order to forget Bhaswati. But he couldn't. Irresistibly drawn to her he returned to Kolkata, but she didn't let him get anywhere near her this time. She was infatuated with Ashis Sinha. Engineer in a well-known company, a settled future ahead – she didn't care a fig for Tathagato. Poor chap tried to steady himself by clutching on to Joyita, but Bhaswati had taken up residence in his heart. With predictable consequences! He began to find Joyita intolerable, lost his mind, took to alcohol, got caught up in all sorts of other addictions. Joyita had never tried to find out why Tathagato had taken to such behaviour, never felt the need to probe. Instead, she added to his woes by making a great show of walking out with her child. In that half-mad condition, Tathagato met Bhaswati again. By then she had spent several years at home with Ashisbabu, he was now stale fare for her. You've seen Ashisbabu, all of you, he's a simple, straightforward person. Our lady queen was no longer satisfied with him. Perhaps it was sexual frustration ..." Lowering his voice, Saurabh glanced once at the driver. "Yes, out of sheer lust, she latched on to Tathagato again. A relationship without commitment. Just for fun. Plus the thrill of being involved in a secret affair ... Dashing off to Digha today, Diamond Harbour tomorrow, Kankrajhor the day after. Milking Tathagato all the time. He was completely trapped, the poor fellow, ensnared in Bhaswati's net. If she had really had the slightest regard for Tathagato, she would have abandoned Ashisbabu long ago, in order to be with Tathagato, I believe Tathagato had grown wise to Bhaswati's game. It is even possible that this was what she and Tathagato were arguing about in the car today. Perhaps Tathagato was very disturbed mentally, perhaps it was lack of concentration that led to this accident. If it had dawned on Tathagato earlier that Bhaswati was only using him for her own pleasure, he may not have had to die."

"That's outrageous!" protested Robin inarticulately. "You've made Bhaswati into a veritable she-devil!"

"I haven't made up anything, I know women very well. Basically they only understand their own needs."

"You have heavy fundas about women, deep theories about them, it seems? How many women have you come across in your life?"

"You don't need to come across too many. For the observant eye, one drop is an ocean of revelation." Saurabh was becoming increasingly agitated. He flung his lighted cigarette out into the darkness. Turning to look face ahead, he muttered: "The entire female sex is incredibly demanding. There's no pleasing them in any way by any means."

Robin looked askance at me. And I at him. We understood something of the bitterness that consumed Saurabh like a fire. Of all of us, it was Saurabh who hadn't quite managed to establish himself. Not that we had scaled great heights, but on the whole, we held good jobs, and were placed more than comfortably above. Saurabh was a clerk in a government office but his wife had queenly tastes. Anita's constant demands made Saurabh reel. The poor man had to resort to all sorts of strategies to make a bit on the side. That he was a little ashamed of his underhand income, I knew. But why should Bhaswati bear the brunt of his rage at Anita? And how fair was it to declare her greedy and self-indulgent?

The car had crossed a town, Ranaghat, probably. Somehow the place had a somnolent air, as if it was half-asleep. A few people could still be spotted at this late hour, labourers, truck drivers and the like. There was even a tiny hotel still open. Not a hotel, a shop. A stall, like a dhaba.

"Shall I stop the car?" Robin asked. "Do you want some tea?"

"Not a bad idea."

Thought was instantly turned into deed. The driver quickly pulled over and got out. So did I. As I lit up, Robin took a peek inside.

"Tadka-roti is also available," he informed us. "Do you want some?"

Saurabh had alighted too.

"It's one-forty," he remarked, glancing at his watch. "It'll definitely take us another hour or so to get there."

"So it will. We have to locate the hospital once we reach Krishnanagar, we don't know that area at all. There's no saying how long it might take … so let's fill up our bellies a bit."

"And there's little chance of our getting anything to eat there either, so late at night."

"But it'll be a relief to reach there."

"Won't be able to relax, though, even tea might be hard to swallow then."

As we argued, the three of us settled down on the benches outside the shop. Robin's driver Surinder just had a glass of tea. Before us were plates of warmed-up tadka and rotis. The shopkeeper, a young lad, also served us onions and chillies. And salad.

Tasting the tadka, Robin remarked: "I must say he's added a lot of chillies!"

"Be glad there's some food for your stomach!" Saurabh was back to his usual manner. Stuffing tadka-smeared roti into his mouth, he said, "Doesn't taste too bad."

"To a hungry mouth, everything tastes like nectar." I bit into the onion. "The roti is quite soft, too," I added, as I chewed.

"They've probably mixed channa dal in the tadka."

"So it seems. If keema had also been added, it would have made it even tastier. I had such beautiful tadka that time, en route from Delhi to Jaipur ..." I stopped abruptly, as soon as the words were out of my mouth. The corpse of a dear friend lay in hospital, we had been so anxious about him all this time, yet at this moment we were avidly discussing a meagre dish of tadka! Such short-lived grief! In a low voice I confessed: "We've made a big mistake, I say!"

"What's that?" Robin looked up.

"Maybe we should have informed Joyita."

"Why? What use is it letting Joyita know?" Saurabh objected almost at once.

"Why do you forget that Tathagato also has a son? The father-son relationship wasn't wiped out, was it? Toton may be young now, but when he grows up he may tell us all, it was your duty to let me see my father one last time."

"Hmm," Robin nodded, "but there's nothing to be done now. Let's wait till the morning."

"Do you know the telephone number at Joyita's parents' place?"

"I may have it in my old diary. We can call Seema for the number in the morning." Robin appeared slightly distracted. In a heavy voice he said: "To inform a son about his father's death ... what an unpleasant task! This Tathagato has really landed us in a spot."

"Or Bhaswati," added Saurabh glumly. "You can never be sure which of them actually put us there."

"Not again!" protested Robin, looking displeased. "Be quiet, will you!"

"Why? Have I said anything illogical?" Saurabh's jaw was set.

I quickly intervened "Why are the two of you locking horns over whether it was his fault or hers! Perhaps nobody is to blame, they were just victims of their circumstances."

"It's possible," shrugged Robin. "Perhaps the car was coasting along normally, and it was the lorry that knocked into them. Randomly, like God. Or the devil."

"I'm not referring to the accident alone. After all, all their lives, Tathagato and Bhaswati ..." As I spoke, my mind was wandering. I was groping in my memory. Inwardly I was turning over the pages of that photo album. "How sharp your memory is I can't say," I pointed out quietly. "Speaking for myself I can't recall the day to day details of college life, that's why it's hard for me to say whether it was Bhaswati who fell in love with Tathagato first, or he with her. But yes, as a young man, Tathagato was undoubtedly a jewel. And Bhaswati was no ordinary person, either. We all used to say they were made for each other. Tathagato was anyway keen on JNU for his M.A. So I can't say with any certainty that he went off there because Bhaswati dumped him or that he escaped in order to ditch Bhaswati. Nor is it possible for me to say why Bhaswati didn't spend two-and-a-half years waiting for Tathagato, or why she fell in love with Ashisbabu. Perhaps they were growing apart, perhaps it was gossip about Poonam that drove her away from him. In such a situation, it's quite natural to lean on a sweet-spoken, responsible person like Ashisbabu … anyway, both Tathagato and Bhaswati sought happiness in marriage, in their own way. It was Tathagato's bad luck that Joyita was a total mismatch for him. They were poles apart. Joyita is rigid about rules, very disciplined. I mean, she's our Robin's type. And Tathagato was Tathagato. Joyita made the mistake of trying to cast her husband in her own mould. That boomeranged on her, and Tathagato became even more wayward. Who knows, maybe he tried to avenge himself by going to pieces. But after Joyita left him, his life became a complete vacuum. He didn't have Toton, was utterly alone in the world … driven by a terrible loneliness. Once he blurted out to me: 'whether I live or die makes no difference any more, Joy! My very existence seems meaningless!' "

Robin narrowed his eyes. "Did he actually say that?"

"What's so surprising?" Saurabh exclaimed. "We know he was very unhappy. It was his agony that Bhaswati encashed."

"Harping on the same thing again!" I placed a hand on Saurabh's back. "And why do you assume Bhaswati was such a bad sort? She suffered a lot as well. A series of miscarriages … relations with Ashisbabu growing stale … And at such a juncture, to encounter Tathagato again. He had become a wreck. Psychologically, she was almost in the same state. They might very well have sought refuge in each other."

Robin was through with his food.

"So let them seek refuge, who's stopping them!" he said with a small burp. "But why be so furtive, baba? Why didn't Tathagato marry Bhaswati? Why didn't he force her to get a divorce?"

"There must have been something. Perhaps they couldn't overcome the mental obstacle."

"And so they committed adultery? Do you support that, too?"

"I don't denounce it. If they clung to each other to be free of a vacuum ..."

"Is this the only way to fill the vacuum? Then why have society, values, social mores?"

"You're mistaken, Robin. Social mores will prevail in the interests of society itself. Yet the Tathagatos and Bhaswatis of this world will want to live on their own terms. Such is reality."

"Nonsense, all bakwaas." Saurabh was rinsing his hands with water from the glass. Running a wet finger over his lips he continued: "Adultery is nothing but sex. And the distance between Ashisbabu and Bhaswati was also based on sex."

"Don't oversimplify things to such an extent, Saurabh. If sex is all a human being desires, then we're no different from cats and dogs. As soon as appetite is aroused or frustration experienced, does a human being immediately start you-know-what with the first person who comes along? With humans, the heart has a major role to play. Heart comes first, then the body. A person for whom the physical urge is all that matters would be no different from an animal. I hope you're not placing Tathagato and Bhaswati in that category! Had that been true, would their relationship have survived for six or seven years?"

But his words didn't seem to appeal to Saurabh. He didn't press the point. The shop owner had served tea, Saurabh was sipping from his glass.

It was almost two-thirty when we returned to the car after settling the bill. Dew was falling quite heavily and it felt rather chilly. Rolling up the windows we leaned back in our seats, all three of us. Stomachs full, we felt drowsy, our eyes grew heavy.

"Ai, Joy, get up, we're there!" Robin's voice roused us from our stupor.

Rubbing our eyes, we saw that the car had halted right inside the hospital compound. Immediately our hearts missed a beat. So we had reached Tathagato and Bhaswati! We had gone to great lengths dissecting them, taking them apart, but now it was our turn to face them!

We alighted from the car, legs unsteady. Why did our knees suddenly buckle? Was it because we had been sitting for such a long stretch? We seemed to be shivering a bit as well. Was the late night breeze so cool, or were our minds making us aware of us of the vast difference between thinking about death from afar and finding ourselves in close proximity to it?

The hospital was a two-storey building. The courtyard was not entirely quiet, fragments of sound floated to our ears. Metallic sounds. Human voices. Perhaps even the rustle of the breeze. There was a shaggy mango tree in the hospital courtyard and on the paved platform beneath it a few people lay sleeping. Only one old man was awake, chin tucked between his knees with a detached air. As if he had completed his quota of sleep on this earth, this old fellow.

Saurabh advanced towards the Enquiry. Robin and I dragged our feet. Somewhere, an infant cried out. Was it a newborn child just entering the world? A nurse marched quickly down the long, straight corridor, the whiteness of her dress very jarring to the eyes.

Within about five minutes, Saurabh was back.

"They have sent both corpses to the morgue," he informed us hoarsely. "The doctor will come at ten in the morning, and the post-mortem will take place then."

"Oh," said Robin drily. "So what do we do now?"

"Wait."

"Did you find out if anyone else has arrived?"

"We're the first… . They said we could go and see them once, if we wished."

A cold current flowed down my spine. I glanced at Robin, then at Saurabh. Drawing out a cigarette, I clenched it between my lips. I was groping for a match. First in one pocket, then the other. Like a blind man.

"So, do you want to go now?" Robin asked in a feeble voice.

Having fumbled with three matchsticks, I had now lit up with the fourth. Swallowing smoke, I ventured: "We'll have to go there, anyway, if not now, then later."

"Yes, even to identify ... Suppose it's not them at all! It maybe some other Tathagato! Some other Bhaswati!"

This was utterly impossible we knew. But at this moment we really wanted to believe it could be. Filling my lungs with burnt tobacco fumes, I said: "Even if it's not them, we'll have to look at them once. Come on, we may as well go in there now."

Though we spoke again and again of going, our feet seemed unwilling to move. As if, by not seeing them, we were trying to keep the Tathagato and Bhaswati we had been analyzing so intently alive. As if, once we came face to face with them, they would be truly dead.

The open field was hardly any distance from the morgue, yet it seemed to take us years to cross it. There was a faint musty smell in the frozen chamber. The light was dim. Yellowish. Enveloped in half-shadows, side by side on the shabby, worn-out table, lay two bodies. Deathly still. Covered up to the neck in white cloth.

Yes, it was them all right. Tathagato and Bhaswati.

"How extraordinary," muttered Robin, "no injury on their heads or faces!"

"Perhaps they were hit in the middle region," said Saurabh in a low voice. "On the chest ... or stomach ... Look at Tathagato's face ... as if all his cares have vanished and he is sleeping in peace."

"Bhaswati's countenance seems to be glowing!" observed

Robin as if to himself. “Anxiety, frustration, unease, no trace of any such emotion. It’s Tathagato who appears …”

But I saw peace on both countenances. As if both had found relief at last, after so long.

No, none of us could see the real Tathagato or Bhaswati even now. What our eyes perceived was an image of what lay within our own hearts. Two human beings, cast in the mould of our own emotions.

Slowly we stepped out of the morgue. Outside, dawn was breaking. The broken moon had vanished from the sky. The birds were stirring.

Within the Furnace

ANITA AGNIHOTRI

ABANIDA had called.

"Be ready by eight, I'll pick you up."

"So early? Couldn't we leave at around nine-thirty?"

The thought of her daily morning chores made Nandini's head spin. If they left at eight, she wouldn't have time to complete the cooking. Jharna's Ma, the housemaid, would leave at nine, if she found the house locked. There was no telling how late they might return …

"When do we get back, Abanida?"

Abanida sounded a little annoyed, his voice sharp.

"Actually, these timings are beyond our control. When to go, by when to return – all this will be determined by those who light the furnace. Make a little effort, just this once …"

Just once, indeed! I've been making an effort since ever so long ago, Nandini thought to herself. And there was her father, another person who had died after a prolonged effort to survive. But some things cannot be said out aloud.

"Very well, Abanida," she said, the hint of a smile in her voice, "I'll be ready at eight, as you say. Till tomorrow morning then!"

All the built-in cupboards of the tiny flat were in complete disarray, and Nandini had not yet managed to restore order. Ma would have been angry at the sight. How beautifully neat and orderly her things had been even in such tiny spaces.

They had been looking for a picture of Baba. Not in advanced age, nor when he was very young, but a picture taken in middle age. When the glory of his youth had faded and his countenance lost some of its intellectual brilliance, clouded by a profundity of thought that had begun spreading its shadow beneath those dark, heavy brows. Where was such a picture to be found? Sixty or seventy years ago, did people in middle-class households ever take photographs? Once or twice Ma, on a whim, had gone to a studio to have their picture taken. How hard it had been, even then, to drag Baba there, all dressed up! Only Ma could have accomplished it. The studio photographer had apparently come to their house on Nandini's fifth birthday. There was a picture of her, close to her father's lap. Abanida and the others selected that picture. In a group photograph, there was an image of her father, standing. And a picture of Ma and Baba, side by side. Old albums, rust-stained envelopes ... Looking for and retrieving Baba's middle-age from a heap of pictures spread out on a floor-mat. Nowadays you see a still camera in every hand, handicams everywhere, a continuous stream of photographs being taken at every ceremony or gathering, whether anyone ever looks at them or not. Fifty years ago, people did not so crave visual images. They were unselfconscious. Ah! Here you are: a few of the books carried Baba's picture, these should do, Nandini said, holding them out. Abanida shook his head. The printing is of such poor quality, you can't make out his features at all.

Who were the people close to the poet, the sculptor had wanted to know. People who had seen him up close when he was that age, who could look at the clay portrait prior to the plaster casting, to comment on the likeness.

So, they had tracked Nandini down to Hazaribagh. Ma was no more. Nandini was a schoolteacher. Dhiman was in Patna. Their only child, Shami, was in the engineering college hostel at Rourkela. In Nandini's lonely household there was only an ancient acacia, a raintree that shed its leaves without pause. On rainy evenings countless fireflies played in its shaggy darkness, flashing on and off, on and off.

At Hazaribagh she was besieged with phone calls, letters, repeated invitations. Come to Kolkata. That childhood home – Nandini still held on to it at a low rent. Amulyakaku was dead. Ma was gone. Amulyakaku had been Baba's friend, the first reader of the countless things that Baba wrote. Amulyakaku's sons, all of them older than Nandini, had no taste for the literary. Two of them held salaried jobs, the third was in business. Every now and then they nagged and complained, asked her to vacate the house instead of increasing the rent, but Nandini had not been able to surrender it, not after all these years. She would visit two or three times a year, sweep away the dust and cobwebs that had gathered in the corners, arrange her father's papers. When Baba passed away in the little room to the east, there had been nobody with him. Ma had died earlier. Nandini was in Kolkata, staying with a friend, forbidden to enter this house. Baba ordered his own meals, delivered from the "hotel," the rice stall at the corner. Jharna's Ma would serve him tea and snacks, morning and evening, and do the basic household chores. In the wee hours, when the tumultuous downpour had drowned out all other sounds in the universe, Death came silently to Baba's bed. Had he looked out for anyone then? For Ma herself, perhaps. When death is close at hand, the past vanishes. Baba could well have forgotten that Ma was already gone.

Had he looked for Nandini? She was the distant past after all! Ten years after she had got married, she had set foot in this house for the first and only time – at the news of Ma's death. Baba was godless and so, bending to his will, was Ma. After her death there were no rituals, only a condolence meeting. Nandini had wanted Baba to stay with her because she felt it was not right for him to live alone. But Nandini was forbidden to visit. When she called, her father answered the phone.

No faith in god, yet he believed in man-made divisions of caste and class. That must be it. Otherwise why had his heart turned to stone when Nandini married Dhiman, forever closing the doors of his house to his own daughter? Why?

I was twenty-five then, educated and employed. Wasn't it possible to talk things over with me?

Nandini stood before the mirror, lost in thought. She noticed how the hair on both sides of her parting had begun to turn grey. Dusk was approaching. The rosy light fell upon the mirror on the wall. The glow of twilight. The mirror had been bought in Moradabad. Nandini had watched her mother stand at the mirror like this, braiding her hair. The seating area was tiny. Just the two rooms, one stuffed with Baba's books and papers. Yet, when she was a child, this room had never seemed inadequate to her. Carrying her in his arms, indulging her whims, Baba would pull books out of the rack and explain their contents to her in his own way. When his own books were published, there would be a separate signed copy for Nandini. When he came home from public functions, he would give Nandini all the bouquets and shawls he had received. And then there was his Writers' Forum. Workshops, bulletins, meetings in various capitals and districts. Baba was a college teacher, but outside his working hours he didn't spent a single moment thinking about college. And he never thought about his wife. Her silent loneliness, the endless cups of tea she produced in the kitchen, the suitcases she packed for his tours, the care she lavished on Nandini's school and college education – neither Baba nor Nandini had ever considered Ma an independent entity. She was the ordinary wife of a famous poet. In this way, gradually losing her social identity, Ma herself had forgotten who she was.

There was virtually no connection those days between money and literary pursuits. But for his college job, Baba would probably have been very badly off. Four or five awards, forty-odd books, the flow of royalties dwindling into nothing. Suddenly in need of money, yet no payments forthcoming from publishers – how often had Nandini witnessed such situations! As a little girl, how she would mentally quarrel with those unknown publishers, her head buried in her pillow! But there was respect. There was joy. When Baba went to Delhi to receive the Sahitya Akademi award, Nandini became aware for the first time that her father had left Kolkata without her. It would have been difficult for him to take Ma and her along, arrange for them to stay with him there. Although she understood everything, Nandini, now a university student after graduating from college, had sobbed all night. She had smiled only when Baba returned and handed her the trophy. Because she had been born when Baba was somewhat advanced in years, Nandini had received more than her fair share of pampering and affection. To outsiders it seemed that she was excessively spoilt.

After her marriage, Nandini left home, left Kolkata, left Bengal. And Baba's writing, too, came to a halt. Like a river changing course, leaving behind an empty channel-bed. Little by little, the likelihood of receiving the nation's highest literary honour began to fade. Then, while he was still alive, people forgot Baba. He lived to be a little over eighty-five, active, physically fit, self-reliant – and utterly alone. It was only because Jharna's Ma came punctually at dawn that Baba's body could be cremated in time.

And then suddenly, on the occasion of his centenary, Baba, his poems, and along with them, so many related memories, had come to life again.

It was almost dark. Walking slowly in the park, along the brick-paved pathway almost entirely overgrown with grass,

Nandini thought of the many times she had come here to play. By herself, but also with Baba. Baba's full-length statue would go up at the corner of this very park. The Writers' Forum was celebrating his centenary. Its current president was Asamanja Nag, MP Money from his MP's fund and from the Forum – the two streams would converge in the construction of the statue. Baba's books were being reprinted, some in the form of centenary volumes.

A poet's statue? And that too a full-length one? Was such a thing possible? Tagore apart, had there been a statue of anyone else? But Tagore was no mere poet, he was much more; for over a century, this poet had also been involved with every medium of self-expression.

"Why not, if a man happens to be a legend! In this case, it is our responsibility to prove that Amalendushekhar was a legend. We mustn't forget that distance in time lends human beings a stature many times greater than their actual size. Especially if the fog of undeserved amnesia screens the man from the present-day world. Do you remember that book, Amalendushekhar's three-part epic, *Puppets of Time*? Of course it didn't ultimately win a national award, but we haven't forgotten the storm it raised!" Asamanja was an extraordinarily good speaker. Courteous, well-spoken, his eloquence sufficient to transform day into night. Among the Forum members, Abinash Mitra remained silent. Asamanja had not appreciated this.

"Do you have something to say, Mitrada?"

"There won't be a problem with protocol, I hope?" said Mitra, clearing his throat.

"No there won't," declared Asamanja, shaking his head. "True, Amalendushekhar had drifted away from us after his Akademi award, become strangely remote. He had never applied for Party membership, but six months before his death, the

Party itself made him an honorary member. So there is no technical hitch."

Gopal Deb, poet and rhymester, was a new member of the Writers' Forum. He had not yet properly realized the importance of the prestige accorded to understand a representative of the people.

"I fail to understand what makes Amalendushekhar a legend!" he exclaimed.

"Have you read his books?" asked Asamanja.

"I haven't."

"Read them, then. Whatever remains to be proved will be established once his statue is inaugurated. The Writers' Forum was Amalendushekhar's creation, and this is the first time in fifty years that we are putting up the statue of someone not in politics and not a freedom fighter. The Writers' Forum has reached every district, inducted members at the block level, that's how all of you have arrived here."

In the past year, Nandini had visited Kolkata three or four times. Travelling from Hazaribagh, she had searched the flat for photographs of Baba in his youth, and for his early writings. She had discussed things with the sculptor, Sudhanya Chandra.

There were some photographs taken in a studio with an ordinary camera. It was Ma who had arranged the sitting.

"Besides a few pictures, there's not much else."

"Not that I expect video footage of a person of his vintage, but we do need some more material. His gait, how he would stand up from a seated posture ..."

"Also the type of clothes he wore, his spectacles, haircut ..." added Abanibabu.

In other words, it was a question of creating a person for the public, almost from nothing. What an impossible endeavour! thought Nandini. What did it matter if Baba's glasses or hairstyle didn't belong to the Sixties? Could a person who had remained all but invisible for the past twenty-five years be resurrected purely from memory? Was it revival or resurrection? Amalendushekhar lay in profound slumber beneath those fathomless waters. This was not a prayer ritual after all, where the deity could be summoned up by the chanting of mantras! The facts of the past must be uprooted, torn up from the opposite shore of time's stagnant, silted up channel, and placed within a human jungle of the early twenty-first century. A park where the carpet of grass had all but vanished, where stalls of illicit liquor flourished at night, where not even the stench of dead peacocks lingered in the empty wire cages, where the young ones didn't come out to play anymore, because via a succession of terminal examinations, they had left, gone away to disport themselves with joint entrance tests.

How often Amalendushekhar had taken his beloved daughter to that park! Nandini had no memory of her parents having gone there together; Amalendu did not feel comfortable in his wife's company on social occasions for he considered her rather foolish and a little unimaginative. Nandini had memories of plucking flowers while being carried in Baba's arms; she even remembered chewing the calyx of rangan, ixora blossom, in the hope of tasting its nectar. She would fill Baba's breast pocket with small pebbles and fragments of mica that she found scattered on the ground. When she was a little older, she walked beside her father, sometimes overtaking him, then coming back, talking nineteen to the dozen, dragging him by the hand, all the way round on the paved path.

"Baba had all his shirts tailored; and his kurtas … Ma bought them from Amrita Brothers at Gariahat."

"And the buttons on his kurta?"

"Mother-of-pearl, very ordinary …"

"Can you identify this shoe …"

"Closed leather chappals, not shoes … Kalachand had this

shop in Bhabanipur . .. Ma said the leather there was good, not expensive either . . ."

"So it was your mother who managed your father's entire wardrobe?"

On the road outside Sudhanyachandra Studio there were countless bougainvillea shrubs. White, pink, orange – outwardly a blissful afternoon. Tears filled the corners of Nandini's eyes, making them ache. She felt utterly worthless, rejected, outcast.

Ma had never been allowed to cross the threshold into Baba's world of intellect and creativity. Society had made her responsible for maintaining Baba's health by cooking for him painstakingly – in summer, neem with eggplant, and shukto; in winter, cauliflower dalna; and in the month of Phalgun, tender jackfruit koftas. Tidying Baba's table, putting his manuscripts in order, dusting the correspondence files; buying his clothes and shoes when required, keeping them handy, ready for use, buttons and drawstrings in place – all were part of Ma's assigned duties. Nandini did not understand all this as a child, but during adolescence she felt a deep compassion for her mother, knowing herself to be the only claimant for her brilliant, talented father's attention and love. In early youth as well, Nandini's position of privilege remained intact. But when she fell in love with Dhiman, she realized that her relationship with Baba had nothing inevitable about it. Dhiman might be educated and employed, but he was from a low caste. Such people, victims of history, might infect Nandini's orderly, beautiful world with their own attitudes of defeatism. On account of this anxiety, Baba refused to set eyes on Dhiman, saw no need to talk things over with him, and like a shyama insect in the month of Kartik, brushed off his beautiful daughter who was so much cleverer than her mother, casting her out of his intellectual fold. Flung swiftly and violently onto the hard paved ground, Nandini realized that in their family hierarchy there was no difference between her caste and her mother's.

What hurt more than being spurned by her father was the discovery that she no longer loved him, no longer respected him, nor felt attracted to him in any way. All along, Nandini had thought of love, not as a particular condition of the heart and emotions, but as a special inner power. For a long time she was tormented by the feeling that by no longer loving Baba she herself had become powerless and impoverished. In the sculptor's company, even the process of reviving these minute particulars about Baba failed to rouse any sense of grief within her. She felt she was utterly redundant.

Now after all these years, Baba's own social group had awakened and was pursuing her. Baba's image, made of clay, limbs made of plaster of Paris – she had observed all this with silent patience, discussing possible minor changes with the sculptor. Once the metal casting was complete, Nandini's job would also be over. She had more or less decided that, once back in Hazaribagh, she would not return for a long time.

"We'll get off here," said Abanida.

If he hadn't spoken, Nandini would not have thought of alighting, though the car had come to a halt. Open drains lined both sides of a narrow brick lane. Leaving the Titagarh highway they had wound their way through sundry alleys to reach this neighbourhood. Row upon row of casting factories could be seen. Beyond the black gates of one was a garment factory. Smoke spiralled up from the chimney into the sky. On the left was a tiny entrance set inside a rusty gate, its paint peeling off to expose the primer underneath. One had to bend and twist the body to enter. Nandini clambered in behind Abanida. Just an hour-and-a-half-long drive, and she was already drenched in sweat. Her throat was parched, but the water in the bottle was so hot that she didn't want to touch it.

Sudhanya Chandra had arrived there early in the morning. As he did every day. Casting requires hard labour and unwavering concentration. Eleven to twelve hours of labour, every day. One can't become a sculptor without tremendous strength and endurance. There stood the statue of Amalendushekhar. A book in his left hand, turning the pages with his right. Nandini must check if the arms were positioned in a lifelike manner. How delicately Baba would finger the pages of a book, lightly and with such simple absent-mindedness! Nandini herself had tried to touch the pages of the book. It was hard to match his gesture …

As soon as she entered the dense, heavy heat made her recoil, almost flung her off her feet. At the far end of the high-roofed tin shed were two large furnaces. Abanida, member of the Writers' Forum Working Committee, had been bubbling constantly like the molten metal itself, so great was his enthusiasm about this construction.

"The fire was lit at five in the morning today … because of our visit!" he whispered.

Those ignited furnaces now roared with flames, both of them; burning within them were bronze and copper foil, fragments, wires … The metal was placed in another container called a muchi, also made of metal; and around it blazed a fire of stony coal. The mouth of the furnace was sealed with heavy sheets of tin, to intensify the heat.

The factory floor was unpaved, uneven; away from the furnaces, at a height, stood the mould into which the molten metal would be poured. To her right as soon as she entered, Nandini had noticed some lifeless, dismembered forms, arranged side by side.

"The one on that side is the torso, " explained the excited team-leader Gopal Ram, after she cast a couple of glances in that direction. "Those two objects you see over there are a pair of feet, and that roundish shape at the far end is the head. The mould is covered in gravel and plaster ..."

A dismembered body.

The men have awakened in the wee hours – Gopal Ram and his army of workmen from the provincial towns of Bihar, ribs pushing their way out of tattered vests and bare torsos, some dressed in just a loincloth, others in faded shorts tied at the waist with coir-rope drawstrings. They light the furnace, these men, and instal the muchi in the roaring heat. Then, carefully but very swiftly, they carry the immensely heavy container of molten metal to the mould placed within the other furnace. Then little by little, the metal is poured in through a funnel.

Fighting waves of intense heat, thirst and sadness, Nandini looked at the severed bodyparts. The plaster-of-Paris moulds had been filled with melted wax, then placed in the furnace. In the heat of the fire, the wax had drained out through the exit-points. Now there remained the hollow interior, waiting to take the molten metal into itself. Such fragmented, broken images of Amalendushekhar had indeed once prevailed – at the Forum, for his readers, before his wife and daughter, within the literary establishment, at the government's court of judgment. Today, a decade-and-a-half after his death, overcoming a spell of forgetful indifference, the nation was trying to piece together a complete image by joining the different limbs and parts, but in this process of social reconstruction, Amalendushekhar was being dismembered, fragemented, dispersed over and over again. In fact, looking at the lifeless pieces, it seemed Nandini was glimpsing the silent pain of existence itself.

Nandini's head began to ache listening to the hiss of boiling metal, standing close to the fire's heat. She remembered the milling crowds in their house and outside in the alley, the day Amalendushekhar left them forever. The shock of the news had shaken society's conscience. In that sea of humanity were Baba's readers, many of them people of his own vintage, or men and women who were older still. They had come on behalf of the Party, the Municipal Commission, the local committee. On various white floral wreaths were attached the donors' names, addresses, telephone numbers. Jharna's Ma, who had summoned people to break the door down when she found it locked in the morning, had invited Nandini in. It was as well that she did otherwise she would have been forced to wait like a beggar in the street, if she had arrived after the huge crowd had assembled. Nandini had rushed to the house upon receiving the news from Bhakti Mashima. Standing on the landing outside, she was wondering whether it would be correct to go inside, violating her father's dictum banning her entry during his lifetime. But following Bhikhu Mashima's instructions about ritual procedure, she carefully poured Ganga water into Baba's slightly open mouth, her hands trembling with fear and hesitation. As she wondered whether this amounted to interference in Baba's own beliefs and convictions, she noticed that countless black-and-white splotches had appeared on Baba's tongue, like fungus in the rainy season. Death was taking possession of Amalendushekhar. The boat was floating away from the shore; Nandini was alone, a vast expanse of water stretching out before her. Standing there, utterly alone, she glimpsed the loneliness that preceded her birth.

Today, gazing at Amalendushekhar's fragmented body placed in wax-filled, gravel-and-plaster moulds on the uneven, unpaved floor of this casting factory, Nandini suddenly felt it was far from clear whether her father was being created or destroyed. In this construction or deconstruction, she had no role to play, for Amalendu had banished his only child from him. Beyond asking after his well-being, he had given her no right to preserve their relationship. Yet, here Nandini must remain; from unbaked clay to plaster-of-Paris, wax, gravel and molten metal, crossing the different stages of transformation she was advancing towards a definite conclusion. She could claim nothing – no love, passion, childhood, nothing. Amalendushekhar's metal statue would remain standing in the solitary corner of her own childhood park, remain there forever, left palm holding a book, right hand absently turning the pages, a metal palm, a metal page, fingers made of metal. Should Nandini come close, the pupils would not dilate in the statue's eyes, the lips would not quiver. Putting down the book, he would not reach out to lift her in his arms, as he had not done for the last thirty years.

A tremendous babble of voices rent the factory air. The leader of the workers had announced that the melting process was complete. It was now time to begin the casting. Nandini watched the feet as they rushed by, clad in rubber slippers, veins standing out. Merged with the crowd of landless Harijan labourers from the remote villages of Bihar, were two elderly persons from DumDum and Belgharia, both almost ready to be discarded.

"What can we do, we aren't trained in any other work," they had said, as a few of them rested in the harsh sunlight of the alley, legs outstretched.. "It's even hotter inside, how does the sunlight matter?" they had laughed, showing their broken teeth.

Now, like animals craving magic wings, they rushed towards the furnace. Four of them picked up immensely heavy iron tongs; two others, bending forward like wild lunatics, delved into the fire's belly to retrieve the shell filled with molten metal; the temperature of the liquid metal is about 800°; in that heat, their almost bare chests would be scorched, so also their eyebrows, foreheads, eyelashes; their sunken eyes would be scalded. But still, they ventured into the heart of the fire. Probing the mouth of the furnace with its lid of red-hot coal, Gopal Ram cried out – *Ha re re . . . !* – his voice resounding with the enormous exhilaration of that heat. Then six of them together, grasping rods fixed at the ends of a pair of tongs, carried the metal-filled vessel weighing two hundred kilograms. The metal had now to be poured into the mouth of the funnel. Carrying the load in this fashion, being matched neither in expertise nor uniform in their gait, some of them almost lost their balance as they jostled each other. Immediately afterwards, they screamed like slaughtered animals, for the shell tilted at an angle, spilling molten metal onto the ground like a flowing stream of fire. The fire scalds their feet, making their toes curl, but they leap up again, regain their balance, swiftly and carefully lowering their burden of tremendous heat into the dying furnace on the other side. The metal must be poured into the funnel, balancing the weight of the shell on a temporary brick frame and tilting it forward. The mould has already been stuffed with enough sand and bricks to ensure that the heat of the metal does not cause it to shatter. Six destitute labourers complete this task at amazing speed, gritting their teeth, for if the metal congeals, if there be the slightest delay, the loss to the owner of the works will be tremendous. Who in this case happen to be the sculptor. The men have been trained to regard their own lives as expendable in the face of any such eventuality …

Watching this ten-minute-long spectacle of metallic fire, Nandini became terrified and desperate, crying out in horror without being aware of it, fearing a labourer might burn to death before her very eyes. "No! No! No!" she screamed in terror. By then, through the funnel's mouth, the metal had entered the hollow interior of the mould. The ashes of the furnace flew about in the air. Emerging into the sun from the immense heat of the factory, the labourers sought to cool themselves. "Water! Water!" they cried as they came out into the open with their burnt, black chests and reddened eyes. As if they weren't alive, as if they were only fire-scorched ghostly spirits, all of them …

Watching the living dead rush out Nandini realized that the men had not been destroyed, after all. In the trapeze act of today's creative endeavour, their lives hung on by a thread, their impending death reserved for yet another day when molten metal must again be poured into a mould …

In the yellow light of the sun, the sight of scars on their bodies, caused by scorches, burns and cuts was hard to bear. Their eyes were bloodshot, ash-filled, brimming with tears. Seeing Nandini's cheeks wet with tears Gopal Ram and the others smiled sheepishly. She realized that her dead love for Amalendushekhar was gradually coming back to life within her. Trying to embrace the agony of Gopal Ram and the rest in exchange for their close encounter with death, she found her heart recovering its natural strength, its warmth and its childlike longing for the human touch.

Contributors

Susheela Sen was a writer and activist who participated in the Swadeshi movement. Her stories appeared in journals such as *Bharatvarsha* and *Kuntalin.* She won the Kuntalin award in 1908.

Giribala Debi (1891–1983) was a well-known writer of short stories and novels. She also published short poems in various periodicals. Her best-known novels are *Ruphina, Hindur Meye* and *Raibari.* Her short-story collection *Trinaguchchha* also won acclaim. She won numerous titles such as Saraswati and Ratnaprabha, and received the Nirupama Puraskar and the Lila Puraskar.

Rokeya Sakhawat Hossain (1880–1932) was a writer, educationist and social activist. She was the founder of the Sakhawat Memorial Girls' School in Kolkata, for the education of Muslim girls. She published essays, stories, satires and a novel. "Sultana's Dream" is a utopian feminist work. *Abarodh Bashini* attacks the purdah system.

Razia Khatun Chaudhurani (1907–1934) was born in Noakhali and grew up in the political environment of the freedom struggle. She published two books: a volume of poems titled *Upahaar,* and a collection of short stories called *Pather Kahini.* Her writings, including her remarkable letters, are collected in *Razia Khatun Chaudhuranir Rachana Sankalan.*

Radharani Debi (1903–1989) also wrote under the name Aparajita Devi. She was a close associate of Saratchandra Chatterji and married to poet Narendra Dev. She wrote poems, short stories, novels and prose pieces on a range of themes, including romantic love and women's role in the domestic sphere.

Sabitri Ray (1918–1985) was born in Dhaka and moved to Kolkata as a college student. She was a politically committed writer, known for her concern for ordinary people. *Notun Kichhu Noi* was her first volume of short stories. *Paka Dhaner Gan* is her best-known novel.

Ashapurna Devi (1909–1995) was born in Kolkata and educated at home. She was the author of almost 150 books, including poetry, short stories and novels. Her works include *Sagar Shukaye Jai*, *Agnipariksha*, *Nirjan Prithibi*, *Pratham Pratisruti* and *Subarnalata*. She was awarded the Lila Puraskar, the Bhartiya Jnanpith and the Rabindra Puraskar.

Sulekha Sanyal (1928–1962) was born in Faridpur, and came to Kolkata as a student. Although she became a communist, her ideas often clashed with those of the Party. *Sindure Megh* was her first collection of short stories. Her novel, *Nabankur*, is remarkable for its radical feminist approach.

Lila Majumdar (1908–2007) spent her early childhood in Shillong. In 1919, her family moved to Kolkata, where she completed her schooling and got a university degree in English Literature. She taught at Darjeeling and Shantiniketan, but eventually gave up teaching to focus on her writing. She has more than 125 books to her credit. *Holde Pakhir Palok* won the state award for children's literature, *Bak Badh Pala* the Sangeet

Natak Akademi Award, and *Aar Konokhane* the Rabindra Puraskar. She also won the Suresh Smriti Puraskar, the Vidyasagar Puraskar, the Ananda Puraskar, and the Bhubaneshwari Medal for lifetime achievement.

Jyotirmoyee Devi (1893–1988) was born in Jaipur, Rajasthan. Widowed at 25, she joined the women's movement. Her stories, poems and novels express the anguish of marginalized women from different sections of Indian society. Her books include *Sonarupa Noi*, *Rajghotak*, *Chhayapath*, *Sarojini*, *Sudhir Prem*, and *Baisakher Niruddesh Megh*. She was awarded the Bhuban Mohini Gold Medal and the Rabindra Puraskar.

Kabita Sinha (1931–1998) was born in Kolkata and educated at the University of Calcutta in English and Bengali Literature. She worked for the Indian government most of her life, particularly All India Radio, as a correspondent, producer, and station director, and began publishing her writings in the 1950s. She received major awards for her more than 50 books (novels, short story collections, and volumes of poetry), and published several books under the pseudonym, Sultana Chaudhuri.

Mahasweta Devi (1926–) was born in Dhaka and educated in Kolkata and Shantiniketan. She is known for her anti-establishment stance and her struggle for the rights of indigenous communities. She has published novels, short stories, essays and autobiographical and journalistic writings. Her major works of fiction include *Hajar Churashir Ma, Aranyer Adhikar,* "Stanadayini" and "Draupadi". She has won international recognition and received numerous awards, including the Jnanpith, Sahitya Akademi, Magsaysay and the Padma Shri.

Bani Basu (1939–) is one of the major writers of contemporary Bengal. *Janmabhumi Matribhumi* was her first novel, published when she was almost fifty, and *Mohana* her first collection of short stories. Her well-known works include the novels *Antarghat*, *Maitreya Jatak*, and some of her volumes of short stories, such as *Samudra*, *Nana Swader Galpo* and *Baranda o Anyanya*. She has won numerous awards, including the Tarashankar Award, the Ananda Puraskar, Bankim Puraskar and Shiromani Puraskar.

Ahana Biswas (1970–) is a well known novelist and poet. She was educated in Viswa Bharati, and is now a Burdwan-based academic. She writes poetry and fiction. Her collection of short stories *Ahanar Galpo* is experimental in theme and technique. Some of her writings proved controversial because of her bold approach to contemporary issues.

Nabaneeta Dev Sen (1938–) was born in Kolkata. She is a well-known feminist writer, and has published poems, short stories, novels, essays, travelogues and autobiographical writings. *Ami Anupam* was her first volume of poems, and *Pratham Prattyay* her first novel. She is also an academic, a specialist in women's writing. She has won numerous major awards, including the Padma Shri, the Bharat Nirman Award, the National Sahitya Akademi Award and the Kavi Puraskar.

Joya Mitra (1950–) has written several novels in Bengali, including *Swarna Kamaler Chinha* (The Sign of the Golden Lotus) and collections of poems, among them *Pratnoprastherer Gaan* (Song of the Ancient Stones), and *Deergha Ektara* (The Long String Instrument). She has translated the works of Amrita Pritam, Bhisham Sahni, Vaidehi and Ajeet Caur into Bengali.

Suchitra Bhattacharya (1950–) is a major novelist and short-story writer. She has published more than 20 novels and several volumes of short stories. Some of her acclaimed novels are *Kachhher Manush, Dahan, Kacher Dewal, Hemonter Pakhi, Neel Ghurni, Aleek Shukh, Gabhir Ashukh, Uro Megh, Chhera Taar, Alochhaya, Anyo Basanto, Parabas, Palabar Path Nei, Aami Raikishori, Rangin Pritibi* and *Jalchhobi.* Her novels and short stories have been translated into many Indian languages, and she also writes for children. She has received several awards, including the Bhuban Mohini Medal, the Nanjanagudu Thirumalamba National Award, the Tarashankar Award, the Sharat Puraskar, and the Bharat Nirman Award.

Anita Agnihotri (1956–) started writing for the children's periodical, *Sandesh*, as a child. A civil servant and social activist, she has spent many years in Orissa and Bihar. She has published several volumes of poetry and fiction, including a lyrical novel, *Jara Bhalobesechhilo*, which she has also translated from the original Bengali into English, and a collcction of short stories and journal writings, *Forest Interludes* (2001).